STARSHIP FOR SALE

Starship For Sale, Book One

M.R. FORBES

Published by Quirky Algorithms
Seattle, Washington

This novel is a work of fiction and a product of the author's
imagination. Any resemblance to actual persons or events is purely
coincidental.

Cover illustration by Tom Edwards
Edited by Merrylee Lanehart

Chapter One

"Benjamin Murdock? The doctor will see you now."

My eyes latched onto the last text message resting at the bottom of my phone's screen. Words of encouragement from my best friend, Matt. *Good luck, bro. I know it'll turn out fine.*

I wanted more than anything for those words to be prophetic. I wanted to feel like everything would turn out fine. But my sense of dread wouldn't leave me. The fear of the unknown. Matt was the lead singer of our band. Not a prophet. Not even a medical student who might be able to make an educated guess about my situation.

Pure hope. That's all he had. That's all I had.

"Ben?" my mother said, her voice as tight as a guitar string. Her calloused hand slid into my open palm and squeezed, offering me what little comfort she could. Always a fighter, mom raised four of us alone after my father died, working two jobs while managing to care for us, leaning on my Aunt Cassidy to help carry the load. She loved all of us—me, my sister and two brothers—more than I had ever loved myself, and I knew it.

Which made the prospect of dying young even worse.

"It's going to be okay, Ben," she whispered, doing her best not to break down in the waiting room. "Do you want me to come back with you?"

I glanced over at her. One of her jobs was in construction, and the elements had aged her face beyond her forty-six years. The wrinkles and wind damage went with her tired brown eyes and thinning brown hair. She had always told me that she didn't care how hard she had worked or how young she might die, as long as she saw all of us to adulthood. None of us were supposed to go before she did.

I nodded, accepting her invitation to go see Doctor Haines with me, though I knew the question wasn't really a request. If I said no, she would put up a fight. And nobody was dumb enough to argue with her.

I switched off my phone, catching one last glance at Matt's text before it faded to black. His was one of a handful of well wishes from friends while more posts of encouragement had come from acquaintances I'd met on social media. As I headed toward the nurse near the door to the back, I wondered how many of his staff would remember me a month after I passed.

A macabre thought for sure. One I probably shouldn't have let take up residence in my head. But I'd spent the last three days since the MRI giving room for the darkest recesses of my soul to creep forward as I tried to figure out what the purpose of my short life had been and what the benefits of a full life versus a short one really were. If the outcome was bad, might that actually be good? I wouldn't have to grow old and wrinkled or lose my ability to see or hear or even walk. I wouldn't have to be stressed over finding work or keeping a roof over my head. Nothing about the world had bothered me before I had been born. Wouldn't it be the same going out?

Desperate coping. Where did that fall into the five stages of grief?

I slipped my phone into the pocket of my jeans, where a square matching its size and shape had pressed out the fibers, giving the denim a slightly more worn look that went well with the other tears and fading. I was hardly a fashionista. Rather, the thrift shop was the best we could afford. Even my phone was a three-year-old model bought off eBay for pennies on the original retail price, but I had learned early never to complain. I was enrolled in university, earning a degree in computer science with a minor in music on a half scholarship. The other half was in loans, eminently affordable as long as I was full-time. As far as Mom was concerned all of my focus needed to be on my classes, not split between study and work that went beyond the occasional gig our band-mate Calvin scored at one of the local dives. Fifty bucks a pop per band member, barely enough to pay my monthly cell bill. That was when I could still play. My coordination and balance had been off for weeks, keeping me offstage. It's the whole reason I ended up here.

I'd spent the last three years telling myself that things would be different after graduation. My CS degree would land me a job at one of the FAANG companies— namely Facebook, Apple, Amazon, Netflix, and Google —with enough of a starting salary to handle the loan repayments and hopefully allow Mom to quit one of her jobs. My aptitude, experience, and non-MIT level education be damned. Or maybe I could get lucky in crypto, learn solidity and catch on with a DAO. Or if all my dreams came true, the band would catch the eye of a producer and a few new stars would be born.

At the moment, none of that mattered. Even my most mundane dreams were under threat. Would I even be here to see my sis get married in a few months?

Life didn't just hand me lemons. It squeezed the damn things into my eyes.

"It's going to be okay," Mom said again as we made the long, slow walk from our seats in the waiting room toward the nurse. Becky. That was her name. Older than me but still young, fresh out of nursing school. Blonde hair and compassionate blue eyes.

"Hey Becky," I said when we reached her. "I feel like I'm on death row. You know, dead man walking." The dark statement caught her off guard, and her face flushed. I could sense Mom's horror as well. "Sorry," I added, correcting course. "I'm just nervous."

"It's perfectly understandable," Becky replied. "You're going through a lot right now. I'd be nervous too."

Our eyes met, and I wondered if she had learned those lines in school. If the compassionate eyes were like makeup, and if she would keep that look as she gained experience, or if she would grow jaded at some point. Nobody went to a neurosurgeon for routine care.

"Thank you for not keeping us waiting long," Mom said.

"Of course," Becky answered. "This way."

We followed her out of the waiting room and into a long hallway with offices and exam rooms on either side. I'd been back here a couple of times already as part of the process, and I knew Doctor Haines' office was halfway down on the left, next to the print of that Van Gogh painting of sunflowers. Thirty feet. I made it close

4

to ten before my vision started blurring slightly and I had to slow down and lean on Mom to help stabilize my balance.

"Damn it," I cursed under my breath. I had spent the last weeks hoping the symptoms would magically clear up. Wishful thinking hadn't helped. Neither had prayers.

"I've got you," Mom said, tears already in her eyes as she helped me along. She was the eternal optimist, and I knew, like me, she expected bad news. I hated doing this to her.

Becky knocked softly on the doctor's closed door.

"Come in," a deep voice said from behind it.

She opened the door, moving aside to let Mom and me pass. Haines rose to his feet behind his desk as we entered. A tall, broad man, it continued to amaze me that he could do such delicate surgery with such large hands.

"Ben," he said. "Missus Murdock." He waved at the two chairs positioned in front of his desk. "Please, have a seat."

I hadn't actually been inside Haines' office before. Only the exam rooms. My eyes danced nervously around, stopping at the photos of his wife and kids that sprinkled the walls between sports memorabilia and more Van Gogh prints. Anything to keep from looking him in the eye.

Mom kept her grip on me as I sat, just in case I lost balance and fell instead. Once I was fully down and settled she moved to the other seat, accepting the tissue Haines offered. I looked at the kindness as a sign of bad news.

I went from avoiding Haines to staring right at him, searching his kind face for any hint of what he was about to say, as if divining the answer ten seconds earlier could somehow change my future. If he hadn't become a surgeon, he probably could have made a killing in professional poker. Or maybe he had just been around long enough, seen enough sick people that we became more like broken objects than broken people.

Dark thoughts. Ugly thoughts. I'd never been so much of a pessimist. But then again, we all knew there was something wrong with my brain.

Becky left us alone, closing the door on her way out.

Chapter Two

I opened the door to leave Doctor Haines' office almost twenty minutes later. I remained surprisingly calm despite the diagnosis he had offered. The treatment options that stood little chance of changing the outcome. All most of them would buy me was time.

And not quality time.

Just time.

Mom stayed behind, still needing to ask as many questions as she could. She had taken the news worse than I expected, practically begging me to do anything to stay alive as long as I could. I didn't question her love or devotion, and at the same time it bothered me that I had to play the strong one. The devastation, we shared. The disease, mine alone.

The decision was also mine, and right now I didn't know what I wanted to do. Beyond the lousy odds, the fatigue, the nausea, the pain, there was also the cost to consider. Since I was still in school I had Mom's insurance, but how much would it cover? How much could we afford?

I knew the answer to that question. Nothing.

I told Doctor Haines I needed time to think. He prescribed me some meds that would immediately help manage my symptoms and improve my overall quality of life, at least for the short term. Moving from the office, back through the waiting room, and down the hallway to the elevator, my every sense felt numb, as if I were pushing through mud. I couldn't get my thoughts under control. I couldn't decide if I wanted to cry, stay strong, or just pretend the meeting hadn't happened. I don't know what I looked like to other people, but the elderly couple getting off the elevator when I reached it looked at me with tender eyes before quickly turning away, not wanting to share my moross state.

The pharmacy was on the ground level behind the lobby, and I reached it less than a minute later. Not much more than a counter inside the hospital, it was staffed by a pair of older women. Their white hair and wrinkled faces were almost unbearable for me to look at as I approached.

"Hi. I'm Ben Murdock. Doctor Haines should have sent down some prescription orders for me?"

"Let me look you up," one of the women said, typing in my name. I could see her eyes narrow slightly at the medications I'd been assigned. No doubt she knew what they were for. Glancing at me, she had the face of someone who knew I was too damn young, but didn't want to embarrass me by saying so. "The pharmacist is filling them now. It'll take about fifteen minutes." She pointed to a row of maroon chairs. "You can wait there. I'll call you over when they're ready."

"Thank you," I replied.

She offered an empathetic smile but didn't say

anything else, so I retreated to the chairs, taking up the first position and pulling my phone from my pocket.

Hey Matt. Bad news. I'm dying, man.

I stared at the words as I hit the send button. Despite the meeting with Doctor Haines, despite seeing them written there, I still couldn't quite believe it was real. Matt's answer came back in a hurry.

Shit. Ru srs? So sry. Can they do anything?

I shook my head as I typed.

Surgery, chemo, radiation. Best case sucks.

He responded even faster this time.

Worst case?

I stared at the screen. My fingers barely wanted to move to type the response.

Death.

My eyes lingered on the word again. I had never imagined writing something like that in relation to myself. Even when I first started getting dizzy, I had always convinced myself this was something I could get over.

How long?

It took me a minute to type the response. My hand started shaking, another symptom. Another reminder.

Few months. A year if I'm lucky.

I could almost picture Matt's face. We had been friends since we were old enough to walk and talk, starting as neighbors in the same Section Eight apartment building. Matt's mother was an alcoholic and drug addict, and she had left the picture when he was eight. He was raised to adulthood by his father. Most people who looked at him saw a rock star wannabe slacker. But Matt had a natural vocal range most singers would kill to have. What he really needed was a better band around him. His loyalty kept him tied to the rest of us, me especially.

Where ru now?

I quickly entered the answer, ignoring the typos caused by the tremors.

Hspital pharmaky. Mom's upstir w doc haindes.

I looked up as a mother and daughter entered the pharmacy. The girl was maybe nine years old, wearing a colorful knit hat even though it was sixty degrees outside. I wasn't so obtuse that I didn't understand right away.

Then I realized she was broken, like me. But even younger. And farther along in her treatment.

She noticed me looking at her and offered an innocent wave. I smiled and waved back before looking back at my phone.

on my way. Don't leave b4 i get there.

I smiled. Matt knew I couldn't drive myself anywhere anymore. I could take the bus, but I had figured he would come running when I gave him the news. Unlike my mother, I could confide in him without having to consider all of the familial ramifications. I could bounce every thought off him without worry. That's what best friends were for.

Ok. I'll meet you in the lobby. Waiting on meds.

The mother and daughter crossed to the chairs and sat, the girl climbing onto the chair next to mine.

"Hi," she said cheerfully. "I'm Eunice."

I looked over at her, thinking I would force a grin but finding a real one at the sight of her smile. "Ben," I replied. "That's a great hat you have there."

"Thank you. My mom made it for me to keep my head warm. I don't have any hair. Do you want to see?"

"Sure."

She lifted the hat off, revealing her bald scalp. "Tada!"

I laughed. "How do you feel?"

"A little nauseous sometimes, but I'm okay. The doctor says I'll get better and be able to go back to school next year."

The innocent words jabbed me in the gut. "That sounds exciting."

"It is!" she laughed. "Are you sick too?"

"Yeah."

Her smile turned into a wide oval and she breathed in sharply. "That sounds terrible. I'm sorry you're sick. You seem like a nice man."

I glanced at Eunice's mother. She wore a similar expression to the woman at the pharmacy counter.

"Is it bad?" the woman asked, sincerely concerned.

I nodded.

"I'm so sorry."

"Thank you."

"I'm sorry too," Eunice said. "I like you, Ben."

I laughed. "I like you too, Eunice."

"Benjamin Murdock," the woman at the pharmacy counter said.

"That's me," I said. "It was nice meeting you. Good luck with everything."

"I hope I'll see you again," Eunice said. "Maybe we can play checkers."

"I hope so," I replied.

The pharmacist replaced the woman behind the counter when I arrived. He had three different bottles in his hands, all of them filled with large pills. "Mister Murdock," he said, placing each one on the counter in turn. "Inflammation. Nausea. Steroid. The first one is the most important, but the second one will help with the side effects of the first. The third will help with the fatigue."

"I'm not fatigued."

"I'm sorry to say, you will be as things progress."

Not something I looked forward to. "Right. Okay."

"Dosage instructions are on the label. If you experience diarrhea or rashes, stop taking the medication immediately and call the pharmacy or Doctor Haines. Okay?"

"Got it," I said.

He left the pills on the counter and retreated to the back, replaced by the clerk. She scanned each of the bottles and put them in a bag.

"That'll be one hundred fifty dollars," she said, ringing up the purchase.

"I have insurance," I replied.

"That's the fifty dollar copay for each prescription. Honestly, you're fortunate your provider covers these at all."

I swallowed hard as I reached for my wallet. My credit card could handle this batch, this month. But it was my first taste of how expensive this whole thing might quickly become. If I decided to do the full treatment, Mom would be bankrupt in no time, her whole life savings gone in a matter of months with no guarantees.

She would do it without hesitation. That was the problem.

I paid for the meds and left the pharmacy, waving to Eunice again on the way out. Making my way to the lobby, I had to slow down when another wave of dizziness passed over me. I found a seat and dropped into it, leaning my head back and closing my eyes while I waited for Matt to arrive.

"Ben."

I must have fallen asleep, because it seemed like I had just shut my eyes when his voice jogged them back open. Tall, lean, and handsome, Matt had longer blonde hair, a strong jaw, blue eyes and tanned skin. He wore a black t-shirt over his muscled chest, a leather jacket over that, matching his designer jeans and black combat boots. He was the one all of the women fawned over, while the rest of us battled through our sets behind him, mostly going unnoticed. I had never minded. Matt had the look of an arrogant pretty-boy but in fact had a heart of gold.

I sat up as he dropped into the seat beside me and wrapped his arms around me, unashamed to hug me in public.

"Shit," he said again. "I…" He trailed off, and when he pulled away his cheeks were moist.

"Let's just get out of here," I said.

"Definitely. Where to?"

"I don't know. You name it," I said, pulling my phone out. I texted my mom to let her know I was leaving with Matt.

He smiled. "I think I know. Come on."

Chapter Three

Matt had left his car parked in one of the handicap spots just outside. A late model Mustang, he had added modified fenders, tires, and rims plus a chameleon wrap to make the thing really stand out on the street. It got a lot of attention from people who appreciated cars like that, and a lot of attention from the police. Matt had mastered apologetic politeness, his natural charisma often getting him out of tickets.

I thought he might need to put the charm into high gear when a patrol car pulled up behind the Mustang while we were walking toward it. The officer got out and approached the car, eying the registration tab before searching for a driver.

"Sorry officer," Matt said, catching him before he could take any further action. "I just stopped here to pick up my friend."

"This is a handicap spot," the officer replied. "You shouldn't be parked here."

"I know, I know. I was only inside for two minutes."

"I am handicapped," I offered in support.

"I don't see a tag," the officer replied.

"I know," I replied. "I haven't had a chance to apply for one yet. It's recent."

He didn't believe us. Why would he? To him, we looked like a couple of kids flaunting the rules. "You don't look handicapped to me."

"I lose my balance sometimes. If you don't believe me, take a look at these meds and then go ask the pharmacist." I held the bag out in his direction.

He eyed it, considering taking up the challenge before nodding. "Okay. I hope you wouldn't pretend to be that sick just to get out of a parking ticket."

"Believe me, officer, I'd rather be pretending."

He nodded, giving me a sympathetic look.

"Thank you, officer," Matt said, opening the passenger door for me. I climbed into the car, exhaling sharply as he circled the front and got in on the driver's side. The policeman returned to his car, driving off ahead of us. "That was close."

"Please, what's your ratio now?"

"Seven stops to one ticket," he answered, starting the engine and pulling away from the hospital.

We spent the next couple of minutes in silence, as I did my best to ignore the reality of my situation and just let myself exist. I didn't want to think about cancer right now. Or dying. But as I stared out the windshield, watching the world moving around me, it was almost more than I could take.

"I can't even begin to guess how you feel right now, Bennie," Matt said, breaking the silence at just the right moment. "Shit, I don't even know how I feel. I just want you to know that I've got your back like I always have. Through everything, no matter what. If you want to talk, we can talk. If you want to cry, I totally understand.

If you want to just chill and be silent, we can do that too."

"Thanks, Matt," I replied. "Where are we going?"

"Do you remember that place we drove past a few weeks ago? The VR arcade?"

I searched my memories for the moment, recalling the futuristic sign, the black tinted windows, and the *Coming Soon* banner hanging below it. "Yeah. Is it open?"

"I drove by again a couple of days ago when I dropped Rachel off at her apartment. The banner had changed to *Grand Opening*. So yeah, I think it is."

"Rachel?" I said. "You didn't tell me about her."

He laughed. "There isn't much to tell. Rachel Portnoy. You met her at one of our gigs a month or two ago. She texted me out of the blue and asked me out."

"She asked *you* out?"

"Yeah. Nothing wrong with a woman who knows what she wants, in my opinion. Anyway, she's cute. Very cute. But not really my type. We had dinner and I brought her back to her place."

"She didn't invite you up?"

"I wouldn't have accepted if she had, but no. We both knew it wasn't working. No hard feelings. Anyway, back to the arcade. I looked it up online. They've got all kinds of simulators and geeky virtual reality stuff like that. Not really my thing, but I know you're into all that sci-fi tech. I figured you might like a chance to blow off some steam."

"I'm not angry."

He glanced over at me. "Bullshit."

"I'm not," I insisted.

"You don't get told you're going to die without getting angry at the world. I don't need to consult a shrink to know that. Maybe it just hasn't hit you yet, in which case we can front-run the emotions and you can decompress before you do something stupid."

"Like hang out with you?"

"Even if I'm wrong and you aren't angry, it might take your mind off things for a couple of hours. We can hit *McRory's* after, have a few beers and hate on everything."

I shook my bag of meds. "I don't think I can drink with these."

"What's the worst it can do, kill you?" he replied, tensing when I didn't laugh at the joke. "Sorry. Too soon, maybe." He quieted down.

"No, you're right. I don't want to spend whatever time I might have being all doom and gloom. Still, beers first, meds later. I'm sure they can wait until morning."

"Are you sure?"

"Yeah. If my appointment was tomorrow instead of today, I wouldn't have them yet, right?"

"Right," he agreed.

"So tell me more about this arcade."

"I don't know what more to say. They advertised a few different games. A mech simulator. A starship combat simulator. Some game where you have to walk through a jungle and shoot aliens."

"Predator?" I asked.

"You're asking the wrong person. I still can't believe things didn't work out with you and Caroline. You're both such nerds."

"How can I be a nerd? I play guitar in a rock band."

"You can take the guitar out of the nerd, but you can't take the nerd out of the guitar."

"That doesn't make any sense."

"Who gives a shit about sense," he said. We both laughed. I knew he was happy to force my better mood.

"Let's just forget about all of this cancer crap for the rest of the day," I said. "I'll deal with my impending doom tomorrow. Right now, I just want to have some fun."

Matt hit the gas, sending the Mustang racing through a yellow light. He swerved around a pothole and sped up even more, forcing a different kind of exhilaration through me. "That's the spirit. Screw cancer. Your wish is my command."

Chapter Four

Matt and I pulled into the parking lot of *VR Awesome!* ten minutes later. With it being early evening on a Friday, the place had already started attracting a small crowd. Only a few spots remained in the lot, all of them near the back, so Matt pulled into one of the handicapped spots in front.

"Do you want another shot at a ticket or what?" I asked. "You can't afford the fine for this."

"I can afford more than you think," Matt replied cryptically. "Besides, nobody wants you getting dizzy before we can even make it inside."

"I'll be fine."

"Not open for debate. It's my ride, and I'm parking her here." He smiled as he stopped in the spot. "You may not have a tag, but you're still a cripple. Even before all of this."

"Jerk," I shot back, taking the comment for the joke it was.

We got out of the car and crossed the sidewalk to the front of the arcade. A group of teenagers waited outside, probably for more of their friends to arrive. The boys eyed Matt's car. The girls eyed Matt. He barely noticed, accustomed to the attention.

"You good?" he said, opening the door for me.

"So far," I replied, walking in and looking back at him over my shoulder. "I appreciate your concern, but treating me differently isn't going to help."

"Sorry, bro."

A small counter sat at the front of the arcade, occupied by a pair of young women who were both in the process of helping other customers. I used the wait to scout out the interior, my eyes dancing from one part of the floor to the next. The square footage was broken up into different segments, separated by a grid of wide aisles marked by dark carpeting. Classic stand-up arcade games like *Pac-man* and *Mortal Kombat* were lined up in the middle of the aisles as dividers between directions of traffic. Glass partitions separated the segments from outside interference and accidents like spilled drinks.

Nearest them, a dozen omni-directional treadmills drew my attention. Their fat fronts hid the electronic guts of the VR machines that displayed the game's environment on the inside of the light weight, helmet visors that went over each player's head. Wires snaked out from the glove each player wore, connecting to different parts of their arm, allowing them to manipulate the virtual world. Racks on both sides of each treadmill held props —a sword, a machine gun, a bow and arrow—that a player could use to add to their specific illusion.

It was all very, very cool.

And for a moment, I forgot I was dying.

"Ben," Matt said. "Earth to Ben."

I looked over at him, finding him in front of the

counter. So enthralled by the VR treadmills, I had lost track of everything else.

"Sorry," I said, joining him at the counter. "This is just so awesome."

"That's what it says in the marketing too," one of the girls replied with a big smile. Around my age, she had a pretty face, with big eyes made larger by the thick purple frames of her glasses.

"Have you tried any of it yet?" I asked.

"Oh yeah," she replied, excitedly. "*Jungle Invasion* is pretty cool, but it's a lot of exercise for a keyboard jockey. If I had known it was coming, I would have started going to the gym a month ago."

"That doesn't sound like a great fit for you," Matt said.

"Keyboard jockey?" the girl asked.

"Actually, I play guitar," I replied.

Her eyebrows went up. "Really?"

I could feel the heat in my face. "Yeah. I think I'll try it anyway, even if I only last a minute or two. If I had known about *Jungle Invasion* a month ago, I would have started going to the gym too."

"Maybe we could go together," she said, causing my face to heat up a lot more. By her expression, I think she was enjoying my embarrassment. I was used to women giving Matt all of the attention.

"Uh, sure," I said. "Why not?"

"Just pass me your number on the way out."

My big smile grew even larger. "Okay."

It was her turn to blush. "Good." She paused to take a breath. "It's forty dollars for an all-access pass," she continued, getting down to business. "Forty-four fifty, with tax."

I reached for my wallet, but of course Matt was

already passing her his card. "Two passes," he said. "It's on me."

"Thanks, Matt," I replied.

She ran the card, scanned a couple of bracelets, and handed them over to us. "Each game has different gear, so you'll be outfitted there before your turn." She pointed to *Jungle Invasion*. Following her point, I spotted a group of twelve players on the sidelines, ahead of a counter stocked with helmets, gloves, and the haptic connectors. "Each game is fifteen minutes, if you can last that long. Eight games in total. We're open until two A.M."

"You'll still be here at closing?" Matt asked.

"Yup. I'll be here all night."

"Good. I don't want Ben to miss you."

"You won't," she assured me.

"If you get a break, maybe you can join us for a round," Matt suggested.

"I would, but they don't let us play when it's this busy."

"In that case, we'll see you later."

"Great. Have fun." She looked from Matt to me. "See you later, Ben."

"I…" I paused.. "I didn't catch your name?"

"Levi," she replied, pointing to her name badge.

"Cool name," I said. "We'll talk later. Matt, let's just take a look at everything first."

"Sure," he replied. We left the counter, walking down the right side of the center aisle. "That was a new experience."

"What do you mean?" I asked.

"It's not often that I feel like I don't exist."

"Jealous?"

He smiled. "Yeah, a little. She really liked you."

"I don't know why."

"Come on. You're a good looking guy. A little nerdy, but you've got your own style. So did she. Two peas in a pod, I think. Plus, you're smart, talented, creative, resourceful."

"If you keep going, I might puke."

He laughed, stopping in the aisle and turning to me. "I just want you to know what I think of you. I never got to tell my dad what I thought of him before he left."

"I hope you aren't comparing me to your dad."

"Inversely," he answered.

I bit my lip, trying not to get emotional in such a public space. "Thank you. But just a reminder. Tonight, I'm not dying. I'll get started with that tomorrow."

"You always have been a procrastinator."

We resumed our exploration of the different games. Half of them were based on the treadmills like *Jungle Invasion*. There was also a car racing simulator, something that involved riding a horse, and a flight simulator where it appeared each person could choose their own style of play.

Reaching the end, my eyes lit up at the final two sections. *Mech War* and *Star Squadron*.

"I see you just spotted your utopia," Matt said.

"I read about these on *Engadget*," I replied, mentioning one of my favorite blogs. "I hoped they were here when I saw *Jungle Invasion*." I scouted the prep areas for both. "*Star Squadron* has a couple of openings. We can jump into the next round."

Matt didn't look too thrilled about actually playing the games. I knew he would have preferred the more physically challenging sims, but even that was a stretch for him. Sure, he liked to mess around with stuff like *Smash Bros.* or *Mario Kart*, but that was the extent of his level of interest. Sometimes it amazed me how we had managed to remain so close despite such different hobbies. But then, we had grown up together, and we both still shared our love of making music.

It was enough.

"Just go easy on me, okay?" he said.

I smirked back at him. "We'll see."

"Let's do it."

Chapter Five

We passed through the entrance to *Star Squadron*, my gaze immediately fixing on the monitors displaying the current action. With five minutes left in the match, only a few of the combatants remained, each side clearly marked by colored outlines around their starfighters. Each ship had a different skin—swept wing, delta wing, x-wing, long and sleek, a little more round—but were all close to the same overall shape and size and likely used the same algorithmic boundaries to determine hits.

They shot back and forth through space in a tense dogfight through what appeared to be the debris field from an earlier battle involving larger starships. The graphics were impressive, not the blocky renders I was accustomed to seeing in larger-scale virtual reality displays. Even standing outside looking in on the world, I could almost feel the tension of the battle as if I were looking through the viewport of an outlying corvette.

Matt laughed when I told him as much. "You're such a nerd. The graphics are pretty cool, though."

The older man in charge of the prep area smiled at

us as we approached. They had gone all out with the props, putting him in a silver flight suit and helmet with a yellowed visor, his beginnings of a dad-gut pressing against the zippered front. "Did you come to enlist in the squadron?" he asked.

"Uh, sure," Matt replied, hesitant to buy into role-play.

The man pulled a green laser pistol from a holster on his waist and pointed it at us. "I need to make sure you aren't spies for the Axon."

"What?" Matt said, confused.

"We aren't spies," I answered, holding out my wristband. "Here are our credentials, sir."

The man pointed the pistol at my band, scanning it. He did the same for Matt. "Congratulations! You've both been accepted into the Centurion Space Force." Head to the barracks to pick up your gear. You'll each need a flight suit and helmet."

"Yes, sir," I snapped, offering a salute. A geeky thing to do, but it drew a laugh from the other players waiting near the so-called barracks.

"Have fun!" the man said.

We made the short walk to the equipment rack. The flight suits were all the same size, big enough to fit over the clothes of all but the heaviest participant, who probably wouldn't fit inside the simulator anyway. Only two suits remained, one red, the other green.

"I think this means we can't play on the same side," Matt said.

"Then you can forget about me going easy on you," I replied.

"Fair enough. I suck at these things anyway. Which color do you want?"

Being the last two players, I had the benefit of

scouting the rest of the lineup before choosing a side. It was hard to judge starfighter simulator aptitude from a glance, but the red team definitely had a more geeky tilt. Probably because of Star Wars. Who doesn't want to say, *Red-5 standing by*?

All of that in mind, I decided to go with green, under the assumption it would give Matt a better chance at victory. I liked games, but I wasn't as competitive as much as cooperative despite what I had said about not going easy on him. It didn't matter if we were on different sides.

"I guess I'm red, then," Matt said as I took the green flight suit off the hangar and pulled it on. Of course it hung off my slender shoulders like a tent, but I was still excited to wear it.

Matt grabbed the red one and slipped into it, his more muscular frame better filling out the material. As a one-size-fits-all, he still couldn't make it look good on him.

We picked up our respective colored helmets and walked over to the other players. I slowed as we approached, lowering my head as a slight sense of vertigo hit me. Matt noticed right away, his eyes flicking toward me, hand reaching out. Remembering what I had said about not treating me like an invalid, he stopped himself, waiting to see if I really needed help. I didn't.

"Hey," Matt said, breaking the ice with the other players. "I'm Matt. This is my friend Ben."

"Nice to meet you all," I added. "Well, everyone on Green, anyway. That excludes you, Door Matt."

A few of the players returned the greetings, a few others were too anxious to do more than wave and looked uncomfortable. I understood the feeling. I had been anxious like that too when I was thirteen. But learning to play the guitar and later starting the band with Matt had fixed that.

"How long until the next match?" the youngest boy asked. Ten years old at best, he looked even more ridiculous in the flight suit than I did. It left me to wonder if maybe the child sizes just hadn't been delivered yet, considering the place was so new.

"It says up on the monitors," an older woman replied. Probably his mother. They were both on green with me. "See." She pointed to the nearest screen. "Looks like one minute."

"This is going to be so cool," the boy said.

"Is this your first time?" I asked.

"Yeah. You?"

"Yup. Have any of you played this one, yet?"

"I have," a teenage girl answered. "Twice last week. It's a lot of fun. You get to choose your ship design and pick a callsign. I guess if you're with a bunch of people you know you can organize your squadron and try to run plays or something, but fifteen minutes isn't really enough time to do more than have a free-for-all with strangers."

"I'm up for strategy," I said.

"Too bad you're a greenie weenie," she answered with a smirk.

She was there with a friend, who giggled as they both turned away from me.

I shrugged it off, scouting out the other three members of my squad. Another dad bod who was probably the little kid's father and a pair of high-schooler guys, likely friends. I had noticed the place was thick with people younger than Matt and me, but then it was still early. The adults would probably take over the late night shift.

The previous game ended, the motion of the simulators settling down as the only two remaining starfighters circled one another under AI control. The players climbed out of their seats and headed toward the equipment rack. A young girl only made it halfway before she turned away from the group, leaned over, and puked on the rubberized floor. She looked mortified when she had finished.

"Cleanup at Star Squadron," the man running the game announced over the loudspeaker, as if it was a common occurrence. He hurried over to the girl. "Don't worry. It happens to someone almost every match."

"Uh, I'm starting to have second thoughts about this," Matt said.

"You don't get motion sick," I replied.

"Under normal circumstances, no. I think I underestimated the motion of those boxes."

"If I can do it, you can do it."

"Can you?"

"Or I'll die trying," I joked.

His expression flattened, uncertain how to react. Then he shook his head. "Is that how it's going to be?"

"It is for tonight. No promises tomorrow. Just give me a warning if you're going to blow, I'll get it on video."

We fist-bumped and went our separate ways. Red against Green.

This was going to be fun.

Chapter Six

The VR simulators were identical for both *Mech Jockey* and *Star Squadron*. A padded seat rested behind a short steering column with a joystick, a throttle, and a pair of foot pedals. The whole thing was about the size of a small go-kart and rested on a set of robotic arms that could raise and lower the platform from each corner. It allowed up to twenty degrees of pitch and yaw to help sell the effect of flying.

The seat also contained a number of haptic sensors to shake the player up whenever they took a hit. The platform didn't have a monitor and wasn't enclosed. Instead, all of the visuals took place through the flight helmet, which had adjustable foam padding inside to help it fit snugly around the head.

I settled in the seat and strapped myself in with a three-point restraint that hugged me almost a little too tightly between the legs. I looked directly across from me to the Red Squadron setup Matt had claimed. He smirked and offered me a thumbs up. I returned the gesture before putting on the flight helmet, messing with it for a minute to make it rest more comfortably. The visor came down far over my eyes, leaving a small gap just below my nose so I could easily flip it up if I needed to make a quick return to reality in the midst of the simulation. After seeing the girl puke on the mat, I understood why the escape was necessary, though I would have preferred a fully enclosed experience.

I didn't leave the visor down. Curiosity got the better of me, and I raised it to look over at the boy, who had taken the simulator next to mine. The helmet was comically big on him, the visor nearly down to his mouth. Again, it occurred to me that *VR Awesome!* wasn't very prepared for younger visitors, but the kid didn't seem to mind. His huge smile beamed from beneath the oversized headgear.

A tone sounded through speakers embedded in the helmet's earpads. "Attention. Debriefing will commence in thirty seconds," a stylized robotic female voice said.

I slid the visor back over my eyes, finding myself staring at what I assumed were the blast doors to a hangar bay. Turning my head back toward the boy, I saw that a rendering of a starfighter had replaced the simulator, a generic pilot inside. I returned my attention to my own cockpit, glancing at my virtual hands before wrapping one of them around the virtual stick, identical to the real thing on the other side of the visor.

A second tone sounded about thirty seconds later. A heads-up display appeared in front of me, projecting a hologram of a woman in a crisp Space Force uniform onto the starfighter's dashboard.

"I'm Commander Abigail Cage," she said. "Welcome to *Star Squadron*."

I heard the boy beside me *woop* in excitement.

"If this is your first mission, raise your right hand so I

can go over the basics with you," Commander Cage continued. "If you're a veteran, tap the thumb trigger on your stick to skip to the next section and standby."

I put my right hand up. I'm sure most of the other players did too.

"So, you want to become a *Star Squadron* ace," Cage said. A shiver went down my spine, my mind already convinced the virtual world in front of my eyes was the real thing, that she was a real hologram, and she was looking directly at me. "You should know, it's a dangerous path you've chosen. A path that's claimed the lives of hundreds of aspiring pilots before you. Are you sure you want to continue?"

"Yes," I said softly. I could hear the woman in the simulator behind me say yes too, though less convincingly.

Commander Cage smiled. "Good. The first thing you need to do is enter your callsign and a passcode. You'll only have to do this once to have all of your career information saved to central intelligence and available whenever you are part of *Star Squadron*, become a *Mech Jockey*, or participate in *Jungle Invasion*, among other challenges."

A holographic keyboard appeared in my lap. I smiled as I reached down to enter a callsign. Online, I always went by Trubblemaker, so I used that here too. As I tapped on the virtual keys, the letters flew out in front of me and dangled in the air ahead of Commander Cage.

I flinched when I hit the enter key and the system told me Trubblemaker was already taken. Who the hell could have stolen my callsign? I had even spelled *trouble* wrong to make it less common. I guess it wasn't as unique as I had thought.

I stared at the keyboard, trying to think of another

callsign. After using that one for the last eight years, I didn't know what else to call myself.

"If you can't decide on a callsign, one will be assigned to you," Commander Cage said as if the system could read my mind. "You have ten seconds to begin entering a callsign."

One I didn't want, that I would be stuck with for the rest of my *VR Awesome!* life. I almost laughed out loud. So, a few months? Big deal.

I let the clock run out.

"Welcome to *Star Squadron*, Hondo," Commander Cage said.

"Hondo?" I replied out loud. "What kind of stupid callsign is that?" I shook my head. It didn't really matter. I typed in Password!23 for the password. That didn't matter either.

"Next, you'll select your starfighter. All ships have the same basic capabilities, but as you gain experience you'll be able to upgrade to less common designs, and better inertial dampeners that will soften the blow from hits. Special unique starfighter NFTs are also available for purchase."

"Of course they are," I muttered as a dozen ship designs appeared in front of my eyes. I didn't care which one I used, so I touched the one closest to my hand. Teardrop shaped, white with green accents, it had a pair of guns on either side of the fuselage and two huge thrusters in the rear. I hadn't seen the design in the prior game.

"Excellent choice," Cage said. I was certain every choice was an excellent one. "If you need to go over the control layout, raise your right hand. Otherwise, tap the thumb trigger on your stick to skip to the next section and standby."

I didn't think I needed instructions on how to work the controls. I'd played plenty of starfighter games before, though they hadn't been in such high-quality VR. I tapped the trigger and rested back in the seat as Commander Cage vanished. Still inside the hangar, I noticed the cockpit's interior had changed to match the skin I'd selected.

Thirty seconds later, Commander Cage returned. "Attention *Star Squadron!*" she snapped. "We've just jumped into the Aurea System on the far side of the Belt. Sensors have detected Axon clone forces on the other side of the asteroid field. Their Dreadstars are launching fighters, sending them through the field to engage. It's up to you to enter the asteroid field and destroy the opposition before they can destroy us. I'm activating your comms now. Prepare to launch."

A click in my ears signaled the connection to the rest of Green Squadron.

"This is so cool," the boy said. "Mom, which ship did you pick?"

"I don't know. I think the one in the bottom right corner," she replied.

The same design as mine, I realized. What were the odds?

"I took that one too," the kid's father said, leaving me more dismayed. I wondered if there was somewhere I could swap out for a different ride.

"I took the X-wing," the boy said. "I'm Luke Skywalker."

Except he hadn't picked Red. Why not?

I turned my head to see the boy's ship. His callsign appeared on the side of the fighter, large enough to read from a distance. *LukeSkywalker1021*. At least it helped me feel better about Hondo.

Emergency klaxons blared in my ears. Warning lights flashed at the front of the hangar. A holographic count-down hung in the HUD. Five seconds.

My heart rate increased, excitement building. I could feel myself smiling, and at that moment I forgot all about my cancer. The hangar bay doors slid open, revealing a sea of asteroids ahead.

The countdown reached zero, the lights on either side of the hangar turning green.

I grabbed the throttle and pushed it forward, the harness around me tightening to simulate the g-forces as my virtual starfighter rocketed out into virtual space and I clenched my teeth to keep myself from whooping until I realized I had no good reason to keep the emotion in check.

"Woooooo!" I cried out, joined by the kid beside me a moment later.

Now, where was Matt?

Chapter Seven

The sharpness of the graphics brought the entire experience to life, even with the small bit of normalcy filtering in from under the visor. Within seconds of launching from the hangar bay, my mind had convinced me I was really out in space, the mock g-force and inertia shifting as I used the stick to maneuver the starfighter, getting a feel for its capabilities. Instead of rushing right into the asteroid belt ahead, I practiced adding and cutting the throttle, changing direction, and adjusting to the feel of the simulator when I pushed the physics engine to the edge. The entire experience felt so real.

It was, as the name of the place conveyed, awesome.

The other members of Green Squadron didn't join me in the practice maneuvers. Understandable. We only had fifteen minutes till the match, and they wanted to get into the dogfight and win the mission. Commander Cage hadn't mentioned what we would earn for coming out on top, but I imagined the system kept track of experience points or something like that.

The other five starfighters left me behind, making

their way into the asteroid belt and vanishing amidst the spinning rocks. The kid seemed the most adept at controlling his ship, his movements more smooth than his parents, easy to spot because their starfighters matched mine. They jerked and overcorrected, sped up and slowed down, and otherwise looked as green as the team they had chosen. It seemed I had been mostly right in my assumption that the more serious players would gravitate toward Red Squadron. Excluding Matt, of course. He didn't care which side he was on.

"Hondo, are you going to help us?" the kid asked through the comms a few seconds after disappearing. "Or just fly in circles like a crazy person?"

"I'm coming, Luke," I replied, giving the kid a thrill by calling using his callsign. "Right behind you."

I changed direction, orienting my virtual ship toward the asteroid belt and hitting the throttle. The bottom right corner of the HUD showed a map of the theater, including red and green triangles to denote the position of all the players. It was probably the most unrealistic part of the cockpit interior, but also necessary. Nobody would have any fun shooting around space for fifteen minutes without finding one another. Well, I probably would.

Entering the asteroid field, I slipped the starfighter smoothly around the variably sized and shaped rocks, which moved on various trajectories that seemed to create obvious paths to circumvent them. Moving faster than my teammates, I caught up to them within a dozen seconds, pulling in behind the bright blue flare from the ship flown by Luke's mother. Her callsign, Daisy, floated above her fighter on the HUD. The kid's father, callsign Bowser, navigated the asteroids a short distance away.

"It looks like we're getting close," one of the high-schoolers said. Callsign *PrattLord*. I glanced at the map, eyeing the opposition. Two of their fighters had jumped out to a huge lead over the others, and I automatically assumed they belonged to the two girls who had played this game already. Three more of the ships were a little further back, while one remained outside the belt, not moving much at all.

That had to be Matt, struggling to work the controls.

"Should we try to work together?" Luke asked.

"Let's just try to blast them," the other high-schooler replied. Callsign *Bloodstain*. "You guys stay out of my way."

I huffed into the comms in response to the statement.

"You got a problem, Hodor?" Bloostain asked.

"Not yet," I answered. "And it's Hondo. Or do you have trouble with basic reading skills?"

"What? You son of a—"

"Young men," Daisy said. "We're on the same team. Can we just play without acting like idiots? We're here to have fun."

"Sorry, ma'am," I replied. I couldn't help it. I hated arrogant assholes. Who didn't, except for other arrogant assholes?

"Fine," Bloodstain said. "But if you're still on the field when Red is dead, you're next Hodor."

"Bring it on, Poopstain." It wasn't the word I wanted to use, but I wouldn't go that far in front of Luke or his mother.

"Oh, I will."

He and PrattLord were at the head of our group, and they reached the girls in the leading Red starfighters first. I saw the flashes of light behind the asteroids they swung around, and then the two enemy fighters ducking beneath them. They cut to the left as a single unit. The two high-schoolers followed recklessly after them, and my gaze shifted to the map.

The other three Red starfighters had changed direction, moving to intercept the idiots on their flank. Clearly, the more experienced player had convinced her team to work with her to win. As much as I wanted to see Bloodstain embarrassed by being knocked out first, I also wanted a chance to go after him myself.

"Bloodstain, PrattLord, watch your flank," I said. "Three bogeys incoming."

"What?" Bloodstain said. "Who do you think—"

"Jeff, give it up, look," PrattLord said, using Bloodstain's real name.

"Luke, let's help them out," I said.

"I'll use the Force," he replied.

"Bloodstain, PrattLord, pull up on my signal."

"I'm not listening to—"

"Jeff," PrattLord complained.

"Fine. Just say when."

I hit the throttle, skirting the asteroids with ease and swooping beneath Bloodstain's plane. Luke followed my lead, sticking close as we moved in to intercept the rest of Red Squadron, who had yet to notice that I had noticed them. The lead Red fighters stayed relatively straight, drawing the two Green fighters into the trap.

"Here they come," I said, adding a little more thrust to close the distance. The asteroids whizzed past on either side, my velocity dangerously close to being too high to prevent a collision. Luke couldn't keep up, taking a hit on the side from one of the asteroids that bounced his fighter off course and marked damage on his ship.

"Crap," he said, recovering and falling in behind me again, too late to help out.

I glanced at the map again, and then watched the

two girls shoot over the top of me and fly slightly ahead. Spotting the other Red fighters, my heart pounded as I realized I had successfully gotten a good angle of attack against them.

"Now!" I said, giving the high-schoolers their cue.

PrattLord broke up as expected. Bloodstain dove downward, right into my line of fire.

"I said up!" I shouted, unable to fire without hitting him. It was so damned tempting, but I refused to start the civil war.

"Too bad," he replied smugly.

My shot ruined, I watched as the three Red fighters changed course to follow PrattLord while the girls turned and shot past us, headed for Daisy and Bowser.

"Frigging idiot," I muttered under my breath. "Luke, you need to try to intercept the lead fighters. Daisy, Bowser, they're coming your way."

"Okay, Hondo," Bowser said.

"I'm using the Force," Luke added, moving away from me.

Bloodstain shot past close enough I could see him flip me the bird on the way by. I could hardly believe the guy's antics. Why did he have to ruin people's fun? I doubted he was even having any fun himself. Maybe he was like Matt, and didn't really want to play? I didn't think so. He was too good for that to be the case. After all, Matt had only just reached the asteroid field, proving how incompetent he really was at playing the game. Bloodstain didn't have that problem at all.

I didn't have any more time to worry about him. PrattLord had three bogeys slowly creeping up on his six as they worked together to take him out. I hit the throttle, changing vectors so quickly I thought the simulator might break as it bucked me to the left. Yanked in my restraints, I managed to swerve past an incoming asteroid and accelerate through a lucky opening in the field. The strip of clear space allowed me to gain on the Red fighters, closing the gap between me and PrattLord.

A glance at the map showed Bloodstain had decided to try to help his friend, falling in behind the Red fighters chasing us. He was too far back to do much of anything, and I might have told him so if I didn't already know how he would respond. Meanwhile, Luke and his family were about to mix it up with the two more experienced players, a skirmish that would likely only end one way. Once they had cleared that part of our squadron, they would be back to finish us off. The only chance we had to even the odds was to take out PrattLord's tail.

"PrattLord, dive on my signal," I said.

"Don't listen to him," Bloodstain remarked.

I ignored him, eyeballing the three Red fighters as they each veered around a larger asteroid to get into a clearing with PrattLord. A few more seconds, and he would be toast. "Now!" I snapped, cutting my throttle and curving toward him. I couldn't be sure he would follow my command until his starfighter dropped away only an instant before red beams flashed through space where he had just been. Holding steady, I could sense my eyes narrowing as the first Red fighter headed directly toward my reticle.

I squeezed the trigger and held, sending a green beam arcing out into space. The Red fighter couldn't change course in time to avoid it, and it split him in half like a hot knife through butter, leaving the two pieces of the fighter to drift before they exploded.

"Yes," I hissed under my breath, not wasting too much time celebrating. I changed vectors again, moving into position to fall in behind the Red players while they continued after PrattLord.

"Lucky shot," Bloodstain said, ever the asshole.

"Nice move, Hondo," PrattLord said. "What's next?"

"Bank hard right and circle back toward me," I replied. "Lead them in, and I'll try to hit them head on."

"Sounds like a plan, man. How'd you get so good at this?"

"I don't know. I play a lot of video games at home."

"So do I. I'm still a little lost out here."

"Bank now, pull toward me."

PrattLord did as I said, nearly clipping an asteroid during his turn. "Yahooooooo!!!" he shouted, his voice audible beyond the VR setup as he scraped past the rock and turned directly toward me. I smiled in response, both to his shout and how well the setup was playing out. Better than even I expected.

"Hondo, we need help," Luke said, drawing my glance at the map. The girls had already taken out Bowser, and were tight on Daisy's tail. He had managed to angle in toward them, but they managed to avoid him.

"Be there soon," I replied as the two Red fighters came around the asteroid. I squeezed the trigger, my green beam lancing the one closer to the obstacle. Like the first, it exploded.

The second fighter returned fire, red beam shooting out surprisingly close as I peeled away. At first, I thought he had just missed me. Then I noticed PrattLord vanish from the map.

"Shit, I'm out," he cursed.

"Damn it," I replied. "Sorry, man."

"Just get that bastard for me."

"Don't bother," Bloodstain said, sweeping in from above and blasting the remaining Red fighter. "I've got him. If you hadn't listened to Hodor you'd still be in the game."

"With three fighters on his tail, assuming they hadn't shot him yet," I snapped back.

"I would have caught up before then. His digital blood is on your hands."

"Hondo," Luke repeated.

Looking at the map, I saw he was alone against the two Red fighters, and they were coming in fast. "We need to help Luke," I said.

"Screw that," Bloodstain replied. "I've got a juicier target. Easy pickings. Let me tie up the game, then I'll take them out."

"Leave that one alone," I said. "Luke is in trouble."

"I don't answer to you, Hodor." He swung his fighter toward Matt and hit the thrusters, shooting away.

My jaw clenched, stomach tensing in response to the choice presented. I could let Bloodstain go destroy Matt and try to help Luke against the other two Red players, or I could leave Luke to fend for himself so I could help my friend, who just happened to be on the other team.

A look at the map showed Matt trying to navigate the asteroids, bouncing back and forth as they collided with his ship. He was clearly no threat to anyone, and the team would be better served by focusing on the two girls. But Bloodstain didn't care. He wanted the easy kill.

Game be damned, I couldn't let him do it.

Chapter Eight

"Luke, I'm sorry," I said as I flipped my starfighter over and maxed out the throttle. In a real starfighter, the force of the maneuver probably would have left me unconscious. But the simulator had explained away the mechanical limits of the platform as *inertial dampeners* that in reality translated to a little extra pressure from the tightening restraints. My fighter slowed to a stop before gradually gaining speed, already at a huge disadvantage because I had to completely change course. Bloodstain was already out of visual range, halfway to Matt while I was still regaining velocity.

"It's okay," Luke replied. "The game is still fun."

Somehow, he was managing to stay out of the enemy line of fire, smartly using the asteroids as cover while he hopped between them, leaving himself vulnerable for only a second or two at a time. The Red players had nearly come to a standstill as they tried to figure out a safe path to reach him.

I would have preferred to agree with the kid that the game remained fun. But Bloodstain had managed to ruin that, turning the entertaining experience into a real battle. I wished I had comms to the Red team so I could warn Matt about the idiot headed his way. There was no chance for me to catch Bloodstain before he reached my friend. He was already at speed, leaving me trailing by dozens of kilometers despite my adeptness at avoiding the asteroids. He would get at least one shot at Matt before I arrived, and judging by Matt's skill behind the stick, one was all he would need.

Desperate for a solution, I tapped on the thumb trigger, wondering if it had a purpose beyond skipping ahead in the introduction since the main trigger was for the lasers. My heart jumped when a second targeting reticle appeared on the HUD, an image of a missile painted in the lower right hand corner. The ship's skin didn't present any outward indication of missiles, but there they were.

My excitement didn't last. I was still too far away to use them. I would still get there too late. I couldn't make my ship go any faster, and I couldn't slow Bloodstain down.

Or could I?

Scanning the asteroid field ahead, I spotted the blue glow of Bloodstain's thrusters, rocketing on a relatively direct path toward Matt's position on the map. Eying the field from his position revealed a handful of asteroids covering the space between him and me, one or two blocking my view of him as I had to maneuver around another. Clearing the rock, my eyes flicked to each of the obstacles, noting their movement as I found an asteroid further ahead of my quarry. If I could hit that one with one of the missiles, maybe I could push it off course and into Bloodstain?

I liked the idea, but not the odds. Sneaking a projectile through the swirling asteroids would be a once-in-a-lifetime shot, like hitting a three-pointer from the other end of the court. But I had seen people do it on YouTube. I had seen people do stuff that seemed a lot more impossible than that.

And really, I had nothing to lose.

I swooped around another asteroid, sparing one more look at the map. The other two Red fighters had Luke nearly outflanked, and would drop in on him at any second. Matt was still meandering in my general direction, gaining speed as he became more comfortable with the controls. Had the other Red players given him shit for his inaction in the fight? I smiled. Not if they had seen how he was flying.

Bloodstain remained in a line as straight as he could follow, slipping around obstacles but maintaining his vector. I didn't know if he knew I was behind him. It seemed to me he would have something stupid to say if he noticed me on the map. The element of surprise would improve my chance to catch him completely unaware.

Coming around one final asteroid, I traced the other rocks between me and the asteroid ahead of Bloodstain that I had singled out. I couldn't target lock it or anything like that, and when I tapped the thumb trigger the first time a warning popped up on my HUD that I had nothing targeted. A second tap confirmed that I really did want to fire, sending the missile zipping away.

I locked my gaze on its green thruster as it darted ahead, already moving much faster than me or Bloodstain. Happy to see it would at least make it to the target ahead of the moron, I leaned forward in my seat, tilting my head as if that would help steer it past the asteroids.

One of the rocks tumbled in front of it, and for a

moment I thought they would hit. But it passed aside just ahead of the missile, close enough I could imagine the fuselage scraping the edge of the asteroid's surface. It cleared most of the other asteroids more cleanly, gaining on the other Green ship.

"Go, go, go," I said softly, lips curling in a primal grin.

Another asteroid moved in front of the missile, catching it before it reached the target.

"No!" I shouted, slamming my throttle hand down on the seat's armrest. I had missed.

My state of mind swung around again as the impact and detonation blew the asteroid apart, sending huge chunks sideways, one of them hitting Bloodstain. The blow knocked the fighter off-course. It rolled, bouncing off a second, smaller rock and spinning until it came to a stop perpendicular to its original path.

"What the hell?" Bloodstain said, his confusion bringing me great joy. He was silent as he regained control of his ship, finally noticing me coming up on him. "You?" he growled. "Whose side are you on?"

"I told you to leave him alone," I replied.

Bloodstain laughed. "What are you two, a couple of queers? Can't stand to have me shoot down your girlfriend?"

Anger raced through me, and I pushed the throttle open again, turning toward him. "Actions speak louder than words, asshole."

"Yeah, they do," he replied, swinging his fighter until we were directly in line with one another.

Adrenaline rushed through me, ready to put Bloodstain in his place as we prepared to charge one another like a couple of medieval jousters.

We didn't get the chance. A red beam sliced through

space from off Bloodstain's left flank, cutting his ship in half and taking him out of the fight.

"What the...?" he said again.

Matt's fighter came out from behind an asteroid as I started laughing.

"You're dead, Bloodstain," I replied.

"You're dead, you bastard," he hissed back.

"You're a ghost. You can't do anything to me now."

"We'll see about that."

Matt turned to face me as I raced toward him. I quickly tipped my wing a few times, hoping he understood what it meant. He replicated the move, acknowledging he knew it was me and holding his fire.

I checked the map again. The two girls had finished Luke off, and were coming my direction. Two against one? I cut the throttle, planning to sit and wait for them.

Matt moved in beside me and came to a full stop.

Two against two.

I tipped my wing. He tipped his. We waited. At the other Red player's speed, we wouldn't wait long.

The Red ships slowed as they approached, confused by the fact that I wasn't moving, and neither was the other remaining Red fighter. I could imagine them communicating with Matt, trying to figure out what was going on. A few seconds later, they regained some of their velocity.

I opened the throttle, pushing toward them. Matt did the same, a half-second behind. We raced headlong toward each other, my eyes on the asteroid between us, missile locked and loaded. It had worked once, why not do it again?

I watched the Red ships on the map, ready to fire into the asteroid and send fragments around it that would hopefully collide with the targets, knocking them out of position and making them easy kills. They drew closer to the rock, my finger tensing on the thumb trigger.

Then someone grabbed me.

Chapter Nine

One second, I was about to take the shot I hoped would end the match. The next, hands dragged my body out of my seat, the wires connecting my helmet to the simulator pulling on my head until they suddenly released and my tailbone slammed into the floor. Unable to see what was happening past the helmet's opaque visor, I heard other people reacting to the commotion and the familiar voice of the guy who stood over me.

"I told you you're dead, asshole," Jeff growled, his foot slamming down on my chest and knocking the air out of me.

I coughed as I lifted the visor in time to see his foot coming in again, kicking me hard in the ribs. From further away, I heard running footsteps coming toward me. It turned out to be the ride's operator rushing toward us, radio in hand calling for help.

"What the hell?" I wheezed, bringing my arms up to try to defend myself. There wasn't much more I could do. "It's just a game."

"Screw you and your game," Jeff exploded. "Nobody makes a fool out of me."

"You're doing a great job of that all by yourself," Matt said, coming up behind him. He grabbed Jeff's shoulder, spinning the guy around.

Jeff threw an awkward right hook that Matt easily dodged, returning the favor by planting his fist in Bloodstain's jaw. I winced at the sound of the impact, and watched in surprise as the guy collapsed like an imploding skyscraper. He hit the floor behind me and laid there, groaning.

"Asshole," Matt hissed, turning to look down at me. "Are you okay?"

"My neck hurts. Ribs too." I pointed when I noticed the other guy, PrattLord, rushing up behind Matt. "Behind you!"

Matt whirled on PrattLord, who skidded to a stop and put up his hands.

"Wait! I don't want to fight."

"What the hell is going on here?" the operator said, finally reaching us. "This is a family entertainment venue. You should be ashamed of yourselves."

"We didn't do anything," Matt said, pointing at Jeff. "He decided if he couldn't outgun me in the game, he would do some damage outside of it."

Jeff stayed down, stunned by Matt's punch. The operator looked at me. "Are you okay, son?"

"I'm fine," I replied, raising my hand. "Matt?" He took it and pulled me to my feet.

Two more male operators reached the scene, moving in beside our guy. "Everyone just stay put," one of them said. "We're calling the police."

"No," I replied, shaking my head. "You don't need to do that. I'm fine. It's over."

"He attacked you," Matt said. "That's not right."

"I said it's over," I replied, looking at the arcade employees. "Can we just go?"

They glanced at one another, uncertain what to say. The older one finally looked at me. "You're sure you don't want to press charges?"

"Yeah, I'm sure. He didn't knife me or shoot me or anything. Just a little fistfight. No big deal. And he got worse than he gave."

Our operator laughed. "He sure did. In game and out."

Jeff turned his head at the comment, embarrassed by the outcome. He still didn't get up.

"I think it's best if all four of you leave," one of the other employees said. "We don't need this kind of trouble here. We're a new business, and we can't afford to have people think this place is dangerous."

"Yeah, I'm sorry," I replied. "I think this place is great. I don't want to hurt your business."

"Me neither," Matt said.

"I'm sorry too," PrattLord added. "For me and on Jeff's behalf." He looked at me. "He's been having a rough time lately. He just lost his mom a few weeks ago. It's really hitting him hard."

The statement hit me hard too. Holding the throbbing in my ribs, I turned to Jeff and extended my other hand. "Man, I'm sorry about your mother. I know how rough that is. I lost my Dad when I was little. No hard feelings?"

His head turned, his eyes locking on my outstretched hand. For a second, I thought he might actually take it.

"Go to hell," he replied bitterly.

I shrugged, retracting the offer. "Suit yourself. I'm still sorry for your loss." I turned to Matt. "Let's go."

"Okay," Matt replied. I could see the distress in his eyes. He had brought me here to relax and have some fun, and not only did it backfire, we had to leave before getting to play any of the other games.

I clapped PrattLord on the shoulder on the way past, offering him silent support. He nodded to me, and Matt and I left Star Squadron, one of the three operators joining us to make sure we left.

"That was some punch," the guy said once we had left the play area. "Are you a boxer?"

"Mixed martial arts," Matt answered. "I have a black belt in karate and muay-thai. I've been studying since I was six."

"That wasn't a martial arts move."

"Sometimes the best approach is the most basic."

"And effective," the man said, smiling. "I've never seen anyone lash out like he did before. He's not going to like being banned from the arcade."

"It's probably the best thing for him right now," I said.

"Are you sure you're alright?"

"I'll have a couple of bruises in the morning, but they'll heal."

"Do you do MMA too?"

"Me? No. Matt's taught me a few moves, but I prefer less physical hobbies."

"Me too," the guy said, patting his rounded stomach.

We made it back to the entrance. Levi looked up when we arrived, surprised to see us on the way out.

"Leaving already?" she asked.

"Not entirely by choice," I answered.

Her surprised expression was too cute. "What happened?"

"It wasn't their fault," the operator said, shaking his

head. "Some idiot got rough with him because they beat him at *Star Squadron*. They agreed to leave quietly to help avoid any other disturbances."

Levi flashed me a concerned look. "Are you okay?"

"Yeah, I'm fine. I appreciate you asking though."

She reached into her pocket to retrieve her phone and held it out to me. "Don't forget to leave me your number."

I smiled at her while my gut clenched. I had been out with other women before, but Levi was the first who had shown such an immediate, open interest. It made me feel special. Handsome. Interesting.

The timing sucked.

I quickly entered my name and number into her phone and passed it back.

"Thanks," she said, smiling as she accepted her phone. She ignored her customer to tap on it, and a moment later my phone buzzed with her first text.

"Got it," I replied.

Matt and I left *VR Awesome!*, making our way to his car. No policeman. No ticket. We climbed in, and I dropped my head against the headrest, exhaling a big sigh.

"I'm so sorry about all of this," Matt said, starting the engine.

"You don't have anything to be sorry about," I replied. "Just my bad luck, I guess. I feel like I really pissed someone off Upstairs, and I don't know how."

"They say bad things always come in threes. You're due for a win streak now."

I laughed, wincing and clutching at my ribs as pain lanced through them. "Well, it can't get much worse. First I find out I'm dying. Then Levi practically asks me out on a date. Then I get into a physical fight playing a

VR sim?" I shook my head. "I think maybe I should win the lotto or something." I pulled out my phone, glancing at the notification of Levi's message.

Dinner Saturday @ 8? 12 Sycamore Street.

"Okay, she actually did ask me out," I corrected. "How do I say no?"

"Don't say no."

"I can't go out with her."

"Why not?"

"Because I'm dying. I don't want to meet someone and fall in love and all that just to croak in the end like some lame Hallmark channel romance."

Matt backed out of the spot and drove slowly through the parking lot. "You aren't dead yet. You should live as much as you can while you can."

"That wouldn't be fair to her."

He shrugged. "Just think about it. Maybe you'll change your mind."

"Okay, but what do I say in the meantime? I can't just ignore her."

"Tell her you're busy Saturday. That you have a gig. Some other time."

I stared at the notification. I couldn't bring myself to do that either so I turned off the phone and shoved it back in my pocket.

"Ah, the coward's way out. That'll help."

"Shut up. I'll text her after I've had a beer or two."

"Sure you will."

"Are we going to *McRory's*?" I asked.

"Yes, sir, we are," he replied. "Hungry?"

"Yeah. Starving."

"I wasn't on Green team comms, but Bloodstain was a total douche, wasn't he?" Matt said, making conversation as we drove.

"He was," I agreed. "Especially when he wouldn't take my hand after you knocked him on his ass. I kind of feel bad for him. He's going to get himself into worse trouble if he keeps taking out his anger about his mother like that."

"Happens all the time."

My phone vibrated in my pocket.

"Shit, she's probably wondering why I didn't answer yet," I said.

"If she's that aggressive, you don't want her," Matt said. "It's probably your Mom checking up on you."

"As annoying as that is, I hope so." I lifted my phone and turned on the screen, looking at the new notification. "Not Mom. It isn't even a number in my contact list."

"Spam? What does it say?"

I read the message out loud. "Starshipforsale.com. The adventure of a lifetime awaits!"

Matt laughed. "Yeah, like that's not totally a scam."

"Of course it's a scam." Still, I continued staring at the message. I hadn't gotten a spam text in weeks. Why now? It had to be a coincidence. Didn't it?

"It's a scam, why are you still looking at it?"

I glanced over at him. "I don't know. I think I'm going to click on the link."

"It'll take you to some porn site or something and they'll steal your identity or put malware on your phone. Why would you do that?"

"Maybe because I never would before today," I answered. "Maybe because I shouldn't."

"That doesn't make any sense."

"Doesn't it?" I asked. "Maybe because it doesn't matter anymore if someone steals my identity or messes up my phone. At least I'll have an excuse for not answering Levi's text." I opened the messaging app to get to the full message with the hyperlink.

"Ben, I don't think you should—"

"Too late," I interjected, tapping the link. The action opened a web browser, which loaded the web site in question. As the page rendered, my mouth began to gape. "What the…?"

Chapter Ten

I stared at the website as Matt craned his neck, trying to get a look. The page appeared as though it had been designed back in the early days of the Internet, with an ugly space background and bold, gold comic-sans lettering across the top.

STARSHIP FOR SALE!!!!

A big block of white text, hard to read against the background followed.

FOR SALE:

*One moderately used, **fully-functional** starship. Originally designed for use in the film **Space Aces Need Love Too**, this starship is both one of a kind and an important piece of movie-making lore.*

SO WHY ARE WE SELLING IT?

Unfortunately, storage fees have become prohibitive. As it's a starship, it requires a moderate amount of both square footage and secrecy to keep it safe. Rather than dumping the spacecraft into the ocean to dispose of it, we'd like to sell it to someone who will get full use out of everything the ship has to offer.

IS THAT PERSON YOU?

There's no way for us to know. But maybe you already do.

BUT WAIT… HOW MUCH DOES IT COST?

Price is negotiable. If you don't plan to take the starship into space, you'll also be responsible for paying all storage fees from the time of purchase. Plus tax.

INTERESTED?

If you're interested in owning this unique item, please reply directly to the message you received regarding this offer.

THE ADVENTURE OF A LIFETIME AWAITS!!!

I read the whole thing out loud to Matt, who was laughing loudly by the time I finished.

"Total scam," he said. "I can't believe you clicked that link. The only real starships come from NASA, SpaceX, and Blue Origin. And there's no way anybody made a spaceship for a Skinemax B-movie, functional or not." He glanced over at me. "It's probably installing malware as we speak, because nobody is dumb enough to believe any part of that ad is real. They didn't even include a picture of the ship."

"I don't believe it's real," I replied. "But the entertainment factor was worth the click, even if my identity is being stolen while we laugh about it." I looked at the screen one more time before closing the web browser. The whole thing was clearly bull-shit, but still, I couldn't help fantasizing about what it might be like if it were serious. The adventure of a lifetime. Who wouldn't want to spend the last few months of their existence gallivanting through space?

"Just try to keep yourself in check," Matt added. "Maybe you feel like the gloves can come off when it comes to taking risks, but just be careful you don't go too far. Not for yourself, but for the people around you who might become collateral damage."

"I don't think there was any harm in risking my own phone's security."

"No? What if they get all the numbers in your contact list and have even more elaborate phishing schemes to unleash on them? Or what if they use your phone to send those texts?"

I looked over at him, suddenly nervous about my carefree reaction to the spam text. "Do you think? Shit."

"In this case, probably not. It's just something for you to think about."

"Yeah, you're right. It was a dumb thing to do."

"I'm sure it'll be fine."

I nodded. "Usually they go after devices that haven't been kept up to date. I always have the latest patches. But I'll be more careful. I don't want to drag anyone else down with me."

Matt looked at me again, obviously concerned about my mental state. He didn't say anything else, returning his attention to the road. I spotted the red and yellow sign for *McRory's* up ahead. The place was both our best employer and favorite hangout, a bar and grill that did live music every Friday and Saturday night. They also just so happened to have the best burgers in town.

"At least I still have my appetite," I said. "I hope that lasts once I start hitting the meds."

"Me too," Matt agreed. He pulled into the parking lot, grabbing the closest open spot. My mind jumped back to the strange text and the web site. I should have just let it go. Maybe it was my mood or the diagnosis, but I couldn't cast it completely out of my mind. Matt got out of the car, but I stayed in the passenger seat, to open up the scam text and quickly tap out a reply.

I'm interested. Next steps?

I closed the app and turned off the screen before Matt reached my door, pushing it open.

"You okay?" he asked, resting his hand on the top of the car door and staring down at me.

"Yeah," I replied. "Just got a little dizzy when I tried to get out."

"Maybe you should skip the beers and take those meds now?" Matt suggested, motioning to the glove compartment where I had stored the pills.

"Not a chance," I replied, hopping out of the seat to show him I was okay. My ribs still throbbed when I moved, but this time I refused to show it. "Tomorrow."

Matt looked less certain than he had during our first conversation about the subject. "If you insist."

"I do."

Since it was a weeknight, *McRory's* wasn't overly crowded, though they always did good business. Matt and I were on first-name basis with everyone who worked there, including the host at the front who also happened to be our drummer, Richie.

"Hey, Mattie, Bennie," he said, smiling when we entered. "How's it going?"

"Good," I replied before Matt could even think to say anything else. "We're both good."

"You sure?" Richie pushed. "You look a little ragged, like you got beat up or something."

All three of us were friends, but not in the same way Matt and I were friends. Bandmates rather than besties, close but not close enough that I was going to tell him anything about my visit to the doctor. He knew about the coordination issues that had kept me out of the band the last few weeks, but nothing more than that, and he didn't care enough to dig for more. Which, it suddenly occurred to me, hadn't surfaced at all while I had been playing *Star Squadron*. Either something about the experience had settled the ticks or I had been lucky enough to not suffer the random twitches during the game.

"That's another story," Matt said. "But he did get beat up."

"What? Dude."

"It's nothing," I said. "You should see the other guy."

"You don't get into fights," Richie said. "Matt, yes. You, no."

"I'll tell you all about it later. Right now, I'm so freaking hungry I can't see straight."

"I hear you." He picked up two menus from behind the counter. "Follow me."

McCrory's had the look of a typical Irish pub. Dark wood, dark paint, dim lights. Being a bar, there were televisions arranged throughout. Some screens showed soccer, others football. People often told me the Shepherd's Pie was the best in town, and I believed them, but I could never bring myself to break up with my first love.

"Hey guys," one of the waitresses, Melissa, said as Richie walked us to our table. "Funny to see you here on a weeknight."

"I need a burger," I replied, licking my lips and swallowing to keep from drooling.

"And a pint," Matt said.

"Two pints," I added. "Whatever's on tap."

"Coming right up."

Richie brought us to one of the smaller booths in the corner. A private spot unofficially reserved for the most favored customers. Red leather upholstery filled in the dark oak benches on either side while a gold-framed photo of the original *McRory's* stared at us from the wall.

"We're still on for practice Saturday afternoon, right?" Richie asked Matt as we sat.

"Absolutely," he replied. "We've got the gig here at nine."

"Sweet." He put his hand out, fist-bumping both of us. "Enjoy the grub, chums."

"See you later, bro."

Matt opened his menu. I didn't bother. Even if I wasn't desperate for a half-pound slab draped in thick aged cheddar and slathered with onion rings and barbecue sauce, I knew the whole bill of fare by heart. I just wasn't interested in any of it.

Melissa returned to the table, dropping off two pints of beer with enough panache that some of the suds flowed over the sides and onto the table. She quickly mopped the spill up with a towel.

"So how are you boys doing tonight?" she asked.

She always called us boys, even though she was only a couple of years older than us. Maybe because we had only been legal in the place for the last few months, though Junior had often served whoever wasn't driving post-closing prior to our twenty-first birthdays.

I had waited so long to imbibe openly and my moment of opportunity was already dwindling.

That thought led me to another, and I pulled out my phone to check the notifications. I hadn't felt it vibrate against my leg, but maybe I had missed something.

"We're good," Matt replied, giving me a slightly annoyed look because I went right to the phone. "Ben got beat up by some teenage jock at *VR Awesome!*. Asshole totally ambushed him because we destroyed him in the game."

"Really? Ben, are you okay?"

"Yeah, I'm fine," I replied distantly, turning on the screen and feeling a sense of dismay that my text to the scam number had gone unreturned. Of course, I should have expected it. But something in me wanted the adventure of a lifetime so damn bad.

"Oookay," Melissa said. "Sorry to interrupt."

I put down the phone, embarrassed. "Sorry, Mel. I'm being an ass. I'm fine, really. Bruised ribs, nothing major. How are you?"

"Loving life," she replied. "I've got a date after my shift."

"Anyone we know?"

"No. I met him on *Tinder*."

"Ouch," Matt said. "Not your best idea."

"Thanks, Dad," Mel said. "He's cute. Besides, we're having a bite right here, so nothing to worry about. But really, thank you for caring."

"That's what I do."

Mel smiled and lifted her order tablet. "Ben, I already know what you want, unless you decided to try something different?"

"Nope."

"Didn't think so. Matt, what's your pleasure?"

"Shepherd's Pie," he replied. "Nice and crispy. And an order of potato skins, extra bacon."

"Sounds delish." She finished entering the order. "You two need anything else?"

"Not right now."

"Gotcha. Be back soonish."

She wandered off. I picked up my pint and took a drink before leaning back on the bench, not realizing how tense I had gotten until I let my muscles relax.

"Another message from Levi?" Matt asked, wondering why I had picked up my phone so urgently.

"No. Though I still need to do something about that."

"Your mom?"

"No. I thought I felt it vibrate, but it was a phantom shiver." I put it face-down on the table and looked up at the nearest television. "Any idea who's playing?"

"I think it's Inter and Napoli," Matt replied. "I didn't get the score before they cut to commercial, but I expect Inter to wipe the floor with those Neopolitans."

"Want to bet?"

"You haven't seen the score yet."

"I only have about eight hundred dollars to my name. I can't bet that much. Five bucks?"

"Sure."

Both of our eyes shot to my phone when it vibrated for real. I reached for it but Matt was faster, grabbing it and turning it to check the notification. My heart immediately started pounding, wondering if the scammer had actually replied.

Chapter Eleven

"It's your mom," Matt said, eying me suspiciously. "She wants to know how you're feeling."

"Can I have my phone back?" I said, leaning across the table in an effort to grab it from him. I jammed my ribs into the edge of the table and jerked back, wincing in pain.

"Why so jumpy?" Matt asked, sliding my phone across the table. "Are you that nervous about Levi?"

"No. I just don't think you should take another man's phone."

"Yeah, right. We've both done it plenty of times before. What's the real reason?"

I picked up my phone and opened the text from Mom.

Ben, I got some more info from the doctor. We can go over it later. How do you feel?

"This is the last thing I want to think about right now," I said, quickly writing her back.

Same as this morning. All's good. Out with Matt. We can catch up tomorrow.

I closed her message, my gaze drifting to the one I had sent prior. Still no response to it. Total scam. Oh well.

"Wait a minute," Matt said, catching on. He shook his head. "You didn't respond to that spam text, did you?"

"Maybe," I replied.

"What? Ben…"

"I didn't see any harm in writing back. If they already hacked me then they already hacked me. And what if there's something to it?"

"We both know there isn't anything to it. Not anything good, anyway." He paused, his initial irate reaction settling. "I know you're trying to ignore everything until tomorrow, but I have to say. This reeks of grasping at straws."

I stared at him and sighed. "Yeah, I guess it does." The tears came to my eyes unbidden. Damn them. "Matt, I'm not ready to die. I've barely had a chance to live."

His eyes welled a little too. "I know."

It was all he said. All he had to say. At that moment, we could either both break down into a pair of bawling idiots or I could suck it up and shove it back. The scam text was just that. A scam. Of course I was disappointed, but I had to deal with things as they were, not how I wished they might be.

I exhaled sharply and wiped at my eyes as nonchalantly as I could. Matt did the same. We sat back in silence, just kind of being there together for a few quiet, peaceful minutes.

"You two have a spat?" Melissa said when she came back with our food. The sight of the burger immediately lifted my spirits. My stomach growled in approval.

"No, just relaxing," Matt said. "I think the rush from the fight just wore off, that's all."

She put the food down in front of us, along with bottles of ketchup and mustard. "I want to hear more about this," she said, sliding into the booth next to Matt.

"Don't you have work to do?" I asked, reaching for the burger.

"Yeah. But you try to look out for me. I want to do the same for you."

"Thank you. There's nothing you can do. Besides, it's over." I took a bite of the burger. One had never tasted better. I closed my eyes to focus my sense on my taste buds, enjoying every nuance of the combined flavors of beef, cheese, fried and breaded onion, and barbecue sauce. So good.

When I opened my eyes a few seconds later, Melissa had left. Instead, a stubbled, square-jawed stranger in an overcoat, tweed suit, and pork pie hat stood next to the table, glaring down at me with sharp eyes. Matt still sat across from him, looking shell-shocked.

I swallowed my bite of burger, embarrassed when I realized I had a bit of barbecue sauce on my chin. I moved to wipe it off with a napkin, only to have the stranger hold out a gilded handkerchief.

"Uh, thanks," I said. "But I think it'll stain."

"Take it," he urged, his hard voice not the kind anyone rejected.

I took the handkerchief and wiped my chin, then folded it to put the mess on the inside and handed it back.

"Keep it," he said.

"Who are you?" Matt finally asked.

The man reached under his coat in a manner that suggested he might pull a gun as easily as the business card he actually produced. He dropped it between us on the table.

Mr. Keep
ss4sale.com

My eyebrows went up. My heart pounded. My head whipped back to the man. I opened my mouth to speak before realizing I hadn't given the guy an address or anything. Damn it, he *did* hack my phone. The scam must have given him access to my GPS and led him right to me.

I suddenly felt lucky he had pulled the business card instead of a piece. More for Matt's sake than mine.

"What's the matter?" Keep said. "You have brain damage or something?"

It was an odd statement that caught me off-guard, and put me even more on-guard. "What? Uhh…"

"You sent that scam text," Matt said, not as intimidated by Keep as I was. "The one my friend shouldn't have replied to."

"Shouldn't have replied to?" Keep said. "Why not? You don't want a starship?"

"Huh?" I said, still trying to catch up.

"All three of us know there isn't any starship," Matt pressed.

"You think you know something, but you really don't know anything, kid. Mind if I join you?"

He didn't wait for Matt to respond before sliding in where Melissa had been.

"Wait a second, Dick Tracy," I said, regaining my courage. "This is all really weird."

Keep snatched a french fry from my plate, eating half and waving the other end as he spoke. "What's weird? I sent you a message, you responded, badabing badaboom. No tricks. No bullshit. It's that simple."

"There's nothing simple about it," I said. "You can't possibly have a functional starship."

"Keyword: functional," Matt added.

"Why not?"

"Because if you had a functional starship, number one, it would belong to the government or SpaceX or something. And number two, you wouldn't be advertising it in the most scammy way possible with a website that looks like it was built twenty years ago."

"You don't like the web site? I thought it was concise."

"Not really my point."

"Well, how would you advertise a starship for sale then, fancy pants?"

"I don't know. I never really thought about it."

"Well, think about it now; I'll wait."

Keep shoved the other half of the fry in his mouth, reaching for another one.

"Do you mind?" I asked. "Those are my fries."

"Didn't your mother ever teach you to share, or are you an only child or something?" Keep said, grabbing a few fries anyway.

"Okay, if I had a functional starship, and this is all conjecture because it's bullshit, I would probably go to the government first. Or maybe Gates or Bezos or Musk, or someone like that."

Keep whistled and shook his head. "Kid, you're too naive. In case you didn't get the hint, we're trying to keep this transaction on the down low. Bringing it to some high profile rich guy is the opposite of that."

"Why are you keeping it on the down low?" I asked. "Assuming this isn't some weird, intricate con job."

"Do you know what would happen if the Feds found out we had a working starship? They'd confiscate it *toot sweet*, and then start asking a lot of questions I really don't want to answer."

"Like where you got a working starship?" Matt asked.

"Bingo!" Keep said.

"Where did you get a working starship?" I asked.

Keep smiled. "Now you're catching on, kid. That's the million dollar question, isn't it?" He shoved the fries into his mouth, speaking with them in there, his voice slightly muffled. "Before I answer it, I need to know if you're serious about purchasing said starship."

"The web page didn't say how much it cost," I said.

"It's up for discussion."

"Well, if there's any possible way that I could afford to buy a working starship, I would do it sight unseen. If I actually believed you. Why are you really here? What kind of con is this?"

"No con. No scam. No tricks. Are you gonna eat that burger? Because you haven't touched it since I got here."

He started reaching for it. I practically swatted his hand away. "I'm eating that burger," I growled.

"Sure kid," he said, settling for another fry instead. "You seem serious about this to me." He looked at Matt. "What about you?"

"If this isn't a scam, which I can't even start to believe it isn't, then yeah, I'm interested."

"Good. You two have names?"

"Ben," I said, my thumb pointing at me. "And he's Matt."

"Ben and Matt. Pleasure meeting you." He held out his hand. I took it, noticing how calloused it was when we shook. Matt accepted his handshake too. "Finish eating, I'll be waiting outside."

"Waiting for what?" I asked.

"Kid, you need to wise up a little or you aren't going to last two seconds out there. Waiting to bring you to the ship. I don't expect you to buy sight unseen. I'm not a crook."

He stood up, taking a few more fries from my plate before heading for the exit.

Matt and I stared at one another in shocked silence for at least twenty seconds. Then Matt motioned to my burger with his head. "You should eat that."

"Yeah," I replied, picking it up and holding it in front of my face. "You still think this is a scam?"

"Yeah. I do."

"I'm going anyway."

"I know. I'm coming with you."

"You don't have to. If anything happens to me, it's not a big deal. I'm already a dead man walking. You have a lot more to lose."

"I'm coming with you," Matt repeated. "Now shut up and eat your burger."

I nodded, bringing it closer to my lips before pausing again. "What if this isn't a scam?"

"Then I guess we're going to have the adventure of a lifetime."

Chapter Twelve

We left *McRory's* twenty minutes later. Butterflies replaced the growling in my stomach, the burger satisfying but dulled by the nervous excitement around what might lie ahead. Matt and I hadn't spoken a single word to one another while we ate, both of our minds filled with conflicting thoughts. On one hand, I could imagine Keep leading us to a large warehouse in the middle of nowhere, pushing open a large door to let the light in and revealing the coolest thing I had ever seen in real life. On the other, I could picture him driving us off into some secluded part of the woods, binding and gagging us, and shooting us both in the head execution style before burying our bodies. I was okay with that possibility for myself. But not for Matt. I would have tried harder to talk him out of coming, except I knew him well enough to know he would never acquiesce.

Matt's loyalty was his greatest strength and his biggest weakness. Although, I guess I was the same way.

McRory's parking lot wasn't very big, and Mr. Keep was easy to find. He waited just outside the entrance, leaning up against the side of a stretch limousine, one hand in the pocket of his trousers, the other clutching a cigarette. He nodded when we spotted us, pulling a pocket watch out and checking the time.

"Your stomachs feel okay?" he asked when we reached him. "Twenty minutes is a quick meal."

"If I hadn't been so hungry, I don't think I would have been able to eat at all," I replied.

"Nervous then?"

"Yeah. Very."

"In a good way, I hope."

"Mixed."

"Because you think I'm going to drive you off into a secluded part of the woods, bind and gag you and shoot you in the head execution style."

"Who…are…you?" I stared at him, wondering if he had done something to my phone that allowed him to read my mind. But that was impossible, wasn't it? As impossible as someone selling a fully functional starship to a pair of 21-year-olds.

"Wouldn't you like to know," he answered, grinning as he straightened away from the car and took one last pull on his cigarette. Flicking the stub away, he opened the limo's rear passenger door. "Let's get this show on the road, shall we? I don't have all night."

"If you don't mind, we'll follow you in my car," Matt said.

"If you don't mind, I do mind," Keep replied. "Sorry, kid. Like I said, I need to keep this venture on the down low. Which means obfuscating the exact location of the merchandise. Which means we all ride together in the back of the car. The windows are tinted on the inside so you won't be able to see where we're going."

"Until we reach the woods," Matt quipped. He pulled out his phone. "GPS?"

Keep dropped the watch, his hand whipping out to grab Matt's phone just as the watch reached the end of the chain dangling from his hip. Matt's cell quickly disappeared inside Keep's coat. "Thank you." He turned to me. "Yours too. No GPS."

I handed him my phone without complaint. "Just let me know if I get a text from Levi, okay?"

"Levi? Who's that? Your girlfriend?"

"Not yet."

He smirked. "I get it. No GPS. No messages. Airplane mode only. Either get in the car now or lose your chance forever. I'm not showing the merchandise to every muggle with a simple curious streak."

"Did you just reference Harry Potter?" I asked. "Does that mean there's magic involved?"

"It's a wonder I haven't magically ditched you two already," Keep answered. "Decision time, chads."

I ducked into the limo, moving to the soft leather seat across the back. Matt joined me there, while Keep took the rear-facing seat directly behind the driver, closing the door as he entered. I couldn't see the chauffeur past the solid partition between us.

Like he had said, the windows were nearly opaque on the inside, allowing just enough light through for the limo to feel less like a submarine than a car. Making out the landscape beyond the car was impossible.

Keep tapped on the partition behind him. The car got underway.

My heart continued pounding, my entire body shaking with nervous excitement. For as badly as the day had started, if this turned out to be half as cool as it seemed, it would make it all worth it.

Well, maybe not all. Nothing could account for dying.

"Wait!" I snapped. "I need to get something from Matt's car."

"This is a non-stop flight, kid," Keep replied.

"Please? It's important."

"I question that opinion."

"It's medicine. I need it for my...allergies." Keep squinted one eye at me, clearly not convinced I was being wholly honest. I didn't want to tell him how sick I was, worried he would decide I didn't make a good fit as a buyer.

"Fine," he decided, tapping on the partition again.

"I'll get it," Matt said.

The car stopped. Matt jumped out on the driver's side and closed the door, vanishing from sight until he opened it again a half minute later, my bag of meds in hand. He tossed them to me and settled in the seat again.

"Better?" Keep asked.

"Much," I replied, shoving the bag into the pocket of my hoodie. "Thank you."

"No more stops. No breaks. No questions until we get there. In fact, it's probably better if you don't say anything at all."

"How long will it take to get there?" I asked.

Keep coughed softly and glared at me, reminding me I had just asked a question. Matt snorted, half grinning.

"Right." I sank down into the seat, glancing at Matt. We made eye contact, his wisp of a smile still tugging at his lips.

This whole thing was crazy. Crazy enough a part of me wondered if I was still at the hospital office, the entire series of events since I had closed the door to Doctor Haines' office taking place in my diseased head.

I pinched myself as hard as I could, the pain enough to make my eyes water.

"What are you doing?" Keep asked.

"Making sure I'm not hallucinating," I replied.

He looked at me like I had two heads. "Kid, if this is your idea of a daydream, I think you need to set the bar a little higher."

Matt laughed. "Yeah. You could have at least conjured up a couple of girls, or made us rockstars or something. Instead, you gave yourself bruised ribs and a meeting with the door-to-door vacuum cleaner salesman that time forgot."

Heat rushed to my face, and I barely registered Keep's indignant look at Matt over the salesman comment.

Wherever we were going, I couldn't wait to get there.

Chapter Thirteen

Despite my excitement, the silent car ride put me to sleep. It didn't help that the limo was essentially sound-proof, with zero road or engine noise seeping into the rear compartment. It also didn't help that Mr. Keep dozed off himself, lowering his pork pie hat over his face and snoring softly in the seat opposite Matt and me.

I don't think Matt slept at all, but I wasn't awake to know for sure. He shook me some time later, and when I opened my eyes I realized the car had come to a stop. Keep was awake too, looking at his cellphone.

"Ah, Sleeping Beauty awakens," he said, glancing up at me. "Did you have a nice nap, kid?"

"I guess so," I replied. "Can I ask a question now?"

"That counts as a question, you know. But I'm in a better mood, so shoot."

"Are we there yet?"

He actually laughed, revealing a perfect smile. "We're there yet," he affirmed. "I was just checking some last minute details. Do me a favor and reach under the seat. There should be a couple of umbrellas there."

"It's raining?"

"That's usually why you would want an umbrella."

Matt smirked, leaning down and opening a small drawer under our seat. One side had a couple of small bottles of bourbon, the other a pair of umbrellas.

"I don't need one," I said. "I'm not going to melt."

"I like your moxie, kid," Keep said. "Out we go."

He pushed open the passenger side door, allowing the outside noise in once more. I heard the rain hitting hard ground, the car, and something else solid enough to cause an echo when it struck, a symphony that surrounded us. I followed Keep out the door, immediately looking around to get my bearings.

Stacks of steel shipping containers. They were laid out in an array of colors with a variety of logos and company names plastered on the sides. The smell of low tide gave away our general location. A port, one of four that were reachable by car within a relatively moderate length of time.

At least we weren't in a forest. Then again, it would be easy enough for Keep to slaughter us and shove us in one of the containers, never to be seen again.

"This isn't very secret," Matt scoffed, closing the car door after he got out. "I don't need GPS to narrow down where we are."

"Is that right?" Keep asked.

"Yes, sir," Matt answered.

"Well, I guess you outsmarted me there. This way, Sherlock." He walked away from the car toward one of the aisles between the stacks of containers.

I sidled up to Matt as we followed, jabbing him in the side with my elbow. "Do you have to be such a jerk?"

"What? He made such a huge deal of tinting the

windows and soundproofing the interior just to bring us to an easily recognizable place. It seems ridiculous."

"At least he hasn't killed us."

"Yet. Besides, it's not like he isn't being caustic himself."

I lowered my voice, leaning in close. "Look, we both know that this thing is going to be too expensive for us to actually buy, unless it's a one-sixtieth scale model tucked into one of these containers. I don't know why Keep doesn't seem to know that too. I'd like to at least get a look at the thing before you piss him off enough to decide not to let us see the merchandise." I said the last part mimicking Keep's gruff voice.

"Maybe he thinks we're crypto-rich or something," Matt said. "Or maybe he hasn't gotten many idiots replying to something that so clearly looks like a scam. Because, whether he kills us or not, until proven otherwise, my opinion is that this is some kind of weird, elaborate scam."

"I heard that," Keep said, stopping and turning to face us. "How many times do I have to tell you yokels that this isn't a scam?"

"Seeing is believing, sir," Matt answered.

"Well, in that case." He waved us over as he retrieved his phone from his pocket. We were at an intersection among the stacks of containers.

"That way," Keep added, pointing to my left. We turned in that direction, able to see a dark shadow of *something* at the end of the row, surrounded by containers on three sides.

My heart raced again. It didn't have the shape of a starship, but at least it was there, whatever *it* was.

"And here...we...go!" Keep said, tapping on his phone.

Light exploded from the object at the end of the aisle, so bright it blinded me, leaving me unable to see its source. I shied away, bringing my hands to my eyes and instinctively ducking my head as though Keep were about to hit me with something or shoot me right where I stood. I could barely see Matt, but he spun to face Keep, hands coming up into a fighting posture though it was obvious he couldn't see a thing.

"Dang it all," Keep said. "A little too bright. Hold on."

The intensity of the light diminished, though I continued to see flashes behind my eyes that I tried to clear with a couple of blinks. Still squinting, I returned my attention to the object, now able to see that it had two large lights below four smaller ones, all of them illuminating the area and giving me my first good look at…

"*That's* a starship?"

Chapter Fourteen

"Is that a bouncy house?" Matt asked.

I stared at the object, confused. "It looks more like Optimus Prime's head."

Nearly forty feet in height and close to that in width, the starship didn't look like a starship at all. Generally oblong in shape, it appeared to be made from what appeared to be hundreds of individual pieces of slightly rusted and worn sheet metal, likely stripped from cars or even the containers that surrounded the so-called ship. A large rectangular protrusion near its base looked like an open mouth, the ridged metal blocking it giving the appearance of a straight, toothy grin. The lights sat above the mouth, between it and a wide stretch of dark material that looked more like plastic than metal and served as a visor for the eyes. Large triangular ears stuck up on both sides of the head, made of the same patch-work metal as the rest, and antennae jutted out across the top of the scalp like hair.

What really stood out to me were the guns.

Two large, double-barreled turrets sat on either side

of the head, just below the ears, while a matching set was positioned on the ears themselves. The mounts for both suggested they could be rotated, which would give them a three-hundred sixty degree range of fire from front to back when in action. Assuming they could even fire at all, which by their battered condition, didn't seem likely. Keep had advertised that the starship for sale had originally been produced as a low-budget movie prop, and that was exactly what it looked like.

"Who's Optimus Prime?" Keep asked, standing beside me as he lit a cigarette.

"You've never heard of the Transformers?" I asked. "Robots in disguise?"

"Maybe it's before my time."

"I think it's after your time," Matt said. "Way after."

Keep shrugged. "If you're saying you think it looks like a robot's head, you're dead on. That is indeed the head of a robot. Or was. Now it's a starship. Badabing badaboom. What do you think?"

"Was the rest of the robot made from scrap metal too?" Matt asked.

"You're a real smart ass, you know that?" Keep said, casting a sidelong glare at him. "Of course, there's a story that goes along with the merchandise."

"Which you won't want to tell us if we aren't interested, right?" I asked.

"Bingo bango boingo! Give the kid a prize." He took a drag on a cigarette I hadn't seen him light, blowing smoke rings into the rain. "I know she isn't much to look at, kid, but she's got it where it counts."

"Geez." Matt's lip curled in disgust. "Where have I heard that line before?"

"What do you mean?" Keep asked.

"Nevermind. Are you going to show us the inside?"

"If you're still interested."

"I am," I answered.

"Ben, hold up a second," Matt said. "Mr. Keep, you've gone to a lot of trouble to bring us here and show us this…thing. You keep saying it isn't a scam. But hasn't it occurred to you that Ben and I probably can't afford a starship? We probably have a thousand dollars between us, and you could scrap that thing for ten times that much. Nevermind paying for the storage which you said you can't even afford, but you have a limo and chauffeur."

Keep looked at Matt like he had two heads. "I don't know what you're talking about."

"I'm saying even if that thing is a real starship, which after seeing it makes the idea more ludicrous than before, we don't have any money. We can't buy anything but lunch."

"Matt," I complained. I had asked him not to ruin things before I got to at least see the ship, meaning the inside too.

"I'm sorry, Ben. But this started as a bad idea, and it's still a bad idea. How can you say you want to keep things on the down low but you'll show the so-called starship to anyone who responds to your stupid text? Nothing about this makes any sense. I feel like there are hidden cameras somewhere and we'll be on YouTube by tomorrow morning.

Look at these idiot kids. I can't believe they fell for that."

Keep sucked some more nicotine and tar out of his cigarette and calmly blew it out, unruffled by Matt's diatribe. A smirk played at the corner of his mouth. "You're his best friend, right?" he asked Matt.

"Yeah. So?"

"So why are you keeping secrets from him, Mattie? He isn't keeping any from you."

"What?" Matt said.

Keep dropped the spent cigarette on the ground and ground it out despite the rain. "He kept you in the loop. Why don't you return the favor?"

"I don't know what you're talking about."

Keep looked at me. "He knows what Keep is talking about," he said as though he was narrating a television show.

"Matt?" I said, "what's he talking about?"

Matt shook his head. "I…how the hell do you know about that, Keep?"

"Know about what?" I asked, growing more confused by the second.

"Do you think I'll just bring just anyone out here without due diligence? Like you said, that wouldn't be very smart of me. Do you want to tell him, or should I?"

"Tell me what?" I snapped, getting annoyed. "Matt, what the hell?"

Matt dropped his defenses, exhaling sharply. "I didn't want to tell you because honestly, with what you're going through it's the last thing on my mind. And how could I tell you something so positive for me when you're dealing with something so bad for you? It's not because I wanted to keep it a secret. There's just no good way or time to say it."

"Say what?"

"I got a letter in the mail two weeks ago from an attorney. The executor of my mother's will."

"Your mother?" I said. "Wait. She's dead?"

"Yeah."

"Matt, I'm sorry."

Matt shrugged. "She didn't give a shit about me, why

should I care about her? It doesn't matter to me that she's gone. Except apparently she managed to fall into some money during the sixteen years since she left us."

I swallowed a growing lump in my throat. "How much money?"

"I don't know exactly, but the deposit to my bank account was four million."

"Your mother left you four million dollars?" I said, shocked.

He looked at the ground, embarrassed by the wind-fall. "Yeah. I guess she did."

"Why didn't you tell me? That's awesome."

"I'd give it all back if it could save your life," he replied. "And maybe it can help with the meds and treatment and stuff. I…" He trailed off, refusing to get emotional.

I stared at him. He had always been more handsome, more confident, more charismatic. He had a great singing voice, a nice car, and attracted the prettiest women. And now he had fallen into millions of dollars from the mother who had abandoned him. And I was dying. I know it was wrong, but I suddenly felt totally shit on by the universe and completely jealous.

Which was exactly why he hadn't wanted to tell me about the money in the first place.

I swallowed the negative emotions, fighting hard to still be happy for Matt. Maybe he thought he could help me, and I appreciated that thought, but there were some things money couldn't fix, and I was one of them. I wouldn't want him to throw it all away on a lost cause.

"I can see you get it now," Matt said, reading my face. He looked at Keep. "You're an asshole for dragging it out of me."

"An asshole with a starship for sale," Keep replied. "Talking to a kid with more money than sense."

"What did you say?" Matt growled.

"If the shoe fits, kid," Keep retorted, still completely calm even though Matt took a step toward him with doubled fists.

I put the back of my hand up in front of Matt to hold him back and turned to face Keep. "Mister Keep, I appreciate you bringing us out here to see your ship. But the fact is, I'm the one who was interested, and whether Matt has money or not, I'm the one who was delusionally hoping this whole deal was real. Even if that robot head is also a starship, I can't pay for it."

"He can," Keep said, motioning to Matt.

"That's his money, not mine. I wouldn't dream of asking him to buy that piece of junk for me, and you should be ashamed of yourself for even thinking I would do that, even if he offered. He can live a pretty good, comfortable life with that money." I glanced over at the starship, still a little disappointed I hadn't seen the inside. "Just take us back to *McRory's*, okay?"

Keep's eyes drifted from me to Matt and back again. He sighed loudly and nodded. "Okay, kid. If that's what you want. I won't say I'm not a little disappointed. I had hoped I finally found the one."

"Sorry to disappoint you, sir," I replied.

"Ben, wait," Matt said.

"Matt, no," I answered. "Let's just go, okay? I've had enough of today already. I want to go home and forget about all of this."

"Come on, man. Don't be like that. Let's at least take a look inside. We came all this way, right?"

The offer tempted me. I didn't bite. I had gotten my hopes up too high on something that never promised to be more than a fun diversion at best. The fact that it hadn't turned out to be a total scam felt like a hollow victory, but a victory all the same.

"No. The whole idea of a robot head starship is ridiculous, and the idea of you even considering buying something that looks like it cost about a hundred grand to build for millions for a guy who'll be dead a year from now is even more insane. So there's no reason to go inside."

I turned away from him, walking back toward the limo, Keep beside me.

"Thanks for coming, kid," he said. "To be honest, you're the first potential customer I've had in quite a while."

"Yeah well, maybe you should think about changing your approach," I replied.

"Ben," Matt shouted. "Ben, wait!" I didn't stop until he caught up to me and grabbed my arm, forcing me to look at him. "I don't have the power to save your life. If I did, I would use it in a second. But what the hell is money good for if it can't be used for something good? There's still something I can give you."

"What's that?" I asked.

"Maybe the adventure of a lifetime?"

I stared at him, knowing from his expression how much he wanted this and how little he cared about the money. I shook my head. "I can't accept it."

"I'm not asking. It's my money, I can spend it how I want. Keep, show me the inside."

Keep smiled as he turned to face Matt again. "Yes, sir. Your wish is my command." He didn't even look at me as he started back toward the ship.

"You coming, Ben?" Matt asked.

I couldn't keep myself from smiling, the excitement

flooding back into me like a raging river. "Hell, yeah, I'm coming," I replied. "But—"

"Enough. Just go with the flow."

I started after them, slowing a moment later when the sound of engines echoed through the stacks of shipping containers.

Mr. Keep came to a sudden stop, spinning around and freezing to listen. His face hardened as his eyes pierced mine, the fear in his gaze obvious.

"Damn it, they found me. Run!"

Chapter Fifteen

Keep's fear transferred to me, and instead of running like he suggested, I froze. My eyes shifted to the end of the container stack to my right, where two pairs of wide, thin headlights appeared, instantly bathing me in blue light. I whipped my head to the left as two more vehicles braked to a stop directly in front of me.

"Ben, come on!" Matt said, grabbing my arm and tugging me toward the starship. Keep had a ten foot headstart on us, and he didn't slow or look back to make sure we were following.

I broke out of my stupor, joining Matt in a sprint for the ship. Splashing through puddles quickly left my sneakers soaked through to my feet, my heart pounding hard.

Too hard.

The flow of oxygen into my head started the domino effect. Within seconds, a wave of vertigo hit me like a jackhammer and I took a knee, planting my hand on the asphalt and closing my eyes to stop the world from spinning. Nausea followed, the pounding in my skull and ringing in my ears nearly loud enough to drown out the motors of the incoming vehicles.

Oddly enough, it was at that moment I realized there was something off about the engines of the cars. They weren't making a sound I could easily associate with an internal combustion engine or even an electric motor. Come to think of it, their headlights had a pattern I didn't think I had ever seen before either.

"Ben," Matt said, stopping and coming back to me. He kneeled at my side, putting his arm around my shoulders. "Are you okay?"

"Dizzy," I replied. "Go on. I'm fine." I tried to get up and nearly blacked out.

"Yeah, right."

"What are you two doing?" Keep shouted from somewhere ahead. I looked up, finding him near the starship's base. A ramp had extended from the mouth, offering entry. "Come on!"

Matt helped me to my feet as Keep reached into his pocket, producing what appeared to be a gun. He aimed it over our heads and pulled the trigger, and I watched as green bolts of light zipped across the gap between him and these new adversaries.

He used the ramp for cover as return fire burned past us, a few of the bolts close enough I could hear them sizzle past my ears.

"What the hell?" I complained as Matt dragged me back to the ground, pushing me flat and smothering me with his body.

"Clicking on a damn scam link," he cursed in my ear. "Great idea."

I turned my head to look at him. How was I supposed to know this would happen? I didn't even know what *this* was.

A loud rumble joined the mix of sounds. This one I did recognize as a regular car engine. The limousine. The flashes of light around us stopped, and when I turned my head, I saw a handful of figures in dark uniforms climbing out of the parked vehicles, none of them street legal. They didn't even have wheels. Instead, they floated a few inches above the pavement as if gravity were a mere suggestion. They were all facing the adjacent aisle between containers, their attention and firepower fixed on the limo charging directly toward them.

Matt pulled me forcefully to my feet, practically lifting me off the ground as he tugged me toward the starship and Mr. Keep waiting at the ramp leading into the starship. I kept my head turned to watch the action behind us, mouth gaping as the limo approached the uniformed men without slowing. Recognizing the kamikaze move and finding their light blasts ineffective against the car, they scattered as the limo plowed into the midst of their vehicles, sending them spinning away. One smashed into the other two floaters that had come from the opposite direction. The other spun into one of the attackers, throwing him against a shipping container. He slid down the side of it and didn't move again.

The rest of their assailants turned back to the limo, opening fire on it at point blank range. The concentrated blasts of light dissolved the limo's windshield, melting the glass. And then the driver.

I cringed at the sight, my nausea intensifying as we reached the ramp. The robot head felt a lot bigger up close than it had from a distance. The mouth was large enough to swallow a jet fighter, and the curve of it loomed overhead.

"About time you two got here," Keep said. "Don't look up."

I didn't know what he meant until I glanced over my shoulder. The lights that had blinded us earlier had regained their intensity. Suddenly unable to see, their adversaries at the intersection threw up their arms to shield their eyes. The additional illumination allowed me to better make them out. Thin and lanky, their black uniforms looked more like fitted superhero suits with Daft Punk helmets covering their entire heads.

"Get inside," Keep said, joining us on the ramp. "This is going to get violent."

Part of the ridged metal slid aside, revealing an entryway into the ship. Keep tried to shoo us through, but I resisted, disgustingly curious about the promised carnage.

The limo's sunroof exploded upward, immediately followed by a spinning, multi-colored blur vaulting out of the new opening. It flew straight for the stunned punks, a fiery red fan sweeping out from either side of it, the razor-sharp edges eviscerating three of the punks in the blink of an eye. The remaining four fired at the blur, their bolts captured by the fans and thrown back at them. They collapsed almost in unison, tumbling to the wet pavement, steaming holes in their helmets.

"Frigging hell," I muttered, swallowing the bile rising into my throat. The multicolored blur turned toward us, finally slowing down.

A diminutive woman took the blur's place. She had pink hair tied in a pair of pigtails, a narrow, mischievous face, a tiny nose and thin lips. Dressed in a yellow shirt and a red skirt with a bright blue jacket and orange high-tops, the combination of her comical appearance and obvious aptitude for killing scared the living crap out of me.

She held a pair of glowing rods in her hands, which seemed to drip pure energy onto the ground, where it evaporated the moisture, surrounding her in steam. She did something to the rods and the charge vanished, leaving them dark. A quick move made them disappear to somewhere else on her person.

"Who is that?" Matt asked. At the same time, I leaned over the side of the ramp and finally lost control of my esophagus, spewing my dinner onto the ground in front of the robot head.

"That's my personal assistant," Keep replied once I had finished puking. The woman literally skipped down the aisle to us. "Alter, these are our customers, Ben and Matt. Fellows, this is Alter."

"Uh, hi," Matt said in a tone I hadn't heard before. It sounded like a mix between completely appalled and wholly intrigued.

I wiped my mouth with the sleeve of my hoodie, keeping my barf breath angled away from her. "Good to meet you, Alter."

She didn't say anything, choosing a curtsy instead. The killing machine from fifteen seconds ago had turned into a demure waif.

"My apologies for the interruption," Keep said. "Like I told you, I've been trying to keep the details of this potential sale from reaching certain avenues. Apparently, my efforts have failed."

"Those people were trying to kill us," Matt said breathlessly, the reality of the situation catching up to him as the adrenaline began to fade.

"Trying, yes," Keep agreed. "Succeeding, no." He gestured up the ramp. "Shall we?"

Chapter Sixteen

When Keep ushered us into the ship, I was still a little shaky, my mind struggling to catch up to what had just happened outside. A series of spotlights immediately activated, bathing the interior in such stunning relief that all the images of disembowelment and death that had been flashing through my head quickly disappeared.

All my negative thoughts drained away with them, replaced by confused awe. While the action outside had gone a long way toward settling any lingering doubts I had about Keep's sincerity over the nature of the robot head, the inside visuals sealed the deal.

The small entrance emptied into a combination hangar/cargo bay, with a metal grated deck under which ran bundles of cables and pipes. The walls were slightly rusted and worn like the exterior, but they were also lined with numerous crates, boxes, and shelves either bolted down or held fast by thick netting. A set of metal stairs ran up both sides of the open space to an overhang, an interior hatch visible through the grated floor. The lights jutted out from the flat ceiling above the overhang, incandescent bulbs that didn't quite feel out of place.

More exciting than that, a smaller craft rested on the deck in front of me. Painted dark purple, it was about half the size of a jet fighter, sleek and slender, with a raised canopy in the center and a bulge in the rear that housed a massive thruster. A pair of gun turrets were mounted under each rounded delta wing, along with a trio of tubes I assumed held projectiles of some kind.

The excitement didn't last. The sight of the weaponry dragged me back to what had just happened outside, turning my stomach over again in an instant. Everything around me felt so surreal, and I wanted so much to stay in that place of amazed, shocked, awe.

But I couldn't.

"Keep, I want to know what's going on," I said, turning to face him. "Right now."

"I'm not sure I understand what you mean," Keep replied, somehow maintaining a straight face.

"Are you kidding?" Matt snapped, his voice rising as he spoke. "Your personal assistant just killed eight people and trashed four cars, which I don't think were actually cars because they were *floating*."

Alter casually moved into place between Matt and Keep, looking up at him with big, innocent eyes.

Keep put up his hands in surrender. "Yeah. An unfortunate interlude. I'll get to that, I promise. But let's finish the tour first, okay? If you're still interested when we're done, then we can talk a little more about the… how should I put this? Complete picture."

"Complete picture?" I said.

"Like a Carfax for starships. I think it's pretty obvious this one has been around the block once or twice."

"Especially considering it used to be on the neck of a robot," Matt said. "One that must have been what? Three hundred feet tall? What did you use it for? Fighting Godzilla?"

"Kid, I think you let your imagination run away from you a bit too much."

"What else are we supposed to do when you won't tell us anything?" I asked. "Those people were after you for a reason. What are you, some kind of intergalactic criminal?"

"I already told you, I'm not a crook. I'm a salesman, trying to make a deal."

"And that's all you are? A salesman?"

"Yes, sir."

"I don't believe you."

"Me either," Matt said. "Honestly, my instinct is to get the hell out of here and call the police, but I think you'd probably kill them too."

"Which should be a good clue for you, Sherlock. If I wanted either of you dead, you would have been ten times over by now. If I didn't care about your survival, I could have left you out there at the mercy of the duke's minions. So please, can we finish the tour?"

"Why bother?" I said. "People are dead because of you. Because of this ship. I don't want anything to do with that."

"For one thing, they aren't people," Keep retorted. "For another, I was well within my rights to kill them. You both saw that it was self-defense. You should be grateful. Alter saved your lives."

"Thank you, Alter," Matt said, glancing at her. She smiled and giggled like a schoolgirl while she curtsied again.

"She shouldn't have had to save our lives," I argued.

"We came here with the thought that we were going to look at a starship, a fake starship, to be honest. Not be attacked by Daft Punk lookakalikes with ray guns."

"Like I said, an unfortunate interlude. My goal has always been to pull off the sale of the ship without a hitch and with zero risk to potential buyers. What can I do? What's done is done. Badabing badaboom."

"I wish you'd stop saying that. It's annoying."

"What is?"

"That badabing thing."

"What badabing thing?"

"You don't even know you're doing it, do you?"

"Doing what?"

I shook my head. "Here's the deal, Mister Keep. Matt and I would like to go home now, before we both end up dead."

Keep glared at me, pursing his lips. "I really think you should see the rest of the ship."

"Why?"

"Because you came all this way. Because you wanted to see it before you were almost killed. Because you might still be interested in the purchase once you see everything that's included."

"Unless there's a machine in here that can cure cancer, I'm not interested."

The way Keep stared at me caused me to freeze.

"Is there a machine here that can cure cancer?" I asked tentatively.

"Not exactly," he replied. "But I don't think you should be too hasty in dismissing the potential of a universe where functional starships and floating cars exist. Do you?"

I had opened my mouth to counter whatever argument he presented. Now it slammed back closed and I glanced over at Matt, who looked equally thoughtful.

"Ah, now I see you're beginning to listen to reason," Keep said. "I'll give you and Sherlock another clue if you'll agree to follow me upstairs."

My eyes met Matt's. He nodded slightly.

"Fine," I said. "We'll follow you upstairs."

"Badabing badaboom! I knew you'd come around. Alter, keep an eye on things outside. If any more of the duke's forces show up, take care of them."

Alter giggled and nodded, skipping the short distance to the open hatch leading outside.

"That girl is not right," Matt said.

"Maybe not," Keep agreed. "But I've often found the most broken people are also the most efficient. This way."

"You promised us another cookie," I said.

"Right," Keep replied. "Consider this. As I'm trying to keep as few people as possible from becoming aware of this sale, how does that relate to the text message I sent to your phone?"

He didn't wait for me to absorb the question, whirling away and scaling the left-hand steps to the over-hang, leaving me and Matt dumbstruck once more.

Chapter Seventeen

"Why me?" I asked as I reached the top of the stairs.

Keep waited for us near the hatch leading deeper into the ship. "What do you mean?" he replied, playing innocent.

"Your clue. You weren't spamming that website to every phone number you could find. You sent it to me. Deliberately. Why me?"

Only the left side of Keep's mouth moved into a knowing grin. "Good question, but we haven't gone further in the tour yet. The more you see, the more answers you get. Fair enough?"

"I guess. But maybe if I had more answers, I wouldn't need to see the rest of the ship."

"And maybe if you had all the answers you'd definitely want to go home. Until you saw the rest of the ship. This way, you get what you want, and I get what I want."

"Not if you don't make the sale," Matt said, coming up behind me.

"Like I said, that would be disappointing. But maybe

I like my odds. Do we have a deal?" he asked, putting out his hand.

I stared at it for a few seconds before shaking it. "Deal."

"Badabing badaboom! Here we go." He stuck his right index finger into a small hole in the wall, up to the first knuckle. Maybe something scanned his fingerprint. A light over the hole turned green and the hatch slid aside, revealing what looked like a generic hotel elevator.

"By the way, the lift doesn't count," he said, stepping into the cab and turning to face us.

I stopped in my tracks. "The hell it doesn't."

"This isn't an official compartment. It's just a transport mechanism."

I slipped into my best rendition of Keep's voice. "The more you see, the more answers you get." I shrugged. "This is more to see."

"Barely."

"You're splitting hairs."

He sighed, clearly getting worn down by the amount of effort it was taking him to show off a working starship. And maybe I was being too hesitant, especially considering my current situation. But I wasn't here alone. And Matt still had a full life ahead of him.

"Fine," he said. "Get in the lift, I'll tell you on the way up. We'll work our way from top down."

"How many decks are there?" I asked, stepping into the elevator.

"Seven, including the hangar here." The hatch slid closed.

"Why me?" I asked again.

"Sorry, kid. You used up your question."

"What?" I said. "That didn't count."

"The hell it didn't," he countered, mimicking me back. "It isn't my fault you asked a stupid one."

"You aren't a very good salesman, are you?" Matt asked. "You definitely need to work on your schmoozing."

"This ship should sell itself. You're just being diffi-cult." He hit the seven on the elevator's panel. The cab started rising.

"I'm being difficult?" Matt fumed. "Me?"

"Okay, okay," I said, getting between them. "We have a deal. If that was a question, fine. I won't make that mistake a second time."

Matt backed down, as did Keep. The silent ride to the seventh floor only took a few seconds, though I didn't feel any of the force such quick acceleration and deceler-ation would suggest.

"Inertial…" I trailed off, stopping before I asked another question.

"Cancellation," Keep finished.

"That's impossible," Matt said.

"Somebody should tell that to the person who designed the lift," Keep retorted. "Would you have also said floating cars were impossible thirty minutes ago?"

"Not impossible. Just unlikely."

"Is that a wide chasm to cross, from unlikely to impossible?" The answer left Matt stymied, which Keep seemed to enjoy. "If you move forward with the purchase, you'll come to find that there are many things you deem impossible that are only impossible because you don't know any better. It's not your fault."

"I suppose that means you're telling us there are other races of intelligent beings out there too," I said.

The elevator doors slid open. Keep stepped out of

Starship For Sale

the cab without answering. Matt and I joined him on the deck.

"Yes, of course there are other intelligent beings out there," he said, turning to face us. "An entire universe of intelligent beings. Some good. Some bad. Some ugly. Badabing badaboom! Some worse than others, like the duke's goombas."

I swallowed another lump in my throat. Keep had said the punks Alter killed weren't people.

"By the way, you just used up your question for this part of the tour."

"Damn it," I replied, still more than a little eager to know the answer to *why me*.

"Better luck next time, kid."

Even so… aliens! The idea was both awesome and terrifying. What had I gotten Matt and myself into?

"You really are a lousy salesman," Matt said, turning in a full circle with his head swiveling up and down. "How is this supposed to make us eager to buy your giant robot head?"

Looking around, I had to agree. The elevator had dropped us on the rearward side of the head's rounded top, looking across most of the open deck. Hundreds of cables snaked across the curved ceiling, some of their anchors dislodged or missing, leaving them drooping down directly in front of us. The connections to the mohawk antenna I had identified outside were all visible here, along with plenty of other junction boxes, circuit breaker panels, and other electricity related hardware. The largest piece of solid machinery sat in the center of the deck, spewing thick cables out around it like an ugly square octopus. A coating of rust covered its metal shell, corrosion obvious around the wires. A faint, high-pitched buzz flowed from it.

"Honestly, my first impression is that regardless of anything else, this ship is an ass-ton of work to maintain," I said.

"Not so, my good man," Keep countered, walking across to the console. He put his finger against the side, wiping it along the metal to show the thick layer of dust that had gathered on it. He held up his grimy finger. "In fact, this will be the only time you ever need to come up here. My purpose in showing you this first is twofold. One, I want you to make an informed purchase, and you'd see this sooner or later anyway. Two, as proof of how low maintenance the ship really is. Set and forget. Point and click. Plug and play. Badabing badaboom!"

"I have questions about what we're looking at," I said. "You can't count those as questions against the tour." I made sure to phrase everything as a statement, just in case.

"That wasn't our deal," Keep countered.

"We can't make an informed purchase if we can't ask questions," Matt agreed, also as a statement.

Keep hesitated for a moment before nodding. "Fair enough. So long as the questions are specific to something on the tour I won't count them against you."

"So magnanimous of you."

"You have no idea," Keep shot back.

"What is that?" I asked, pointing at the central console.

"That is the PCS. Primary Control System. The brain. All of the ship's systems flow through that box, which monitors their status, adjusts power requirements, and handles hundreds of other tasks completely transparently."

"Is it artificial intelligence?" Matt asked.

"Something like that," Keep replied. "It's not that

important. You won't need to touch it. Shall we go to the next deck?"

"Sure," I said.

We took the elevator to the next deck down. I moved to block the doors before they opened, turning to face Keep and locking eyes with him.

"Why me?" I asked for the third time. "That's the question for this space. That's the one I want answered. Why did you pick me?"

Keep's mouth spread into a wide grin, though he didn't let his lips part to show any teeth. "Why you?" He lifted the pack of cigarettes from his coat pocket, sliding one out and sticking it in the corner of his mouth. "Why you?"

"I'd also appreciate it if you didn't smoke," I said.

"What's it matter to you, kid?" he asked, dropping the pack back into his pocket but not immediately lighting up. "You're already dying, right?"

"Matt isn't," I pointed out. "And besides, it bothers my eyes. The customer is always right, you know."

"Not always. By the way, you just answered your own question."

"I don't understand."

He pulled the cigarette from his mouth and dropped it back into his pocket. "Okay, let's take a look at what's behind door number one, and then I'll spill some beans."

Chapter Eighteen

"Is that what I think it is?" I asked, bending over to look through the small window to the interior of a thick metal cylinder that rested in the center of Deck Six. It wasn't the only thing on the deck, just the most interesting. Additional machinery filled the open floor plan, wires running from the PCS on Deck Seven into the various pieces of equipment, the function of which I couldn't begin to identify.

The largest of the structures rested on either side of the elevator, a pair of thick columns wrapped by wires, pipes, and tubes. Square boxes affixed on their outer sides each sported a chunky cathode display that jutted out and downward, showing numeric soup on a green monochrome screen.

Additional screens circled the center cylinder, offering more information about the state of things to anyone who actually knew how to read it. Mechanical keyboards rested on small ledges beneath the screens, allowing interaction with the system.

"What do you think this cylinder is?" Keep asked.

I moved aside to let Matt take a look. The window in it was only a few inches square, making for challenging viewing.

"If I didn't know any better, I would say it's the sun," Matt said. "Only miniaturized."

"Then it's almost what you think it is," Keep said. "It's called the Star of Caprum."

"That's—"

"Impossible, right? You really need to stop saying that." He smiled. "Not Earth's sun, of course. *That* would be impossible. But it is a star in a box, a lead box that protects the crew from radiation."

"So this is the ship's power source, and those…" I turned and pointed at the two columns on either side of the elevator. "…are the main engines. I take it the other machines are related to...life support?"

"Bingo!" Keep snapped. "You nailed it. Badabing badaboom. Deck Six is home to what I call the essentials. Critical systems. Power, life support, gravity. You name it. Like I said, it's all self-regulating. You'll never need to touch it, or even understand how any of it works."

"So would it be fair to call Decks Seven and Six the brains of the starship?" I asked.

"More than fair," he answered.

Matt straightened up and turned to face Keep. I could see by his face he was becoming more intrigued by the ship. "You promised us answers."

"I did," Keep agreed. "Though to be honest with you, I'd much rather give them when we get to Deck Three. Maybe you have a different question?"

"No," I replied forcefully. "No more games. No more stall tactics. Why me?"

"Okay, kid," Keep said. "I'm going to put it to you straight. I've been trying to sell this ship since before you were born. Do you want to guess how many potential buyers I've had?"

"Zero?"

"Bingo! Zero. Zip. Zilch. Nada. No one. Do you know why?"

"Because everything about this screams scam?" Matt said.

"Enough commentary from the nosebleeds. It's because, as much as I'd like to get this ship off my hands, I can't just sell it to anyone. I'm looking for the right kind of buyer. An individual like yourself, with high upside potential and not much to lose on a risky play. But that isn't good enough. I need someone who understands loyalty and sacrifice, plus isn't a total schlub behind the controls of a starship."

I flinched at his last sentence. "You watched us play *Star Squadron*."

"If we were on Deck Three, I could show you the recording for proof," Keep confirmed. "I didn't actually observe your game from the beginning, but I did tune in once the criteria started the alarm bells ringing. You're the kind of buyer I've spent a long time waiting for. There was just one problem."

"I'm broke."

"Bingo! It's one of the most common reasons why prospective clients fall through. For what it is, the merchandise is extremely reasonably priced. But I do have certain expenses that need to be covered."

"Like parking?" Matt asked.

"For one. But there's more to it than that."

"Because nobody sells a starship just to sell a starship," I said.

"Not true. Lots of starships are bought and sold every day. Just not to someone from Earth."

"And you need someone from Earth because…" I trailed off, proud of myself for making sure to use statements instead of questions.

"That's a long story."

"We're listening."

"No. You need to see the rest of the ship first. I answered your question. Why you? Because you fit all of the criteria I've had in place since I smuggled the ship in. Except for one." He jabbed a finger at Sherlock. "He has the missing piece."

"You mean the money," Matt said.

"Exactamundo."

"*Star Squadron* is a pretty new game. You couldn't have been watching the players for long."

"No. But starship simulation games are hardly new. I've been tracking gameplay since *Wing Commander*."

"What?" I said in disbelief. "No way."

"Yes way. The trouble back then was finding confluence with all of the other traits. That got easier with online multiplayer, and I started getting closer to the perfect candidate. But of course funding is always an issue. So was the high upside potential but not much to lose. Most people at that stage of their lives have already burned all of their upside. But not you, Ben."

"I don't know what kind of upside you mean."

"Just so you know, I see how you're framing questions as statements so they won't count against you. No more backstory until we move on."

I smiled sheepishly, glancing at Matt. His excitement over seeing the first two decks of the ship had faded somewhat with Keep's response to my question. His role in this as purely the coin purse had obviously left him feeling uneasy. Maybe that shouldn't have bothered me, but he had pushed me forward when I balked at using his newfound cash as collateral. He couldn't just reverse course so quickly.

"Lead the way," I said.

We returned to the elevator. I noticed Keep hit the button for Deck Four rather than Five.

"You skipped one," I said. "You told us you were working top-down."

"Deck Five is storage," he answered. "Spare parts, tools, mops and cleaning agents, that sort of thing. Kind of boring, really."

"Or there's something on Deck Five you don't want us to see," Matt said. "After you made a point to tell us we'd see everything eventually anyway."

"Not so, Sherlock. As a professional salesman, it's become obvious to me that I need to punch up the wow factor if I'm going to land this deal. Looking at scrap metal and paint isn't going to get me there."

"Now I know you're lying. Nothing inside or outside this ship was recently painted."

Keep sighed and reached for the elevator controls. "Fine. If you really want to stop on Five…"

"Wait," I said. "If we're skipping around now, I want to go to Deck Three. I want to see the footage of the *Star Squadron* match."

Keep's eyes lit up. "Badabing badaboom! I think that's an excellent idea." He tapped the Deck Four button a second time to cancel it before the doors opened and he selected Deck Three.

"Ben," Matt said, trying to warn me not to skip Five.

"We'll circle back to it," I said. "We won't make a decision until we've seen everything."

He nodded reluctantly, still willing to humor me at least. I was sure he could tell my interest in the ship continued to advance while his receded.

Was he overly cautious, or was I too impulsive? Keep was right. I don't have much to lose. But Matt did, and I had to take that into account.

When all was said and done, would we both be happy with the results?

Chapter Nineteen

I knew something was off as soon as the elevator doors parted. The first two decks were well-defined if messy, and had easily fit into my mental construct of the available space in the robotic head's interior. Deck Three, on the other hand, was in obvious defiance of that construct. The corridor that stretched out from the elevator was easily two times longer than the space that should have been available. It stretched nearly forty feet until it reached the lower of the two transparencies I had identified from outside the ship.

"Bigger on the inside," Matt said, glancing at me. "Like Doctor Who."

"Doctor who?" Keep asked, looking back and forth between Matt and me.

"Yes, Doctor Who," I replied. "He's a character in a British television show. He has a starship, the Tardis. It looks like a phone booth on the outside, but the inside is full-size. I'm surprised you aren't familiar with it."

"Oh. Doctor Who," Keep said, as if he'd known who the character was all along. "Of course. I've seen that one. Funny, I never made the connection. Anyway, this isn't like that. The inside of the ship isn't any larger. It's the perspective that's changed."

"What do you mean? This corridor is twice as long as the ship is wide," I countered.

"It isn't twice the size. We're half the size."

"What?" Matt said, lifting his hands in front of his face to look at them. "That's…" He trailed off before he said it. "I don't feel any different."

I looked back at the elevator, its proportions relative to us remaining the same as it had been on the other decks. "The elevator hasn't changed."

"It's also half the size," Keep stated.

"The ceiling is the same distance above us."

"Deck Three is actually two decks. Three-Below and Three-Above. You can only reach the upper level via a stairway at the end of the corridor, in the primary living space."

"I'm sorry, I have to say it," I said. "That's impossible."

Keep didn't crack a smile. He shrugged instead. "And yet, here we are."

"Okay. How does it work?"

"What, do you want me to recite the technical specifications? It works, kid. That's really all that matters."

"I'm not so sure about that. What if I'm on this deck and someone blows out the window up there and I'm pulled out of the ship? What size will I be?"

"Half size. You would need to go through the expansion process to be restored to full size, and that occurs in the lift shaft. But that's a contrived case. If someone were shooting at you, I would think you'd be on the flight deck, not down here."

"And who would be shooting at us?" Matt asked.

"Is that your question?"

"It's one question," I said. "There are a lot of compartments on this deck I want to ask about." From here, I could make out multiple doors and archways off the main corridor, not even counting the living spaces in Six-A.

"Okay. Badabing badaboom. Let's head to the living area first. The primary display is there."

We started down the hallway. Unlike the interior of the ship we had seen so far, the corridor was clean and brightly lit, and felt more like being in a luxury apartment building than a robot's head. Thick maroon carpeting covered the floor, and framed prints of classical masterpieces lined the walls between open archways and what had to be doors to the bedrooms.

I glanced through some of the open archways. In one, I spotted a room I believed to be a break room based on the arrangement of tables and cabinets. We also passed a gym, stocked with weights and other equipment that looked to have been deposited there more like fifty years earlier, judging by their totally outdated designs.

"Did you decorate this place yourself?" I asked as we reached the end of the corridor.

The living area was slightly sunken, three steps leading down to a hardwood floor, the center covered by an orange shag rug, over which sat a long, lime green chesterfield sofa and glass topped coffee table. A pair of cloth recliners capped the sofa ends, standing lamps beside them and a crystal chandelier hanging overhead. A grand piano sat in the corner on one side of the room, while the primary display hung from a wall mount positioned next to the window on the other side. The stairs, I quickly noticed, were behind me along the side of the piano. A door occupied the matching space on the display side.

"I scooped the furnishings up at garage sales. I didn't have a lot of money to spend on comfort. Do you like it?"

"Not really," Matt said. "It's very…"

"Retro," I finished for him. "I think it's fine. You don't buy a starship for the interior design, right?"

"What do you buy a starship for?" Matt asked. "Oh, that's right. The adventure of a lifetime." He didn't sound as excited about the prospect as he had when he goaded me into continuing the tour. "Who would be shooting at us again, Mister Keep?"

"You mentioned someone called the Duke before," I said. "Who is that?"

"One question at a time," Keep replied. He pointed at me. "I'll answer yours first. Duke Halver Sedeya. He's trying to stop me from selling the ship, and consequently, his minions and forces are the most likely to shoot at you, as they already have."

"So if we buy the ship, we'll be heading out there with a target already on our backs?" Matt asked.

"Part of the reason why a reasonable proficiency flying a spacecraft is part of my selection criterion."

"And you're basing that solely on a video game?"

"Certainly. It's not as if I can base it on real world starship piloting experience, now can I? This may be a surprise to you, but simulations are approximately seventy three percent accurate in predicting real qualification and aptitude. Not ideal, but we take what we can get. Badabing badaboom! Hold on, let me pull up the footage."

He picked up a chunky black remote from the coffee table and pointed it at the display, the buttons on the remote clicking loudly with each press. It took him three tries to get the display to turn on, at first showing white noise.

Putting the remote back on the table, he took his phone from his pocket and tapped on it about a dozen times. Finally, a capture of the *Star Squadron* match appeared on the big screen.

"That one is you," Keep said, pointing to one of the three identical ships on the Green side.

"Wow, how original," Matt said. "Good choice."

Keep let the footage play, surprising me when audio of Green's comms blasted out of speakers mounted around the room. I watched from an outside perspective as I clashed with Bloodstain, tried to save PrattLord from destruction, and generally looked pretty good out there, if I did say so myself.

"I'm not sure this is a good test of skill," Matt said. "It looks great, don't get me wrong. But we were playing against other newbies, not skilled space fighter pilots. I don't think there's a good direct comparison."

"Matt," I said, annoyed by his comment. Watching the match now, I was proud Keep had texted me based on the performance.

"I know you're teetering on the edge of having a total death wish, but let's try to keep things in perspective. What if I buy this ship, we go to space, and subsequently get blown to bits? I think we have to consider that a very real possibility after what happened with Baron Von Asshat's minions outside."

I shrugged. "At this point, I'm okay with that. Matt, come on. This is a freaking starship. A real starship. Nobody gets this kind of opportunity. We can go to space! Man, I'd rather spend twenty minutes out there and get blown to bits than die in bed at home, sick and frail."

"I get that," Matt said. "I do. But something about this isn't sitting right."

"What you need is a little more information," Keep said. "I assume you believe me about why I contacted you?"

"Yeah," I admitted. "I suppose. So why doesn't Baron Whats-his-name want you to sell the ship?"

"To understand that, you need to understand where it came from."

"A giant robot," Matt answered.

"Not exactly, Sherlock," Keep replied. He picked up the big remote again, clicking on it to change the channel or something, leaving the screen blank. Tapping on his phone again, an image of thousands of stars appeared on the monitor. "This is space."

"Clearly," Matt said.

"More specifically, this is the Fertile Quadrant of the Manticore Spiral, so named because it's the most dense cluster of planets which birthed intelligent life in the known universe."

"Cool," I said, staring at all of the stars. The image was too zoomed out to see individual worlds in it. "How many planets are we talking about?"

"Over a hundred," Keep replied.

"Very cool."

"Approximately four hundred years from now, nearly fifty thousand humans will leave Earth on board an arkship destined for the Trappist-1 system to become the first extraterrestrial human settlers. On the way there, they'll accidentally travel into a hole in spacetime and wind up in the Manticore Spiral nearly three thousand years in the past, at a time before most of the intelligent life in the Quadrant has discovered spaceflight. Armed with their already advanced technology, they'll spend the next two millenia expanding across the entirety of the Spiral as the predominant species, and create the seat of power from which they still rule today."

"Wow," I said, mesmerized by the backstory.

"Wait," Matt said. "You're saying you're from the future? A time traveler?"

"No, dummy," I replied. "He said the original humans who settled the Spiral came from our future, but they ended up around twenty five hundred years in our past."

"Okay, but all of them originally came from the future," Matt said, looking at Keep. "And since you're human, that means you originated from someone who is from Earth, but who hasn't even been born yet."

"That's right," Keep confirmed. "That doesn't make me a time traveler. My point of telling you that is to explain how humans wound up halfway across the universe."

"I get it. But how did you wind up back here? Halfway across the universe is pretty damn far away."

"I'll get to that. Moving on."

Keep tapped on his phone. The display zoomed in, flying toward the stars as though it were a spaceship itself, until some of the planets came into focus. A blue outline highlighted one of the worlds. The word *Caprum* appeared over it.

"The Atlas Hegemony is quite large. As a result, it's overseen by a governance similar to the feudal system of Earth's middle ages. The leader of the Hegemony, Empress Li'an, is responsible for all of the higher-level operations of a massive civilization. Primarily, selecting families to raise to the nobility and introduce into the line of succession, mediating some disputes, providing security across the Spiral, and generally living a lavish lifestyle few of us can ever hope to aspire to."

"But you aren't bitter," Matt quipped.

"When the Hegemony's mediation processes fail, the end result is often war, the scale of which depends entirely on the nature of the dispute and the alliances forged between the ruling nobles. Caprum was my home world, Duchess Dryka, my liege. I was her advisor in all matters of state, a poor replacement for her father who was killed when she was only eight years old, poor kid. I was Baron Dryka's man-at-arms. A trained soldier, turned statesman, turned salesman. Badabing badaboom." He laughed sardonically, using his phone to highlight another planet, relatively close to Caprum. "This is Sarton, Duke Sedaya's seat. It was the Duke who caused all of this. My world is rich in levitite, a mineral used in a large number of applications and as a result extremely lucrative. The Duke hoped to gain access to the mines through marriage to the Duchess, but because of the difference in age he had to request permission for the union from the Empress, which she firmly denied. Usually, these types of disagreements lead to war. The Duke's path to power was worse. Far worse."

He turned to face us, his hardened expression threatening to break down.

"He didn't care about a quick victory. After all, Ninaya was only eight. He had time to bide. So he set about corroding us from the inside out, using his lack of morality and his powerful influence to convince trusted allies to turn their backs on Caprum while at the same time secretly putting a bounty on the Duchess' young head. A large portion of my own soldiers participated in the coup, and they would have succeeded in slaughtering Ninaya if not for the few courageous loyal-ists who helped me escape the palace with her and get her off-world. I wasn't so lucky. Duke Sedaya's forces captured me, tortured me, and as the Duke claimed Caprum for his own, exiled me to the planet Demitrus."

He tapped on his phone. A third planet gained a colored outline. It sat at the far tip of the Spiral, a visibly immense distance from Caprum. The name of the world, Demitrus, appeared over it.

"Demitrus is the home of the Acheon," Keep said. "A race of intelligent insectoids who earn their place in the Hegemony by allowing their planet to be used as a massive dumping ground. It sounds bad, but the Acheon are expert engineers and builders, and use the scrap as both living space and to produce repurposed goods for trade, including starships."

"Like this one?" I asked.

"Bingo! The Acheon don't like humans, though they accept that allowing dumping on their planet includes discarded people. Colonies of exiles litter the landscape like the billions of kilograms of trash, scavenging what they can from the scrap the Acheon don't use. It's a hard life, made harder by the harsh environment on Demitrus. But I had two things to keep me going."

"Reuniting with the Duchess," I said. "That's one."

"Yup," Keep agreed.

"The Star of Caprum," Matt added.

Keep raised an eyebrow. "Now, there you are proving your nickname, Sherlock. How'd you guess?"

"You gave it a proper name, which means it's rare if not unique. And I figured the Duke has a good reason to be after you."

"Wait a minute," I said. "If he's after the Star, and

the Star is part of the ship, then if we buy the ship he'll be after us."

"Yes. But also, no," Keep said.

"What does that mean?"

"That's one of the reasons I need to sell the ship. The Star is included in the sale. As it's property of the Duchess and I'm still her legal guardian despite our separation, it's all legitimate in the eyes of the Hegemony. To attack or otherwise seize the Star from you without cause would put Sedaya on the wrong side of the Royal Guard"

"So, we'd be safe," I said.

"As safe as anyone can be in the Fertile Quadrant," Keep qualified. "I can't guarantee Sedaya won't hire mercenaries to try to take the Star from you."

"Ben," Matt said, his tone of voice causing me to grimace. "Can we talk for a minute? Alone?"

"No," I replied. "I know what you're thinking. You don't want to get involved in all of this."

Matt sighed. "You know I love you like a brother, Bennie. But this is all too much. It seemed exciting and harmless enough until people started dying. It was a little concerning, knowing we'd have people gunning for us. But Keep's talking about us stepping into the middle of something a lot bigger. We're already in over our heads, and I'm not too thrilled about the idea of drowning."

"It sounds exciting to me," I said. "A little scary, sure. But this is like something right out of a movie, and not *Space Aces Need Love Too*. This really could be the adventure of a lifetime."

"I hear you," Matt said, his face falling. "And yeah the idea of going to another galaxy is mind blowing. Mister Keep, your story is interesting as hell, really. I hope you were a good soldier, because you're definitely a lousy salesman. Learning more about what we'd be in for didn't help at all. It's my money, and I don't want to get mixed up in all of this. I don't want you mixed up in this either, Ben. You're going to get yourself killed. I'm sorry, but it's time to go home."

Chapter Twenty

I dropped onto the couch behind me, lowering my head into my hands. I knew the final word was coming. I knew what it would be. But that didn't help temper my disappointment.

"Mister Keep, I think the limo that brought us here is totalled," Matt said. "I assume you have another way to get us home."

"I can get you home," Keep replied, voice tense. "But you should know, just because I'm still fighting for the Duchess and Caprum, that doesn't mean you're expected to do the same. As soon as the sale is completed you're free to do whatever you want with the ship, and with the Star. You can even sell it to the Duke, if that's your decision. Though I'd prefer you didn't. Not only would it leave the ship without a power source, but the Star would be more dangerous in Sedaya's hands than anywhere else in the universe."

"As long as we have the Star, we'll be in danger," Matt said.

"Life is a risk," Keep replied. "From the moment you

wake up one day to the moment you wake up the next, any one of a billion things could end it. Truthfully, the Fertile Quadrant can be a dangerous place. But you wouldn't be defenseless."

"You mean the guns? And that smaller ship in the hangar?"

"Yes, and yes. And you'd also have Alter."

I perked up at that. "What do you mean?"

"Alter comes with the ship, assuming you're willing to keep her on. It's her home. The only place she feels at peace. She'll defend it, and its owners, to her last breath. And let me tell you, that's no small benefit. Before she met me, Alter was one of the most infamous assassins in the Quadrant, though few people knew it."

"I don't know whether to be impressed or scared shit-less," I said. "Assassin?"

"A killer for hire."

"I know what an assassin is. I just…other than making short work of Sedaya's minions, she seems kind of sweet and childlike."

"She's many things, kid. Foremost of which is a valu-able asset."

"And you're sure she'd want to stay on with us?"

"Positive. Like I said, this ship is her home."

"How did she wind up here?"

"She was living in the hollowed out remains of the superstructure when I discovered it, exiled to Demitrus like I was. Even when the Acheon began repurposing the remains of the robot head into a ship, she refused to leave. When the ship was completed, I found her waiting for me on the flight deck in the co-pilot's seat."

"I think we're missing a chunk of time," Matt said. "How did you go from being exiled to Demitrus to convincing the insect aliens who hate humans to build you a starship?"

I smiled at the question, my hopes rising as Matt put himself back into the game. Because the idea of having Alter on board made him feel safer, or because he thought she was cute. I hoped for the former. The latter would only cause problems down the road.

"Easy peasy," Keep replied. "I had the Star."

"How did you sneak it past Sedaya?" I asked. "If the Star is that valuable, he must have known you had it?"

"Nope. He thought the Duchess escaped with it. He had me searched, of course, and not gently. But I knew he would want the Star, so I had my body modified to create a compartment to store it beneath my skin, under an old battle scar."

"That's disgusting and amazing at the same time," I said.

"The Acheon had to cut me open to retrieve it. I promised them use of it until they finished building the ship. I never planned to end up with a robot head, but that's what they picked." He smiled, revealing uneven teeth, a seemingly rare occurrence. "Or maybe they just wanted to get Alter off their planet." The smile vanished as quickly as it arrived. "I knew Sedaya had spies on Demitrus. All of the most ambitious Barons do. I knew word of the Star would reach him, and that when it did he would come. The Acheon knew it too, which motivated them to work faster. They finished just in time. Alter and I had to make it through three squadrons of the Duke's fighters to escape."

"Wow."

"Like I said earlier, she may not look like much, but she's got it where it counts. Badabing badaboom!" He stared at Matt. "What do you think? Does having one of the most ferocious bodyguards in the universe help change your mind?"

"You probably should have led with that after she wiped the floor with the Duke's mercenaries, but no. This isn't the kind of adventure I'm looking for."

My face probably matched Keep's. Frustrated, disappointed, desperate. "You haven't seen the rest of the ship," I said.

"I don't need to see it," Matt replied.

"There's one more thing you should keep in mind," Keep said.

"No. I'm done. I can't see how any of this is worth the risk."

"Just one more thing? Humor me, kid."

"Fine. What is it?"

"This ship is powered by a star you can stick in your pocket. This deck shrunk you to half your original size without you knowing it. I came to Earth from the other side of the universe. And you don't think technology exists out there to save your best friend's life?"

Matt had opened his mouth, ready to argue. He clamped it shut, face flushing as he looked over at me. I had read stories about people who had donated a kidney to a friend in need. How much was he willing to give? I didn't expect anything. I didn't deserve anything.

But damn, I wanted it.

Matt's throat shifted as he swallowed a huge lump in it. I stared at him, realizing then that I was looking at something I had rarely seen before. He wanted to say yes. I could see it in his eyes. The reason why he hadn't was simple.

Fear.

While Matt had always been more adventurous than me, this situation had reached the edge of his comfort zone. I couldn't say I didn't understand. How much of my carefree attitude came from knowing I was already living on borrowed time? Or knowing that maybe I could extend the term limit of that loan by heading to the Manticore Spiral? What kind of pressure was he under knowing he almost literally held my life in his hands?

The silent tension shattered when Keep's phone rang. He picked it up immediately, bringing it to his ear. His hard, flat expression shifted as his eyes shifted between Matt and me.

"That was Alter," he said, lowering the phone. "More of the Duke's forces are on the way. If you want a chance to get out of here, I need a decision. Now."

My heart raced, hands clamming up as I quickly overloaded with anxious dread. I didn't want to leave. Like Alter, I would rather go down with the ship.

Matt glanced at me one more time and I saw the icy fear melt, his decision silently made. "How do we finalize the sale?" he asked. "We never even talked about the price."

Chapter Twenty-One

I couldn't hold back the massive grin that came with my sense of relief. I couldn't stop the happy tears from filling my eyes, and it took all of my willpower to keep from jumping up and wrapping my arms around Matt. It didn't matter that a second group of not-people were on their way to try to seize the ship again. I was certain Alter could handle them. It mattered that he had said yes, primarily because it could save my life.

"Four million," Keep said without missing a beat. Everything Matt had inherited from his mother's passing.

"Come on, man. I still have to pay taxes on that money," Matt replied.

Keep laughed out loud, joyous that Matt had decided to go for it. It was strange to hear. "Taxes? Who gives a shit about taxes where you're going?"

Matt's face reddened again. "All right. Four million. How do I pay you?"

I appreciated that he didn't balk at the cost. What good was Earth fiat where we were going, anyway?

"I'll take care of the withdrawal once the contract is signed," Keep said.

"What do you mean? I don't need to send a wire? Or fill anything out for the transfer?"

"That isn't necessary." Keep tapped on his phone, bringing up a white screen. He turned it toward us. The text was so small I could only make out the header.

BILL OF SALE FOR STARSHIP IDENTIFIER CUL8T3R

"You mean you could have drained my account any time you wanted?" Matt asked. "How?"

"I strongly recommend not clicking on hyperlinks from strangers in the future," Keep replied. "Especially when the resulting web site contains malware that replicates to all devices in a person's contact list without them knowing and collects credentials to every app on said device. Including their mobile banking apps. Badabing badaboom!"

Matt's eyes whipped back to me in a harsh glare. I smiled sheepishly. "Sorry. But it all worked out in the end, right?"

His deer-in-headlights look returned. "I hope so."

"I don't think we have time for you to read the whole contract," Keep said. "Basically, it says you're paying me four million United States dollars, official fiat currency on Earth, in exchange for this starship. Once the document is signed, you're responsible for all fees incurred from the point of sale forward. It also says you agree to allow Miss Alter Miyaga to reside on the ship in perpetuity, or until such a time as she chooses to disembark. That decision must be presented in the form of written notice with her signature." He scrolled the full contract, showing how much legalese had been added until he reached the signature field. "Just sign here, I'll transfer the cash, and we're good to go. Badabing badaboom!"

"How do I know you didn't include some line in there that says ownership reverts back to you after some amount of time or something? Or that prohibits us from selling the Star of Caprum?"

Keep shrugged and held out his phone. "You're welcome to read the document in its entirety."

"Matt, he hasn't misled us on a single thing so far," I said. "Even when we thought this whole thing was a total scam."

"Thank you, Ben," Keep said. "I swear on the honor of my position as Steward of Caprum that the contract is exactly as I've described, with no further limitations or hidden clauses. The most important part is that Alter is allowed to stay."

Matt looked over at me a final time, struggling to contain his panicked excitement. He stretched a shaky finger to the phone, using it to sign his name on the bill of sale. Keep added his signature under it.

"A copy will be stored in the ship's database," Keep said. "Should you ever need to present proof of ownership to the Royal Guard." He held out his hand. "Congratulations, Matthew. You just bought a starship."

"Yes!" I shouted, jumping off the sofa and rushing over to him as he took Keep's hand, so nervous he could barely shake it.

Keep put his hand out to me next, and I shook it vigorously. "This is going to be awesome," I said. "The adventure of a lifetime."

"I wish you both all the best on your journeys from here into the wider universe. I know you'll make the most of the opportunity presented to you. If you could escort me out?"

"What?" I said. "You're leaving?"

"Of course."

It was my turn to go deer-in-headlights. "We haven't even seen the flight deck. You need to show me how to fly this thing."

"It's simple. Not much different from flying the *Star Squadron* simulator. Alter can help fill in the gaps."

"She's a pilot?"

"She's a lot of things. You'll see. You'll be grateful to have her."

"I already am if she can help get us off the ground."

"We should head for the hangar," Keep said. "Alter is waiting for us there."

"Sure," Matt replied. "Let's go."

"Matt," I said, stepping in front of him. "Thank you. I can't even begin to tell you how much this means to me."

"I know," he answered. "First order of business, we try to find someone who can help make you well. Permanently. Okay?"

"Absolutely."

"Second order of business," Keep said. "First thing you need to do is give her a name. All she has right now is an identifier, which is a mouthful to say." He tapped on his phone a few times before holding it out to Matt. "This is yours now. It comes with the ship. It allows remote access to pretty much everything. There's a fancier one on the flight deck, but I couldn't carry that one around Earth with me. I already entered the screen to put in a name."

Matt took the phone. A standard model, except it seemed the OS had been replaced with custom software. A blinking white cursor on a black background and a keyboard sat on the screen.

"I have no idea what to name the ship," he said. "Can't this wait?"

"It can," Keep said. "But you should give it some thought."

"How about Optimus Prime?" I suggested. "That's what it looks like. His head, anyway."

Matt shook his head. "Not doing it for me."

"Mr. Roboto?"

"Not a robot."

"Tardis?"

"Taken."

"Probably not in the Manticore Spiral."

"Copyrighted then. Keep thinking while we walk."

We headed back down the hallway to the elevator. It was a little disappointing to me that Mr. Keep didn't have time to finish the tour, but I imagined Alter could make up for whatever he missed.

When we boarded the elevator, I tried to focus on my senses, trying to notice the change as we were returned to our original size. The whole idea of being shrunken seemed so wacky, I wasn't convinced Keep hadn't played us, at least in that one respect. I didn't feel a thing, and when the elevator opened to the hangar everything looked properly scaled again. If the change was imperceptible, I guess it didn't matter.

Alter remained at the open hatch with the larger hangar bay blast doors, standing stiff as a board, hands at her sides as if she was the door. She didn't move a muscle as we descended the stairs and passed the smaller starfighter, coming up behind her.

Being almost two heads taller than her, I quickly realized why she hadn't moved. A dozen more of the uniformed and helmeted Daft Punks stood at the bottom of the ramp, blasters pointed at her. They seemed hesitant to pick a fight, or maybe Alter had promised Keep would come to them.

"Alter," he said, drawing a quick glance back from her. "You can step aside."

She smiled, raising her hands into a clawed position and growling at the punks before hopping backward. the Duke's minions flinched at the threat, drawing an amused giggle from her as she slipped in between Matt and me.

Keep replaced her in the doorway, hands raised in surrender. "Which one of you is in charge?"

Chapter Twenty-Two

One of the helmeted individuals stepped forward. "That would be me," he said, his voice stiff and robotic. Was that the reason for the helmets? Keep had said they weren't people. Were they robots? "Duke Sedaya sends his greetings, Avelus Keeper. He demands your forfeiture of this vessel and all property within it under threat of death."

"Of course he does," Keep said. "Bad news. You're too late. This vessel is under new ownership and all property within has also been transferred with it. The contract is binding and legal in accordance with the Hegemony Code of Law."

The punk didn't have a face, so I couldn't see his reaction. He didn't move at all for nearly five full seconds before responding. "And I assume you have proof?"

Keep looked back at Matt. "Can you help me out, Sherlock? I need to show this asshat the contract."

Matt seemed hesitant to move into the line of fire.

"I can do it," I said.

"No, I've got it," he replied, stepping up to the doorway and handing the phone back to Keep.

"I'm transmitting the contract now. It's already filed in both the ship's log and with the Hegemony."

The punk remained stiff for a few more seconds. "Contract received." He paused again. "It appears the contract is as you say." His helmet shifted slightly, indicating he was looking at Matt. "You are the new owner?"

"Yeah," Matt said. "Co-owner, with my friend."

"An original Earthian, no less. You've always been a sly one, Keeper. You may have outdone yourself this time."

"What does he mean?" I whispered to Alter.

She glanced at me and smiled cutely, but didn't provide any additional information. The reaction sent a wave of anxiety through me. *She* was supposed to help me fly the ship?

"Maybe if it hadn't taken you so long to catch up to me," Keep replied. "I'm sure Duke Sedaya will be pleased with your complete incompetence and failure to achieve his goals."

The lead punk growled under his breath, proving he probably wasn't a robot, though I still couldn't be sure. For all I knew, the guy looked like Pumpkinhead under there. He definitely seemed to have emotions though.

"This isn't over," he said. "As for you, Earthian. The Duke has no quarrel with you. I'm sure he would be willing to pay you exorbitantly for your vessel, or at the very least the star that powers it. I can easily arrange a personal meeting."

Matt looked back at me, and I shook my head. I wasn't ready to just hand over the keys to the kingdom before we had even taken the ship out for a joyride.

"We'll get back to you on that," Matt answered.

"Very well. I'm transmitting the Duke's personal hypercom identifier to you. I suggest you use it. The Spiral isn't kind to those unfamiliar with its ways, and Master Sedaya can be a powerful friend."

"I'll keep that in mind."

"Very well. You have forty-eight hours, Earthian. After that, all bets are off."

The lead punk spun on his heel and raised his arm, a signal to the others. They lowered their blasters as one, turning and marching back to their cars behind him. Keep didn't move while they left, so neither did I.

"I hope you can explain all that to me later," I said, glancing over at Alter again. I flinched when I realized she was gone. How had she slipped away without me noticing? A chill ran down my spine when I remembered what Keep had said about her. She wasn't just an assassin. She was the most infamous assassin in her galaxy.

And she lived on my starship. Crazy.

Keep returned to the hangar once the Duke's forces left the scene. "Well, that was a smooth shave," he said, exhaling sharply and reaching for a cigarette. "A few more minutes and I think they might have tried to blast their way in."

Another chill ran down my back in response to the statement. "I didn't get the impression that the Duke's lackeys plan to leave us be. At least, not unless we sell the Star to him."

"It's out of my hands, kid," Keep said. "It's your property, you can do with it what you will."

"It sounds like we have two days to decide," Matt said. "Assuming forty-eight hours means the same thing to him that it does to us?"

"It does," Keep confirmed. "Since the original human settlers of the Spiral were from your future, they normalized everything based on Earth values. Hours in a standard day, the metric system for measurement, and English as the primary language."

"How convenient for us," I said.

"Of course, that bunch prefers to speak Niflin, their native tongue, and let the translators do the work. They think their mouths are too good to make such nasty sounds." He craned his neck. "Where'd Alter go? I had hoped to say goodbye to her."

"I don't know. She disappeared while the Duke's guy was busy being condescending," I said. "I guess you can call her?"

He held up the phone, handing it back to Matt. "No dice. She probably high-tailed it out of here so she wouldn't have to see me go. I'll get in touch with her once I have a new PHD."

"Let me guess. Personal Hypercom Device?"

"Bingo! Good call, kid. Anyway, now that this bit of business is done, I have other important matters that have been on hold for a long time. Namely, catching up to the Duchess. Congratulations again on your purchase. And thank you for hanging in there with me through the turbulence. You won't regret your decision." He thrust his hand out at me again. We shook for a second time.

"Will we see you again, Mister Keep?" I asked.

He shrugged. "Who knows? It's a small universe." He turned to Matt. "You're a good friend. I know how much you sacrificed. There's a lot of power in putting others before yourself."

Matt shook Keep's hand too. "Thank you, sir. Best of luck to you, wherever you go next."

"You too, kid." He returned to the doorway, pausing there. He paused. "Oh. I almost forgot." He retrieved our cells from his pockets and handed them back. "One more thing. I highly recommend you lift off as soon as possible. This place charges per hour, and it's your tab now." He turned to leave, reaching the doorway.

"Mister Keep, wait," I said, stopping him. "How do we get from Earth to the Manticore Spiral? Come to think of it, how did Sedaya's mercenaries get from the Spiral to Earth?"

"Elementary, my dear Watson," Keep replied. "You haven't been on Earth for about three hours now. Welcome to Caprum, in the Fertile Quadrant of the Manticore Spiral. The last place the Duke ever thought to look for me was right under his ugly little nose." He put up his hand in a wave. "I'll see you two around. Try to stay out of trouble."

He walked down the ramp, leaving Matt and I staring at him, frozen and speechless.

Chapter Twenty-Three

"I think we should go up to the flight deck," I said after nearly a minute had passed. "We need to get off the ground and stop paying for parking. Especially since you just spent everything you had on this baby."

Matt glanced my way, still dumbstruck by Keep's last words. Somehow, we had traversed the universe within a few hours riding in the back of a limousine. I knew what he was thinking because I couldn't stop thinking about it too.

Impossible!

And yet, here we were, though I couldn't guess why Keep's homeworld had so many shipping containers from Earth or why it smelled like low tide out there. It was another of a million questions I had for Alter once she turned up again.

"Yeah," he finally said, breaking out of his stupor. "Let's go up to the flight deck."

"I want to thank you again," I added. "I still can't believe this is really happening. No matter what happens to me from here forward, you've made my whole life."

He smiled sheepishly, embarrassed by my praise. "It's no problem. I'm happy to do it." He looked back at the doorway. "Do you have any idea how to close the hatch?"

I scanned the wall beside the larger hangar door, looking for a switch or a button. "Maybe the controls are on the phone?" We looked at the main screen together. It surprised me that the layout wasn't that different from a modern smartphone, with screens of labeled icons that handled different functions. Could it be that Keep had modified the original program to make it easier for us Earthians to use?

"That one, maybe?" I said, pointing to a lock icon that read *security*.

He tapped on it, opening a list of settings. We scanned it together, not finding anything that fit our purposes exactly, though it seemed we could lock every hatch on the ship by switching a single toggle. I imagined that would include the elevator, which we needed to get to the flight deck.

"Not that," he replied, backing out of the screens. "I don't see one labeled *hatch control*."

"It can't be that hard," I said, scanning the wall again. "Maybe the manual control is upstairs."

"Maybe."

We ascended to the overhang, where I checked the wall next to the elevator for additional controls. The ordeal reminded me of when Mom moved us from the Section 8 apartment to a small house just outside of the city. It took nearly a week before I knew where all the wall switches were, and close to two months before I hit the right one every time.

"Oh shit," I said out loud, reacting to the memory. "Mom."

I picked my phone from my pocket and turned on the screen. Of course the cell had no service. The nearest tower was some non-zero number of light years away. Though it seemed Levi had texted me again before we left Earth.

If you changed your mind you should just be honest. It isn't cool to ghost. Loser.

I cringed at the words. Now she thought I was just another asshole. It was probably better that way, since I couldn't write her back now even if I wanted to. I couldn't write to my mother either, which bothered me a lot more. She would worry about me when I didn't get in touch with her.

"Damn," Matt said, recognizing the situation. "You didn't get a chance to explain anything or say goodbye."

"You didn't either. With your Dad, I mean."

"It'll be a couple of weeks before he notices I'm gone. Maybe longer. He spends most of his time at his girlfriend's place these days."

I exhaled my frustration. "Keep got us here some-how. There must be some way to send a message back to her. I just want her to know I'm okay."

"If there is a way, we'll find it."

"I don't know why Keep had to hurry off like that. We're fish out of water here. We can't even close the hatch."

A soft, echoing thunk sounded from the front of the hangar. Both our heads swiveled to the smaller door, which had slid closed.

"Huh, it worked," Matt said.

"What did?" I asked.

He held up the phone. "I found a setting for voice control. Keep had it disabled."

"Like Alexa?"

"Yeah, but I guess you don't need to say anything first?"

"That's dangerous. Are there more settings?"

Matt tapped on the screen a few times. "It looks like you can enter a custom trigger. What do you think? Should I make it Alexa?"

"No way. That's boring. And common. We should personalize it."

"Do you have any ideas?"

"It's your ship."

"No," Matt said forcefully. "I put the money in. I signed the contract. But this is our ship. Fifty-fifty. I wouldn't have done it otherwise."

I grinned at the response. "I'm grateful for you."

"You already said that. Enough sap for one day."

I laughed. "Fine."

We stared at one another, trying to come up with a trigger word.

"Honestly, I think it's too soon," Matt said. "We haven't really bonded with this place yet. Like when I first got the Mustang, it took time for it to earn a nickname."

"Big Stang Theory," I said. "You're probably right. Let's leave the trigger word off for now. It probably doesn't matter while it's just the three of us onboard."

"So weird to suddenly be living with a woman," Matt said as I tapped the elevator control.

"So weird to suddenly be living with a trained assassin," I replied. "At least she's on our side." The elevator doors opened and we stepped inside.

"I don't think she's on our side. I think she's on the ship's side."

"Same thing."

"Not really. What if we decide to give Duke Sedaya a

call and sell him the ship? We probably have to include her living situation in the bill of sale like Keep did. She won't come with us. She'll stay here."

"I don't know, Keep said the Duke was the one who dumped her on Demitrus. She probably wouldn't want to stick around if he dropped in. Not that it matters. We aren't going to sell the ship or the Star to him. Right?" Matt looked at me. I didn't like his face. "Right?" I repeated.

He shrugged. "Probably not. But I don't think we should just dismiss the possibility outright. According to Keep the guy has a lot of power, and a lot of money. Maybe we could trade her in for something better and have enough cheddar to live like kings in the Spiral. Maybe he could even set us up with our own planet. Make us nobles. That could be cool."

"Except Sedaya is a creepy asshole who wanted to marry an eight-year-old girl, and when he didn't get his way, he stole her planet and chased her away."

"It seems to me that's just the way politics work here. We need to go with the flow. Besides, we might enjoy our futures more if we didn't have his Niflin breathing down our necks. We're free to do whatever we want."

"But we're in this fifty-fifty, right?"

"Right."

"So we'd have to agree."

"Yeah. I'm not going to make unilateral decisions."

"What's the tie-breaker?"

"Alter, I guess. Unless you want to fight me for it?"

"Only if you'll video game me for it."

He smiled. "Alter it is."

"Well, I doubt she'd agree with selling the ship to the Duke, and I'm not with you on that either."

"I know. Like I said, we shouldn't just dismiss the

possibility. We have forty-eight hours before we have to worry about it, so let's not worry about it…yet."

"Agreed. Deck four, please."

"So polite," Matt said.

The elevator doors closed, opening a few seconds later to dump us out in a corridor dimly lit with dangling incandescent bulbs and lined with slightly rusted metal bulkheads. Four closed hatches led to a larger blast door at the far end.

The flight deck.

I couldn't wait to see it.

Chapter Twenty-Four

I practically ran down the passageway in my eagerness to see the flight deck. Expecting the doors to open as I approached, I nearly collided with them when they failed to budge, coming to a quick stop. "Open the flight deck hatch!" I ordered gleefully.

They still didn't move.

"Open the flight deck hatch!"

Nothing.

"The flight deck is secured," Matt said. "Hold up." He tapped on the phone as he approached. "There's a setting for biometrics. Put your thumb on the screen." He turned it to face me, showing me the thumbprint pattern. I placed my left thumb against it, and the lines of the pattern turned green. "That should give you full clearance if I'm reading this thing right."

I glanced at the bulkhead next to the door, finding the biometric scanner there and putting my thumb against it. A small green bulb above it flashed and the flight deck hatch parted in the center.

I hurried through, eyes wide as I took in the arrangement. A long console sat just behind the transparency at the front of the ship, following the curve of the robot head about fifteen feet to either side of center. Two pilot stations were about ten feet behind the window, separated by a narrow center console fronted by a large display angled toward the stations. It currently displayed what looked like an animated screensaver of a...a kitten rolling around on a carpet?

Each pilot station housed a seat upholstered in distressed brown leather in the middle of a set of controls. It surprised me to realize that the setup didn't just resemble the simulator from *VR Awesome!* It matched it, right down to a stick with both a primary and thumb trigger, a full-handled throttle, and a pair of foot pedals at each station, along with a helmet that plugged into the system. I suddenly had the feeling that Keep hadn't just plugged into *Star Squadron* to search for qualified pilots.

He had helped design the game, or at least the simulator itself.

A shiver ran through me at the thought of his involvement. A VR game to test potential pilots for aptitude. When I had read about the simulator in *Engadget*, it had mentioned the rigs were also available for private sale, the cost of which wasn't disclosed. In other words, if you had to ask, you couldn't afford it. No doubt people with the funds to buy the ship had purchased one for their personal use, and maybe that's where Keep had hoped to find a buyer. After all, he had said he spent twenty years searching and had never had a hit before. Desperate times may have called for desperate measures.

And both he and I had gotten incredibly lucky.

The flight deck didn't begin and end with the two pilot's seats. A second row of seats rested behind them in the form of a faded and worn leather sofa that had been modified with three point restraints and bolted into the deck. Behind that, just to the left of the hatch, stood a cylindrical device composed of dozens of narrow bands of metal and lights, a wired harness, and a floor that matched the omnidirectional treadmills I had seen at the arcade. Directly opposite the device, on my right side rested a large box similar to the mainframe on Deck Seven. I figured it was either a backup control system or subprocessor that helped move data from the brain to the flight deck and vice versa.

Like the corridor I had just passed through, the deck's illumination came from incandescent bulbs hung from wires wrapped around wiring and pipes that traveled along the top of the flight deck before vanishing into the superstructure.

"Geez, Ben," Matt said, entering behind me and looking around, deflated. The hatch slid closed behind him. "I'm so stupid. We've totally been rugged. Hard."

"What do you mean?" I asked, turning to face him. "This is so cool."

"What? Look around, bro. This room looks more like a cheap erotic film set than a functional flight deck. He even used the same rigs from *VR Awesome!* as the pilot seats."

"Because he used them to vet potential pilots," I replied. "He helped make the VR rigs. It's the only thing that makes sense."

"Are you mental?"

"Are you?" I retorted.

"The passenger seat is a frigging sofa. What if Keep arranged this elaborate hoax to bilk me out of four million dollars? I mean, all of the bad guys were wearing helmets, Keep left, Alter is MIA. It fits."

"Did we not experience the same Deck Three? You know, the one that was twice the size of the ship?

"How do we know that was Deck Three and not some extra room hidden beneath the ship?" He shook his head. "I can't believe I'm so damn gullible." He lowered his voice to mimic Keep's. "You haven't been on Earth for about three hours now. Welcome to Caprum, in the Fertile Quadrant of the Manticore Spiral." He spat out an angry breath. "Yeah, right. I'm an idiot, so desperate to save your life or at least give you one last adventure that I just let some conman steal my inheritance. Damn it!" He shouted the last part and slammed his fist down on the subprocessor.

"I think you're overreacting," I said. "For one thing, even if this is a rug that's been pulled out from under us, you aren't an idiot for trying to make what's left of my life something special."

His eyes whipped up, finding mine. His jaw clenched, and the anger fled from him. "Maybe not for that," he agreed. "But the rest. How much do you want to bet that when you put that helmet on and use the controls to *fly* the ship, it'll all just be more virtual reality bullshit?"

"I don't believe it. We both saw what Alter did to the Duke's mercenaries. How could they fake that?"

Matt laughed. "Haven't you ever seen a movie before? They probably practiced the whole setup a hundred times, just waiting for the right rubes to—"

He clammed up instantly when the flight deck hatch slid open again and a woman stepped through.

"Who are you?" I asked, staring at the woman. She had shoulder-length, dirty blonde hair and piercing blue eyes, and wore a loose-fitted silver flight suit pulled in at the waist by a black utility belt. A holstered gun hung from the belt on her left side.

"Co-pilot Alter reporting for duty, sir," she said, coming to attention and saluting as if she were in the Air Force.

"Alter?" I replied, squinting my eyes in a futile effort to find the childlike waif I had watched kill half a dozen individuals in a matter of seconds. Maybe there was a little resemblance in the eyes and the general shape of her face, but otherwise she seemed like another person entirely. She had even somehow managed to grow in height, the top of her head closer to the midline of my neck than the bottom of my shoulders. "You look…"

"…different," Matt finished. "Completely different."

"I'm sorry, sir," Alter replied, glancing at him. "I'm not sure what you mean."

"The last time I saw you," Matt pressed. "You had pink hair and were at least six inches shorter. You can't be the same woman. What kind of game are you playing?"

She shook her head. "I'm not here to play games, sir. I'm here to help prepare for everything that lies ahead."

"And what lies ahead?" Matt asked.

She smiled, and I thought I saw a flash of Alter's grin in it. "I don't really know. But you're in the Manticore Spiral. You're unaffiliated, and you own a killer starship. Whatever we do, I'm sure it's going to be a hell of an adventure. Shall we get to it?"

Chapter Twenty-Five

I smiled widely, casting my best *I-told-you-this-wasn't-a-rug-pull* look at Matt before following Alter to the pilot seats. She dropped into the one on the right, so I claimed the one on the left. Matt trailed behind us, plopping himself into the middle of the sofa and pulling the restraint over his head, snapping it into the receiver at the front of the cushion.

"This had better not be fake or—"

"Or what?" I broke in, looking back at him. "Did you not notice she has a gun strapped to her thigh?"

Matt's attention shifted to Alter, proving he hadn't noticed. "Okay, I get your point," he said flatly.

"How would you like me to refer to you, sir?" Alter asked, looking over at me.

"What do you mean?" I asked.

She rattled off a few titles. "My Lord. Captain. Supreme Leader..."

"Oh. How about Ben?"

She paused as if she was considering the request. "Very well. Ben."

"And Matt," he added, jamming a thumb over his shoulder.

"Ben and Matt," she repeated.

"And please don't call us sir," I continued. "That makes us sound like a couple of boomers."

"Boomers?"

"Old people," Matt explained.

"Understood. In that case, permission to speak casually, sir?"

"Granted, especially since I have a few questions I wanted answered before we lift off. And don't call me sir," I repeated.

"Since you're new to the Spiral, I imagine you have more than a few questions," Alter replied, her military-like stiffness fading. "But I do highly recommend leaving the planet as soon as possible. We only have six minutes before our last paid hour is completed, and as far as I know, neither one of you has any electro to pay for a prolonged stay."

"Electro?" Matt asked. "I guess that's the currency here?"

"Yes," Alter answered.

"If we don't have any electro, how are we going to pay for supplies?" I asked. "Food, clothes, that sort of thing."

"We have enough to last a few days."

"Well, I guess that's something," I said, suddenly feeling a lot of pressure. The thought of Duke Sedaya's hypercom identifier sitting in the ship's datastore crossed my mind, but I rejected it. We had to try to make a go of this. For forty-eight hours, at least.

She pulled her helmet over her head and lowered the visor. Unlike at *VR Awesome!*, it wasn't completely opaque.

I matched her, donning my helmet and lowering the visor. I flinched, confused when the entire front portion of the ship disappeared, giving me a full view of the stacked containers around us. When I raised the visor, the inside of the ship reappeared ahead of me.

"This is a serious upgrade from the simulator," I said, raising and lowering the visor a few more times, amazed by the augmented reality.

"You haven't seen anything yet," Alter replied. "You have the stick, Ben. I'll take care of launch control and help guide you if you run into trouble."

Butterflies filled my stomach, my hands turning clammy on the controls. My heart pounded with excitement, and I couldn't wipe the stupid grin off my face if I wanted to. "How do I start the engines?"

The toggle on the console, just above the throttle," she replied.

I leaned forward, eyes fixed on the toggle as I flipped it up. The lightbulbs overhead flickered, the floor vibrated, and a slight hissing sound passed through the superstructure. A green light flashed below the toggle.

"Reactor online," Alter said. "Thrusters online." A different light on the console fleshed red. "We have a problem. Standby."

My excitement turned to despair almost instantly as I looked back at Matt. Thanks to the visor, I saw right through him. I saw through everything as if there was nothing between me and the shipping containers behind the ship. Lifting the visor, I could tell he was nervous.

Alter raised her hands, tapping at the air. Looking forward again, I didn't have any kind of augmented reality controls hovering in front of me. "What are you looking at?" I asked.

"Systems control," she replied. "I'll teach you how to

use it later." Her head swiveled toward me. "Did you think taking care of a starship would be easy?"

I swallowed hard. "Yeah, kind of. Mister Keep said the ship was low maintenance."

Alter laughed. "That's because he isn't the one who maintained it. Don't worry, Ben. You have me."

She had just finished saying that when she pulled off her helmet, unbuckled herself, and jumped out of her seat. "I just need to go to Deck Seven and make a minor repair. I'll be back in a minute."

She hurried off the flight deck.

"This isn't how I expected things to go," I said.

"And yet, somehow I'm not that surprised," Matt replied. "Even if this thing is the real deal, it's been parked here for twenty years."

"Do you think what we paid would even cover the parking for that much time?"

"I don't even know how he plans to spend four million United States Dollars on the other side of the universe. Or how he can access my bank account from here."

"Maybe he just saved your info and didn't really make the transfer," I guessed. "He obviously has a way back to Earth. He could always convert your fiat to gold or diamonds or whatever else is valuable here to bring back and sell."

"Hearing the words coming out of your mouth, I feel like I'm in the middle of the weirdest dream I've ever had. Even scarier is that everything you just said makes sense."

"I know. It's unbelievable." The red light on the console stopped flashing. "I guess it really was a minor problem."

"Starship Identifier CUL8T3R," a woman's voice

echoed in my ears. "This is the Hestus Spaceport Bursar. Our sensors have detected primary thruster power up. As per our agreement, all accrued storage fees are due at the time of primary thruster ignition. I'm transmitting the final invoice to you now."

I swallowed hard again, for a completely different reason. Accrued storage fees? Didn't our contract cover all payment through the current hour? "Uh. Thank you, ma'am," I replied. "We're, uh…we're reviewing the invoice now."

"What's going on?" Matt asked, unable to hear the bursar since he wasn't wearing a helmet.

"Accounts receivable wants us to settle the tab. Keep's tab."

"We're not supposed to pay his bill."

"Tell that to them."

Matt sighed. "Hopefully Alter can clear this up."

The bursar's voice returned. "Be aware, CUL8T3R, that failure to pay prior to departure will result in the distribution of an automated notice of delinquency. A bounty will be placed on your vessel for ten percent of the accrued fees, which looking at your final bill is rather substantial and will make you a very attractive target."

I cringed at her statement. She had already taken the attitude that we didn't intend to pay the bill. How much did Keep owe?

"Understood, ma'am," I replied. "Standby." I looked at Matt again. "I don't know what's going on, but if we don't pay up we're screwed."

The flight deck hatch slid open. Alter hurried in, the front of her flight suit streaked with grime. "Problem solved," she said, slowing when she noticed my expression. "Is the light still blinking?"

"No," I replied. "It's not that. The Hestus Spaceport

Bursar is requesting payment. I don't even know how to look at the invoice, nevermind send whatever money Keep left for us to cover it."

"Okay," Alter said. "Stay calm." She returned to the co-pilot's seat, leaned over and tapped on the center console display. The kitten screensaver vanished, replaced by an interface almost identical to the one on Keep's phone. Expertly navigating the system, she pulled up the invoice in no time.

My eyes nearly rolled back in my head when I saw the number at the bottom of it. I didn't know the spending power of one electro, but seeing two commas gave me goosebumps, and not in a good way.

I glanced over at Alter. She didn't seem concerned by the cost, at least not at first. She tapped on the *transmit payment* button on the bottom of the invoice, confident the funds were available.

My gut dumped when the dreaded dialog appeared over the invoice.

PAYMENT DECLINED. INSUFFICIENT FUNDS.

"Shit," Alter cursed softly. "That son of a bitch."

"He took the money and ran, didn't he?" Matt said from the back seat.

"That can't be right," Alter said. "He wouldn't do that."

She cleared the dialog and hit the button again, receiving the same result.

"Damn it," she hissed.

"Starship Identifier CUL8T3R, our systems have flagged your payment transmission as declined," the bursar said, her voice only audible to me. "The space-port authorities are being dispatched to ensure you remain grounded until payment arrangements can be made."

"Understood, ma'am," I answered. "We're experiencing…uh…technical difficulties with…uh…with our datastore. Please standby. We'll have the funds transmitted in a minute."

I looked at Alter, my expression no doubt displaying every ounce of the panic I felt. "What are we supposed to do?"

Alter tapped on the display, navigating into what looked like a bank account statement. I glanced from it to her face, watching as her eyes narrowed, her cheeks flushed, and her hands balled into fist.

"That son of a bitch!" she shouted, barely restraining herself from punching the display. I looked back at the statement, my eyes drifting to the total in the bottom right corner.

The number had one comma at least. But only two digits on the left side. The line item directly above the totals showed a withdrawal of nearly two million electro.

Matt leaned forward to get a better look at the screen. "I told you," he said, shaking his head in disgust. "Rugged."

Chapter Twenty-Six

"Keep took all of Matt's money," I said, a mix of fear and anger making my voice shake. "And he took the money that was supposed to pay for the ship's storage. Is that right?"

"It looks that way," Alter said. "We have just enough in our account to take care of regular costs for a week or two, depending on what kind of expenses come up. We definitely don't have enough to pay for twenty years of storage."

"But it's in the damn contract," Matt complained. "He's legally bound to pay the fees."

"How could he do this to us?" I said, catching myself when I realized Alter had shared the last twenty years with him, and he had just thrown her under the bus with us. "How could he do this to you?"

"I don't know," Alter replied. "I always believed him to be a man of his word. A loyal servant to the Duchess of Caprum. Honorable and loyal. I don't know what he's thinking or planning." She tapped violently on the display, returning it to the home screen. Picking up her helmet, she yanked it forcefully over head. "I guess this is where our adventure starts."

"What do you mean?" I asked.

"If we stay here, they'll confiscate the ship and put it in the impound yard until the storage fees are settled. You'll lose the ship and be out on the streets of Hestus, one of the largest cities on Caprum. I'll lose my home. Or we can launch illegally and take our chances."

"I think we should take a minute to consider both options," Matt said.

"What?" I replied. "You paid for the ship. It's ours, fair and square. Keep owes them the money. Keep should pay it."

"So, we let them take the ship while we go find Keep. We make him give us back the electro he took from the account, and then we settle up." He pointed at Alter. "You're supposed to be some kind of assassin or something. Don't tell me you can't find him."

Alter flinched at the word assassin as if she had been shot. "I don't do that anymore," she said flatly. "But yes, I could potentially locate him given enough time."

"We don't need to start out with a bounty on us. Or a second bounty on us. That's just nuts."

"There's a problem with that idea," Alter said. "Once the ship is impounded, anyone with the money can claim it."

"Like Duke Sedaya?" I asked.

"If he gets to it first, yes. Or anyone else who can afford the fee. There are professional dealers who just wait for opportunities to buy impounds at cost. If it takes more than a few hours to track down Avelus, it'll be too late."

I turned my attention to the ship's exterior when a new light appeared near the wreckage at the end of the row of containers. A small, boxy vehicle floated into view. "Alter, look."

"The spaceport authority," she said. "If they reach the hull they can tag the ship. It'll be impossible to get anywhere like that."

"I think we should take our chances and find Keep," Matt said.

"Seriously?" I replied. "Since when are you so passive?"

"Since being aggressive is a direct threat against my life," he shot back. "You might already be dying. I'm not quite ready to go that way."

"You're dying?" Alter asked.

"Well, I think we should launch," I shouted back at him, ignoring her question. "And Alter's the tie-breaker. That's what we agreed."

"I'm rescinding our agreement."

I laughed. "That shit worked when we were eight. It's too late. Alter, do we stay or do we go?"

She didn't hesitate. "Go."

"Better buckle up. Stick and throttle?" I asked.

Alter smiled. "Stick and throttle."

My heart leaped again as I grabbed the control, advancing the throttle. The interior hiss rose in pitch, and the starship began sliding forward. I pulled the stick back too, a sense of weightlessness and imbalance hitting me as the forward view shifted from the spaceport authority vehicle approaching us to the dark sky above it.

"Shields!" Alter shouted, flipping one of the toggles on her side.

The entire ship shuddered as I added power and pulled the stick all the way back. The sudden acceleration shoved me back into the seat. A loud tearing sound screamed across the flight deck as we crashed through the metal beams supporting the expanse of rooftop over-head. We pushed through that too, shearing away the metal and revealing a true, blue-red sky dotted with light clouds as we emerged.

I held the stick steady, the ship rocketing upward as I glanced over my shoulder. The visor cleared all of the obstacles to the rear view, including Matt, allowing me to see the obliterated roof of the warehouse. Other similar structures lined the area around it, while starships of every shape and size dotted the surrounding open space. Smaller vehicles darted back and forth among them.

"Wooohoooo!" I cried out in excitement, opening the throttle all the way, increasing our velocity. I was flying a real spaceship, launching it towards space. Bounties be damned, I couldn't think of anything that could be more fun.

"CUL8T3R, you are in direct violation of your storage agreement," the spaceport bursar said. "You have been marked for delinquency. Bounty notices are being transmitted now and the Caprum Defense Force has been alerted. As of this moment, both the ship and its crew are considered fugitives in violation of Hege-mony law. Good luck out there. You're going to need it."

The comm fell silent, the woman's last words echoing in my head and sending a fresh shiver through my body, stealing away the exultation I had felt at the starship's launch. Glancing over at Alter and seeing the resolved set of her jaw gave me a little bit of comfort, but the sudden turn of events was the last thing I had expected.

Thanks to Mister Keep, only three hours in the Manticore Spiral and Matt and I were already fugitives. So be it. If that was the way things were going to be, then there was nothing left to do but escape.

Chapter Twenty-Seven

I fixed my eyes forward, watching the clouds quickly approaching, our rate of speed continuing to increase. Similar to the mechanical limitations of the simulator, the ship seemed to be dampening the gravitational forces acting on us as we accelerated. It was a gentle nudge instead of an all-out jackhammer shove.

Alter tapped a button in front of her, and a three-dimensional view of the sky around us appeared in the corner of my field of vision.

"Who is that?" I asked, spotting five red triangles entering the edge of the map.

"Caprum Defense Force," Alter replied. "Their goal is to stop us from escaping the planet's orbit."

"Can they?" Matt asked.

"That depends on how well we fly. And how well we shoot."

"I don't know if I can shoot at them," I said. "Unless their ships are unmanned?"

"They won't have any problem shooting at us," she answered. "And they don't care that we're alive in here. I know it isn't fair, Ben. I can't believe Alvus did this to you and to me. But you need to decide right now what kind of person you want to be here. You too, Matt. The Manticore Spiral can be an amazing place, but if you aren't up for it you *will* get eaten alive."

On the map, the five triangles were gaining quickly, closing the distance between us in a hurry. I didn't need to ask Alter if we could outrun them. Clearly, we couldn't.

I considered her words. I didn't know if she had just given us a pep talk, a challenge, or what, but I knew she was right. We weren't in Kansas anymore. We couldn't judge life based on what we had known or experienced on Earth. I didn't know what kind of person I wanted to be now. I didn't even know what my options were. But I was absolutely sure I didn't want to go down within five minutes of blasting off. And I didn't want Matt or Alter to go down with me.

"How do I work the guns?" I asked after a tense pause.

"You need to access fire control," she replied. "Raising your hand will activate the command overlay. It will be the largest action item in the cloud."

I wasn't sure what she meant until I released the throttle to put my hand up. Immediately, a group of words appeared between my hand and the exterior view, slightly transparent so I could still see through them. The largest item in the word cloud was FCS. Fire Control System. I punched the transparent image, entering a screen that displayed the ship from the top down, all of the guns I had seen from the exterior highlighted. A turret on either side of the head. above the mouth, another pair tucked under the ears. Currently, they were all set to manual control, with a button below the schematic labeled *activate*.

"You can set the guns to auto if that makes you feel better about shooting at the ships chasing us," Alter said. "But the ship's brain came from a junk hauler dumped on Demitrus over a hundred years ago, so it isn't the quickest or the most accurate. You can also split control between pilot and co-pilot, or handle it all yourself."

"How do I aim backward on my own?" I asked. "Or rotate the guns?"

"Activating in manual will open a split screen with a rear view. The turrets will move with your eyes when you follow a target. The thumb trigger will activate the ear guns, the primary trigger the face turrets. Unfortunately, you can't shoot the batteries individually."

"Okay," I said, barely noticing the view beyond the fire control screen as we exited the clouds and continued launching toward a quickly darkening sky. I tapped on the two rear cannons until the labels beside them changed to 'co-pilot.' "I'm giving you the rear guns."

"I have them," Alter replied.

"What about the shields?"

"The barrels of the turrets push through the shield barrier. While they hold, the gun positions are the weakest link in our defenses."

"What do you mean *while they hold*?" Matt asked.

"The power for the shields comes from the Star of Caprum, which is good. That power flows through seventy-year-old nodes spread across the surface of the ship. Too much power to the nodes will burn them out. They'll need to be replaced to be useful again. Each burned out node leaves a portion of the hull vulnerable."

"So there won't be a single, giant failure?" I said.

"More like death by a thousand cuts. The end result is the same."

As if on cue, a warning tone echoed in my ears and three of the five triangles flashed. A moment later, a three dimensional wireframe of the ship appeared under the map, orange dots showing where the blasts hit. Small green dots appeared in a polygonal arrangement around the hits.

"The dots are the internal temperature of the nodes," Alter explained before I asked. "When they rise to dangerous levels the nodes will be in danger of failing and the dots will turn red."

"How long will that take?" Matt asked.

"Long enough for us to get out of here," Alter replied confidently as a few more hits registered against the same part of the shields. "But it's better not to fly in a straight line."

"Right," I said, embarrassed that I had forgotten to pilot the ship while she had been explaining everything. I pulled the stick left, the ship reacting agilely and cutting in that direction. Bright beams of energy flashed past the front of the ship, proof that I had dodged a hit.

"Good," Alter said. "Keep it up."

I yanked the stick back the other way, pushing it forward as I did. The ship turned and dove, and for the first time I caught a glimpse of the defense force fighters on our tail. Similar to the smaller ship in our hangar, they had a lot more sharp angles and a drab gray paint job. The logo of a scepter on a yellow background adorned the fuselage.

The look only lasted two seconds before the fighters zipped past the ship's rear. Looking over my shoulder, I watched Alter's return fire launch behind them, her aim a little off. Unlike the fighters' energy beams, our guns spat out small, fiery red balls like a machine gun.

"I'm rusty," Alter growled, annoyed with herself for missing. "Try to get us headed back toward space."

"Got it," I said, adjusting course to angle toward the space.

The CDF fighters broke formation, each choosing a different path but all of them staying on our tail, spreading out to make it harder for Alter to hit them. I continued to wobble the stick back and forth, up and down, keeping the ship constantly changing planes and vectors while still rising toward space. My heart pounded a million miles per hour, my mouth completely dry, every muscle in me tense. Even so, there was a part of me enjoying the hell out of the ride.

Matt couldn't say the same. As I pushed the ship into another hard evasive maneuver, he slumped back on the sofa, his face tinged a sick green. His hands gripped the edge of the cushion so tightly I thought he might puncture the old leather, his eyes clamped shut as if he could will it all away. I felt bad for him. He had gone through all of this for me, only to be proven right all along. The sale of the starship *had* been a scam.

Just not the one we expected.

Warning tones again filled my ears. A quick glance at the wireframe showed more hits to the same part of the rear, the shield nodes gaining a yellow hue.

"You need to keep them off our tail," Alter said, doing her best to line up another shot.

"I'm trying. This is my first time flying a real starship, you know."

I pulled up hard, increasing the approach angle toward space, desperate to clear orbit and escape the planet and the starfighters chasing us.

"On second thought, hold steady," Alter said. "Cut the throttle and break to the port side when I give the word."

"Okay."

I held the stick in place, my other hand on the throttle, ready to cut it on Alter's command. The map on the HUD showed the CDF ships closing from three directions.

"Hold it," Alter said, her voice reflecting her increased concentration. "Hold…it…" She adjusted the cannons and opened fire, sending a wave of fiery blobs across the rear of the ship. "Now!"

I jerked the stick to port and cut the throttle. The maneuver threw me sideways against the restraints, nearly causing me to lose control. The ship's frame whined and popped with the strain, and Matt made a gurgling sound that indicated he wouldn't be able to hold his dinner much longer.

The CDF fighters behind us tried to evade, but she had covered the entire rear with the energy balls, leaving them nowhere to turn. Three blobs was all it took to sever the wing of one of the craft, four blobs nearly slicing the fuselage away from the other. Both fighters smoked and peeled away from the fight, their continued operation in question as they quickly vanished from the map.

Alter wasn't done. The quick change of direction put a third fighter in her crosshairs, and she unleashed more blobs, sinking them into the upper portion of the ship, forcing it to peel away. The last two fighters dodged instinctively, breaking their angle of attack to recalibrate.

"Get us to space," she barked. "Punch it!"

I pulled all the way back on the throttle, shoving me

back into the seat again as the thrusters opened up and the hiss turned into a muted rumble.

"The switch all the way to the left above the throttle," she said. "Flip it."

I reached for the toggle, switching it on. The light roar became a louder growl and we shot forward again as if I had hit the afterburners. The two remaining CDF fighters opened fire again, a couple of blasts hitting the strained shields. But we continued accelerating, putting distance between them and us as we reached the thermosphere. The view outside the ship gained an orange hue as heat built up along the front, the shields the only thing preventing hull rupture. Looking further out into space, I could see other craft of various shapes and sizes in orbit on different planes above the planet.

"Look at the size of those things," I said absently, my attention landing on a pair of vessels that had to be at least a mile long. At the same time, I noticed a pair of medium-sized vessels suddenly emit the blue glow of thruster trails.

"Royal Sentries," Alter explained. "They won't get involved in this small matter. But those two corvettes will."

The two large ships I had taken particular notice of were gaining speed, their path carrying them toward us on a collision course. "Can we get past them?" I asked.

"That depends on how well we evade their disruptor cannons. The projectiles are slow and dumb, at least compared to beams, but one hit will disable all the shield nodes, a second will disable the ship and leave us adrift. I can take the stick if you prefer."

I looked out at the two corvettes angling toward us from both flanks. I wanted to keep the stick. To be the one to try to get us through the blockade and away to freedom, not a bystander to the action. I was sure I could do it. I had gotten us away from the ground-based defenses so far. And this was my adventure. My…

I spotted Matt in my peripheral vision. He had fallen unconscious, vomit running down the front of his shirt. All of a sudden I felt like the most selfish turd in the universe. A total asshole. My friend had just given up everything he had for me, and I had let him. And now we were in deep, deep shit and he was out cold covered in his own puke.

And I thought I could handle this?

"Alter, you have the stick," I said, my entire body turning cold. I had made a mistake. A stupid, horrible, selfish mistake. Matt hard warned me earlier about catching people I cared about up in my unstable emotions, and then I had gone ahead and done exactly that. He tried to warn me again, and I still hadn't listened.

And now?

I just wanted to go home.

Chapter Twenty-Eight

Unfortunately, there was no going home. At least not yet.

Right now, the only thing I could do was let the cold grip of gut-wracking, selfish guilt embrace me as I held on for dear life, worried about Matt unconscious on the sofa behind me. Right now, there was nothing I could do for him, except help Alter fight our way out of this mess.

She didn't flinch, or show any sign of nervousness as she took control of the ship. She immediately changed course, taking a more direct path toward the corvette on the starboard flank. I realized why almost immediately, ashamed my nerves had canceled out years of playing strategy video games. By moving directly toward one ship, it limited the other's ability to shoot at us without the risk of hitting a friendly.

At the same time, the maneuver still put us closer to one of the corvettes and its guns. Maybe the disruptor rounds were slow, but every kilometer closer we came to the vessel gave Alter less time to react and evade.

"Ben, take the rear guns," she said calmly, raising her hand from the throttle to pass control of the cannons to me. A box appeared in my HUD to acknowledge the transfer, and I reached up to tap it. Immediately, the forward view was replaced by the rear despite the direction of my head. I quickly scanned for signs of the CDF fighters, only able to see them because the system outlined them against the backdrop of Caprum.

Seeing any planet from outer space live was cause for distraction. It momentarily pulled me back into the wonderment of what was happening and away from Matt's distress. Looking at the blue marble, I immediately noticed how the position of the continents was off, the sky had a slightly deeper blue, and there was a lot more reflective silver and gray amongst the green and brown landscape, indicating a highly developed world.

My gaze shifted to huge tracts of dark patches along that landscape, massive scars as if a giant dragon had once held the entire planet tightly in its claws and dropped it into place. I opened my mouth to ask Alter what had caused the marks before remembering we were running for our lives and I was supposed to be watching our six.

Nothing there. The two remaining fighters had fallen way behind our boosted ascent and had seemed to be continuing the chase out of obligation rather than with any intent to catch up. So why had Alter asked me to take the rear guns?

"Hold on," she said. "The corvettes are starting to fire."

Every part of me wanted to switch back to the forward view. To see what we were about to fly into. I struggled to resist the temptation, certain she had passed me the cannons for a reason. As we began juking and jerking through space, my body was pushed and pulled in every direction despite the ship's countermeasures.

The fear that this adventure would end only minutes after it started expanded in my mind, sending shock-waves of alarm throughout my body. My hand quivered on the stick. My heart pounded so hard I could barely breathe.

In the corner of the HUD, the view of our defenses remained fixed, the shield nodes all intact. Even the ones that had turned yellow had shifted back to green.

The seconds passed, the ship shuddering from the constant change in direction. Maintaining control of the rear cannons, I continued to resist the urge to return to the forward view to see what was happening in front of us, even though I knew Alter had things there well in hand. This was her home. Keep knew she would do everything she could to keep it from being destroyed. How could I *not* trust that?

"It'll be harder to dodge their disruptor fire once we're on the other side of the blockade," Alter said. "And we can't activate the hyperdrive until we're clear of orbit. You need to track and shoot any of the rounds that look like they're going to hit us."

"Maybe you should take the rear guns once we're past?" I replied, my voice shaky. I hated that my nerves were so obvious, but she didn't seem to either notice or care.

"No. You can do it, Ben."

She said it like she really believed it, even though at that moment I didn't. Instead of arguing, I refocused on the view behind us, tensing slightly when the corvette appeared at the bottom of my field of vision. It passed so close below us it felt like I could reach out and touch it.

The ship was at least ten times the size of ours, the gun batteries narrower and more plentiful. The cannons across the top rotated to track us as we passed, the speed of their motors unable to match our velocity once we made it directly overhead. It didn't stop the corvette from shooting at us, but it did reduce the intensity of the lethal bombardment that came our way, at least until we shot across the corvette's bow.

Their port cannons were already in position, and they opened fire the moment we reached the other side of the small blockade, sending dark projectiles at us like shotgun shells. The fire control system painted dozens of incoming rounds sprayed across space.

I wasn't sure which ones were a threat, so I did my best to catch them all, benefitting from the added time our growing distance and matching directional velocity afforded us. I tried to track individual targets with my eyes to line up the cannons, quickly discovering that method was too slow. Only Alter's flying saved us from the first volley, her maneuvers carrying us through the spread.

A more severe warning tone shrilled in my ears, sending my gaze to the ship's wireframe. The area just below the main thrusters flashed red, the shields reporting as offline, hit by one of the rounds.

"Shit!" Alter snapped. "Ben, I need your help."

"On it," I replied, redoubling my focus. I didn't try to hunt the rounds again. Instead, I tested using the stick to move the cannons, pleased to see that the second method of targeting was available. Alter should have mentioned it earlier.

Control through the stick improved my performance immediately. Instead of trying to track individual projectiles, I fired bursts of energy blobs at incoming clusters, spraying the field behind us in a controlled manner. The fiery blobs swept through the disruptor rounds, burning them away one after another, only a few making it through to zip harmlessly past. I could sense the victorious smirk working its way across my face, my confidence growing as I blasted the disruptor rounds with shot after shot.

"Almost there," Alter said.

I didn't relent, spraying a blanket of cover fire behind us that absorbed every round coming our way. With the opposing forces finally dropping back, Alter eased up on her evasive maneuvers, the change so smooth it could barely be felt.

"Cease fire," she said. "Hyperspace in five. Four. Three."

I took my finger off the trigger, new excitement building at the thought of traveling faster than light. It was too bad Matt wasn't awake to experience it firsthand.

Alter's countdown reached one almost at the same moment that one of the disruptor rounds moved into the rear view from out of nowhere. Instinct took over, and I wrapped my finger around the trigger, eyes lining up a shot, the turrets swiveling to adjust.

Spacetime bent around us, Caprum distorting as though it were in a fisheye lens before being pinched, suddenly shrinking away into nothing as though it had never been there at all. For the briefest moment, I thought the disruptor round would vanish with it.

But it didn't. Caught in the bubble or field or magic or whatever that Alter called hyperspace, it stayed with the ship, its trajectory carrying it toward the hole in our shields.

"Alter, one of the rounds made it through. We're about to—"

I didn't get to finish before the projectile hit the hull, sending a shockwave of energy rippling across the exterior. All of the shield nodes on the wireframe switched to red just before the entire HUD vanished, as did the rearview. I found myself looking at the front of the flight deck through the tinted visor. The pilot station had gone offline, and as I turned my head to look at Alter the rest of the flight deck went dead too, leaving us in total darkness.

Chapter Twenty-Nine

"Shit," Alter cursed sharply, her voice my only way of judging her position. "Shit, shit, shit, shit, shit. How did you miss that one?" Her voice stabbed me like a knife, accusing me of failure.

"I didn't see it," I replied. "It came out of nowhere. I'm sorry."

A single light flashed on the flight deck, coming from the subprocessor in the back. It was enough for me to make out Alter's angry face as she ripped off her helmet and released her harness, pushing herself out of the co-pilot's seat.

I hadn't realized the gravity had been lost with the power until she floated free of her station, using it as an anchor to push herself toward the exit. She twisted neatly when she passed Matt, avoiding globs of vomit as they coagulated and floated away from him.

"What do we do?" I asked.

Reaching the exit, she tapped on her boots before putting her feet back on the deck. The soles must be magnetized, because she stuck to the deck as if the gravity had returned.

"The disruptor took out the main systems," she replied. "The emergency backup is online, but I need to go to Deck Seven to manually reboot the primary controller." Pulling open a panel beside the hatch, she used a hidden hand crank to roll the door open just enough to slip out. She paused between the two doors, looking back at me. "It's not your fault, Ben. You did your best. The good news is that we got away from Caprum in one piece."

"What's the bad news?" I asked.

"Getting hit while in hyperspace is less than ideal. Losing power shut down the hyperdrive, dropping us well short of our original destination. If I had to guess, we're probably about halfway between Caprum and Sarton, Duke Sedaya's homeworld. I'll be right back."

"Wait," I said, reaching for my helmet. "I want to learn how to reboot the primary." I picked the helmet off and let it float away. The wire connecting it to the pilot's station anchored it when it reached its apex, holding it in place. I removed my harness, almost giddy when I pushed off and began to float.

"This isn't a good time," Alter answered. "I can teach you everything when we reach a safer location. Just wait here." She vanished through the hatch, leaving it hanging open.

I pushed off the pilot's station, trying to copy her weightless maneuver. Instead, I found myself headed toward the ceiling, my body turning as I flailed, not accustomed to the different physics. The effort rolled me over, and I hit the ceiling with my back, sticking there like Spiderman.

"Ben?" Matt said, eyes opening slowly, looking up at

me from the sofa. "I had the weirdest dream." He paused, staring at me. "Why are you stuck to the ceiling?"

"I'm not stuck," I replied, pushing myself back toward the deck. "There's no gravity right now. Are you okay?"

"Wait. No gravity?" He looked around before groaning. "Damn it. That wasn't a dream, was it? We really did buy a starship."

"We really did. Are you okay?" I repeated.

"I'm not sure now." He looked down at his shirt, where the vomit had left a stain. "I barfed on myself."

I touched down on the deck in front of him, grabbing the pilot's seat to hold myself in place. "I'm afraid so. Look, your puke is floating around the flight deck." I pointed to one of the blobs drifting across the deck.

"Gross," Matt replied. "We aren't dead. That's good. What happened?"

"We made it to hyperspace, but one of the Caprum Defense Force's shots hit us and knocked out the power. We're on backup right now. Alter went to reboot the primary processor, which should bring us back online and fix the gravity."

He stared at me, face still pale. "This isn't what I signed up for."

"I know. I'm sorry."

He sighed. "I don't know why I let you talk me into this."

"Because you care about me."

"Not anymore."

I paused, the guilt still gnawing at me. "I shouldn't have let you do this. I put your life in danger, and it's not right. I'm a selfish asshole."

He shrugged. "What's done is done. We can't change it, so there's no use crying about it."

I forced a smile. "I'm still an asshole."

"Yup," he agreed. "So, just to recap. We're dead in space, flat broke, and both Caprum and Duke Sedaya have bounties out on this ship."

"That sounds about right."

"That's a problem. What's the solution?"

It was just like Matt to put the past where it belonged and focus on the way forward. "I haven't had any time to think about it."

"Me neither, but I know what my gut is telling me. We can either let someone else take this ship from us, or we can beat them to the punch and put ourselves in a better position."

"You're talking about contacting Sedaya again. We've already had that discussion."

"You got to have your joyride to space," Matt snapped angrily. "Look around. We barely made it out of there alive, and now we have not one, but two separate prices on our heads and we've only been here for three hours. You felt guilty about that two seconds ago."

I froze in place, biting my lower lip. He was right. I had worried about him until I knew he was okay before switching back to selfish mode. "What about Alter?"

"We can't make every decision about how it affects her. We didn't take her on willingly, she was part of the package."

"She saved our lives, or at least a trip to the gulag. She's the only reason we made it out of there."

"And I'm fine if she wants to come with us. That's her choice." I opened my mouth to argue, but he didn't let me speak. "Come on, Ben. Sedaya wants the Star. He also runs Caprum. We can turn it over, get a new ship plus some spending money and have him cancel all of our debts and issue a pardon or whatever he needs to do to leave us free and clear. We can rocket around the Fertile Quadrant looking for a cure, and once we find one we can fix you up and go home. Or we can be penniless fugitives until some mercenary or bounty hunter catches up to us. Which one of those sounds better to you?"

I stared at him in silence. Of course, there was only one good answer. But I hated that answer even more now than I had the first time he brought it up. That was the biggest difference between Matt and me. My mother had taught me to dare to dream. His father had taught him to survive.

I looked past him, through the hatch to the corridor leading away from the flight deck where emergency lights offered a dim view. No sign of Alter.

"Okay," I said, the word sour in my mouth. "Call him."

Chapter Thirty

Matt's hands shook slightly as he navigated to the phone's hypercom screen, which immediately displayed a search function on top and what probably should have been a long list of saved identifiers below. Instead, it appeared that Keep had wiped the hypercom datastore clean, leaving only the single ID that he had collected prior to his departure from the ship.

Duke Sedaya's ID.

"You're sure about this?" I asked as Matt's thumb shifted to tap the entry.

"If you have a better idea, I'm open to it," he replied.

We both knew I didn't. I used the lack of gravity to jump over Matt and the sofa, pushing off the ceiling and twisting in the air to come down behind him, unable to hold back my smile when I stuck the landing. My initial confusion over the weightlessness had faded fast. It was all a matter of physics, anyway.

"Show off," he said, pressing down on the entry. "How long do you think it will take to—"

He stopped talking when a man's face appeared on the phone's screen, causing us both to flinch. The connection wasn't great, the image grainy and indistinct, but it only added to the creepiness of the visage looking back at us. Frankly, Sedaya looked like a frostbitten elf. His face was pale, long, and narrow, with a tiny nose, high cheekbones, deep set purple eyes and too-blue lips. His long white hair and pointed ears only solidified that view. But hadn't Keep said he was human?

He looked back at us curiously, an expression of rage crossing over his expression.

"You're not Avelus," he said, his voice too soft and high to match his otherwise evil and unfriendly look. The tension in his jaw relaxed as he seemed to realize the state of things. "Ah. You're the buyers."

He said the word buyers like a cobra spitting venom. Maybe because Keep had managed to sell only minutes before his lackeys arrived on the scene? The timing was good for us, bad for him. At least, I thought it had been good for us. If only I had known we were about to be fleeced.

Matt and I just kept staring at him. Our nerves and surprise prevented us from speaking.

"You're Earthians, aren't you?" he said.

"Y…yes," I stammered out, fighting to regain control of my anxiety.

"We got your hypercom ID from one of your people," Matt said bluntly, kicking his shock to the curb. "He told us you were interested in negotiating for the Star of Caprum, and suggested we could make a deal."

"I see."

That was all he said, silently staring at us as the seconds ticked away. I glanced over my shoulder, making sure Alter hadn't come back yet.

"Are you interested?" Matt asked.

"You just made the purchase," Sedaya replied. "Why do you want to sell so quickly? Greed?"

"What?"

"I just checked the hypernet. It appears a bounty has been placed against your registered identifier. You left Caprum without settling your debt to the storage facility."

"That wasn't us," I said. "Mister Keep said he was covering the prior charges."

"Was it in the contract?"

Matt and I looked at one another. "We didn't have time to read the whole contract," he said. "Your goons were coming, and Keep said we had to make a decision."

Sedaya's laugh rattled like an old lawnmower. "I can't believe Avelus went to Earth to look for a buyer. Or that he settled on you." He shook his head. "You're too young for this."

"Too young for what?" I asked.

"To be an unaffiliated entity with a starship."

"We don't know what that means."

He laughed again, a hint of pity behind the cackle. "I recommend you learn. Quickly."

"We were hoping you could help," Matt said. "Settle our debts, clear the bounty, pay us back what we gave Keep, and send us back to Earth."

"Is that all?" Sedaya said.

"And if there's medicine here that can cure cancer, get us some of that," I said.

"You're sick?"

"Dying. It's terminal. Unless someone here can fix it."

"I see." He froze again, staring at us in silence. Based on the last time, I had the sense he was accessing the hypernet, either offscreen or in his head or something.

The power came back on, the overhead lights flickering to life, the gravity returning. The force was unfamiliar after spending the last ten minutes without it. I winced when my flight helmet crashed to the deck, and again when Matt's vomit splashed down beside the co-pilot station.

Alter would be back soon. We needed to wrap this up.

"We'll give you the Star," Matt said, obviously thinking the same thing. "And the ship if you want it."

Sedaya's amusement fled his face as if it were a candle snuffed out by the wind. "I control over twenty-one worlds in the Fertile Quadrant. My navy is composed of over three hundred ships, not including the countless mercenary units and bounty hunters who drop everything when they receive a work offer from me. I'm the most powerful man in the Manticore Spiral, second in influence only to the Empress herself. That you've spoken to me directly is an honor reserved only for a select few." He leaned away, his angry demeanor settling slightly. "I'm not heartless or merciless, so I'll make you a counteroffer. Give me the Star, and I'll return you to Earth after your debt to my Caprum has been repaid in the levitite mines."

I swallowed my heart for what felt like the dozenth time, body shaking, cold sweat clamming my hands. This was going all wrong. Everything had gone all wrong. I wouldn't live long enough to pay back any debts. I had a sense from the way Sedaya had made the offer, Matt might not either or if he did he would be an old man by the time he went back to Earth.

"I see," Matt said, his voice almost as cold as the

duke's had been. It took me off-guard. I hadn't heard that tone from him in a long time. Since the one and only time his mother had called, trying to reconnect. "I'm guessing from your smug attitude that you probably know where we are, and you've got a goon squad moving in on us while you stall to give them time. I may be young, Baron, but I'm not a total idiot." He smiled at Sedaya, the same charismatic grin he used often. Normally, it looked friendly and approachable. Right now, it oozed so much cool confidence it became scary. "You had your chance to get the Star, but you chose to be a contrarian miser instead. Come and take it from us then. If you can."

Matt tapped on the phone, disconnecting before Sedaya had a chance at a rebuttal.

"What the hell did you just do?" I whispered, finding my breath hard to come by.

He looked back at me, more resolute than pale. "I don't know, but damn it felt good."

"You called Duke Sedaya, didn't you?" Alter said, sneaking in behind me and causing me to jump. Turning to look at her, I was surprised to see her hair had gone from blonde to black and was tied back in a long ponytail. She had also changed her flight suit from the stained, loose silver to a more fitted gold. Somehow, that had made her face look smaller and more pointed, too.

"Yeah," Matt replied. "We thought—"

"He rejected your offer, didn't he?"

"Again, yes."

"And threatened to come after you?"

"I'm not sure he got to that part yet," I said.

"He's an asshole," Matt said. "So high on his own supply. I hate people like that."

"I could have told you that would happen and

stopped you from getting further on his bad side if you had given me the chance. Both of you are new to the Quadrant. You have no idea what you're doing. So maybe you should consider looping me in?"

"We knew you wouldn't be on board with giving Sedaya the ship, considering your history with him," I said.

"And knowing that, how could we know you would give us honest advice?" Matt added. "Since we are so new to the Quadrant, we're unintentionally gullible."

Alter's eyes flicked from me to Matt and back, their intensity piercing. "Well, now you know from Sedaya himself that he won't buy the Star. And that he'll have no problem seizing it. I'm sure he has ships already on the way." She circled the sofa, heading for the co-pilot's seat. "The primary is back online, all systems should be operational within the next minute. Ben, take the pilot's seat. Matt…" She paused next to her station, looking at the deck and making a face. "There's a storage compartment next to the elevator. Go get a mop."

Chapter Thirty-One

"Wait a second," I said from behind the sofa. "This is our ship. We're in charge."

Alter looked back at us. "Okay. Since you've handled everything so well. What should we do?"

I winced at her sarcasm. It wasn't only her look that had changed while she was gone. Her whole personality seemed sharper. More biting and bossy.

"I think I should go to the pilot's seat," I said. "Because someone affiliated with Duke Sedaya has us pinpointed and is headed our way."

"Good idea," Alter said.

"And I should probably get a mop," Matt said. "Before too much of my puke goes through the grating and damages the wires underneath."

"I agree."

Matt removed his harness and jumped off the sofa, legs a little shaky from the ride into space. He held onto whatever support he could find as he made his way from the flight deck in search of the storage closet.

"We should have a cleaning robot or something," I

said as I returned to the pilot's seat. "I mean, over two thousand years to advance in technology and we're still using mops?"

"Sometimes simple tools are the most efficient," Alter said. "Nicer ships have cleaning bots. This ship has me. And mops."

"You fight, you fix things, you clean. Do you cook, too?" I joked, strapping myself in.

"There's no need to cook. The assembler has an adequate list of predefined meals it can produce."

"Assembler? Is that like a replicator? Do you know Star Trek?"

"I've seen it. Yes, it's very similar, but a bit more limited. Science, not wishful thinking."

She pulled on her helmet, so I did the same, noticing the transparency in the visor had cracked when it hit the deck, leaving a thin line down the middle of the view from my left eye. Annoying, but not unusable.

Tapping on the virtual interface, Alter pulled up an enlarged version of the grid she had activated during our escape from Caprum.

"This is an enlargement of the general public access starmap of the Spiral," she explained. "Keep probably showed it to you downstairs."

"Yeah, he did."

"We fell out of hyperspace here," she said, zooming in even more, so that Caprum and Sarton were almost quarter-sized. The ship was only a speck, sitting closer to Caprum near a small moon. "That's Keishan, one of Caprum's outer moons. It looks like we were pulled into orbit while the power was out." She continued zooming in while different datasets appeared above the map, their values constantly changing.

"Is that good or bad?"

"Normally, not too bad. Today, bad."

"Oh. Why?"

"Keishan is a barracks for Sedaya's strike force. If I'm right, we should see their rapid response unit pop up on sensors right. About. Now."

Her timing was flawless. Three red triangles appeared on the zoomed in grid, emerging from the far side of the moon.

Matt returned to the flight deck. "Alter, I found a mop and a bucket. Where do I get water?"

"Forget it," she said. "You took too long. Better buckle up."

"Damn it," he cursed softly as the mop clattered on the deck. "Are we going to get shot at again already?"

"No. Sedaya probably doesn't want to destroy the ship before he has the Star. At least not yet. The incoming unit is most likely a boarding party. Anyway, I'm prepping the hyperdrive. We should be clear before they arrive."

"What's involved with preparing the hyperdrive?" I asked.

"First, you need to pick a destination," she said. "I'm not particular right now. Anywhere-but-here is good. Once that's done, the primary will route a path to avoid any obstacles. That's why every ship has a broadcasting identifier. Otherwise, the odds of collision go up. Believe me, you don't want to run into anything when you're moving at hundreds of times the speed of light."

"So the hyperdrive is FTL, not like a space fold or a wormhole or something like that?" I asked.

"The hyperspace field compresses spacetime. Anything already in the field maintains its velocity. Anything moving into the field is accelerated to the velocity of the field."

"What if a random particle of space junk hits the field?"

"Compressed to the point of obliteration. Something the size of a starship, however…" She trailed off.

"Got it. I think."

"When the route is set, the light on the console above the throttle turns green. Right now, it's flashing orange to show it's processing."

I found the light on my station. "Shouldn't it be done by now? Sedaya's ships are getting close."

"It's probably slowed by the reboot. Once it turns green, flip the switch beneath it and the hyperdrive will be activated. It takes about ten seconds for the field to form. That's how the disruptor round snuck in before we left it far behind. A one in a million shot, really."

"I seem to be hitting all the long odds lately," I said. "What about the ships?"

"If they try to board us, they'll regret it." she replied, flashing me back to the short work she made of the first of Sedaya's mercenaries to reach the ship.

"I bet they will," I said. "Can't we just shoot them?"

"Too risky. The added energy expenditure could cause a short that would send us back to emergency power."

My gaze drifted between the flashing light and the red triangles, over and over as the ships continued closing on our position. After what we had already been through, I really didn't want to get into another fight right now. If we couldn't go home yet, I wanted to take the duke's advice and learn as much about this place as possible, as soon as possible.

With her helmet on and visor down, it was hard to make out Alter's state of mind from her facial expression. But as the gap continued shrinking between us and the duke's forces and as the hyperdrive light persisted its dogged flashing, I noticed how the muscles of her hand tensed as it rested over the switch to activate the drive. When her other hand raised toward her helmet, preparing to pull it off to head elsewhere to defend the ship, I found myself keyed up again, though it wasn't quite as severe as before.

I was getting used to being under threat. I didn't know if that was a good thing.

Seeming to sense our predicament, one of the three ships jumped ahead of the others, gaining velocity to reach us more quickly. A few tense, rapid heartbeats later, the hyperdrive light finally went green. Alter flipped the toggle almost before the color change, as if her perception was a few hundredth of a millisecond faster than mine. While there was no obvious interior change, the activation caused an immediate reaction from the ships trailing us.

The two behind the lead jumped forward, trying to catch up. A warning tone sounded in my ears just before the lead picked up speed, closing the gap much faster.

"Shit, he harpooned us," Alter said, pulling her helmet off. "Ben, you have the stick. I have to go deal with this."

"Do you need help?" Matt asked.

"Those are some of Sedaya's most experienced soldiers. Are you an experienced soldier?"

"No."

"Then there's nothing you can do. Wait here."

She removed her restraint and climbed out of the co-pilot seat to run from the flight deck, leaving me alone at the helm. I still wasn't completely comfortable with flying the ship by myself, but at least my stomach didn't take its usual nosedive. It felt good to be gaining some confidence in my abilities.

"I'll tell you something," Matt said, moving from the sofa to her abandoned seat. "If we're going to be out here for any length of time, I don't want to be dependent on her to come to our rescue every ten minutes."

"Agreed," I said. "Matt, I'm sorry things—"

"Forget it," Matt said. "I'm done worrying about what I can't have right now. All I need to be happy at the moment is to get under Sedaya's skin as much as possible. He reminds me of my boss at Burger Shack."

"Brad?" I asked.

"No, he was okay. The other one."

"Carl?"

"Yeah, him. Guy thought because his dad owned the place he could treat people like shit." He pulled on Alter's helmet, getting his first look at the augmented view. "Oh, wow. This is kind of cool."

I looked over my shoulder, the visor allowing me to see through the ship's flight deck to Sedaya's ship outside. Tall and narrow, it had a pair of thrusters on the top and bottom of the fuselage and a small cockpit in the center, right above the thick cable that held us captive. Four sets of guns sat at equal distances from each other between the cockpit and the two thrusters on each side, proving that if they had wanted to blow us up, they certainly could have.

The other two ships were falling further and further back as the lead ship winched itself closer. The hyperspace field continued forming around us, the universe gaining that strange curve I had noticed before. It cut the two trailing ships off from us completely.

"What's going on?" Matt asked as a hatch opened in

the remaining corvette's bow, just below the grappling line. Dozens of punks in dark spacesuits jumped out, flying through space toward us.

"It looks like we're about to be boarded."

Chapter Thirty-Two

"We need to go help Alter," Matt said as the attackers floated across the gap between their ship and ours.

"Are you kidding?" I replied. "You heard what she said. These are experienced soldiers. Besides, she handled them before. She can take care of it."

"Those were mercenaries. These are trained fighters. Not the same."

"Yeah, exactly. They'll kill us even faster than the other guys would have."

"That goes for Alter too."

"You don't know that."

"You don't know that I'm wrong."

The first soldier reached the ship's stern, one of his boots stomping down on a camera and blotting out part of our view. Intentionally? I didn't think so until he moved his foot and replaced the camera with some kind of dark goop. A second soldier reached the ship, repeating the maneuver and causing us to lose more of the rear view.

"These guys know exactly what they're doing," Matt

said, pulling his helmet off. "If we don't help Alter and she loses, we go to the gulag. You'll be the lucky one to die there in a few months while I'm pick-pick-picking away at hard rock for the rest of my life."

"You don't know it's that kind of mine."

"That's not the point. Come on." He released his harness and jumped out of the seat.

I hesitated before taking my helmet off and standing up. "Matt, we don't have any weapons. You might be Bruce Lee, but I'm more like Peggy Lee."

"There's an armory on Deck Two," Matt said. "We can grab something there."

"What? We never went to Deck Two."

"Why do you think it took me so long to find a mop? I went to the other decks to see what was there. I stayed in the elevator, but the door's labeled." The hatch slid open ahead of his approach.

"So, what's on Deck Five?" I asked, running to catch up to him. I didn't really want to go down to the armory, pick up a gun, and try to shoot someone. But I didn't want Alter to die trying to protect us either. And I definitely didn't want Matt to end up in the levitite mines. It was the least bad in the basket of shitty options.

"Storage, like Keep said, I think."

"You think?"

"There were boxes and metal parts and sheet metal piled almost up to the elevator doors."

We reached the elevator, waiting a couple of seconds for the cab to arrive. A muffled bang echoed from somewhere else on the ship.

"We need to hurry," I said, rushing into the cab when the doors opened and sending it to Deck Two.

We pushed through the doors as soon as they began sliding apart, sprinting the short distance between the elevator and the heavy blast door with a brass tag bolted to it. The word Armory was etched on it in childlike scrawl.

"This can't be the armory," I said, looking at the writing.

The door swung inward, revealing Alter behind it. She had changed again, returning to her original, clownish doll appearance. She smiled widely when she saw us, giggling as she held up a pair of rifles, giving us only a split-second's notice before tossing them our way.

"You knew we were coming down?" I asked, catching the weapon in shaking hands and nearly fumbling it.

Matt caught his cleanly, turning it over to examine it. I had gone to the range with Matt and his father once, where his dad had let us shoot his pride and joy, an AR-15. This gun was about the same size, but a lot lighter and much more sleek and round. Instead of a wider body and narrower barrel, the whole thing was the same diameter front to back, with a huge opening in the muzzle that looked big enough to fire a bazooka shell. The stock, just behind the thicker-than-normal grip, bulged out like a hernia. There was no magazine well or anything that suggested the weapon fired bullets. Instead, a simple switch sat on the side, currently in the locked position.

Alter didn't wait for us to finish looking over the guns. She skipped past, drawing the two rods from her back and spinning them like a cheerleader's batons.

"Should we follow Insane Clown Posse?" I asked.

Matt flipped the switch on his gun, causing it to emit a light hum. "I don't know how she knew we were coming down here after telling us to wait on the flight deck, but I don't think she expected this many soldiers to come aboard either, which is a good indication she needs our help."

"Or maybe she just wants us to feel useful?" I suggested.

Alter skipped into the elevator and turned around. Seeing us still near the open armory door, she made an impatient face and used the batons to wave us in as if we were a pair of airplanes.

We ran to the elevator, and I stepped in front of her. "Which floor?" I asked.

She sighed as she slipped between us, clipping the button for Deck One with her baton. The hangar. Of course. As far as I knew that was the only way in or out of the ship.

"You *are* Alter, right?" I asked in the breath it took for the elevator to drop one deck. I was starting to feel as if there was an army of different women hiding somewhere on the ship.

She glanced back at me over her shoulder and winked. The door slid open at almost the same time a second bang sounded, this one much, much louder than the first.

Smoke already filled the hangar, though it wasn't thick enough to fully obscure the movement of the soldiers entering through the main hatch. And yet, the air wasn't being sucked out of the space the way it was in movies. The way it should have been. In fact, the air wasn't leaving the hangar at all.

I knew better than to try to ask Alter about it, especially now. Not that I had the chance. Before I could even finish thinking about the lack of exposure to space despite the open hatch, she ran out of the elevator and vaulted the overhang's railing, jumping to the lower deck.

Into the middle of a dozen soldiers.

"Shit," I said, a step behind Matt as we rushed forward.

The thick smoke down there made things hard to see, but when Alter's two rods lit up in their fiery glow they were impossible to miss. Dark shapes spun toward Alter. She hit the closest with one of her weapons before he could lay into her. He collapsed in a heap on the deck, and she used his body as a springboard to jump out of the middle of the soldiers. An energy blast barely missed her.

She hit a second soldier with her baton on the way past him. He cried out before collapsing like a deflated balloon. Hitting the deck, she slid under the purple starfighter, using it as cover as a rain of blasts trailed behind her, the little starfighter taking the hits.

Matt reached the edge of the overhang and aimed his weapon down, squeezing the trigger and sending a thick toroid of plasma at one of the shapes. It hit the soldier in the chest, burning through his suit. He screamed, hunching over for a moment before Matt turning his attention to the next target.

I aped Matt's attack, reaching the railing and taking aim at one of the soldiers. My finger froze on the trigger as I wondered if he had a wife and children. If he was a nice guy. If he really wanted to shoot us or was just following orders.

While I hesitated, he spun on his heel, swinging his rifle up toward me. His bolt would have put a hole in me if Matt hadn't shoved me aside, knocking me on my ass. He sent a return volley that took the soldier out of the battle.

"Come on, Ben. Get with the program," he hissed,

kneeling over me and watching for the soldier. "They want to kill us. We need to kill them first."

I stared up at him. His entire demeanor had changed, from the carefree rocker I knew to a tense warrior. The shift felt almost as dramatic as Alter's turn from pilot to clown. He had gone into life-or-death mode. What was my problem? Was I hesitating because my options were death or death?

I collected myself and pulled into a crouch beside him. Beneath us, the soldiers continued firing on Alter, trying to track her as she circled the starfighter and leaped out from behind it. She swung the baton to bat one of the bolts fired at her into a soldier we hadn't seen climbing the stairs toward us. She stabbed a second soldier in the chest, letting go of the baton and turning him around in front of her to block the bolts tracking her.

Matt returned to the railing around the overhang, crouching down to again shoot at the soldiers below. A couple of them fired back, missing Matt because they didn't have a good angle of attack.

Another soldier emerged from the smoke on the opposite stairs on the other side of the overhang, his rifle trained on Matt. I didn't think about it. I turned my rifle toward him and squeezed the trigger, holding it down. He grunted in surprise as the plasma stream knocked him back down the steps. I froze in surprise, half-tempted to throw the gun to the deck and retreat to the elevator, but then Matt's words came back to me.

They want to kill us. We need to kill them first.

It really was that simple.

I hurried over to Matt. He stood beside me at the railing, both of us firing over the side until the enemy gunfire faded to nothing. Looking down, I no longer saw any dark shadows moving among the smoke. Only the top of Alter's head, the rest of her obscured in the smoke. I knew the fight was over when she deactivated her batons.

"I think we won," Matt said, glancing over at me. "You saved my ass, man."

I smiled back at him before dropping the rifle and turning away. I had already puked up my burger earlier, so this time all I could do was dry heave.

A gentle pressure came down on my back as I choked out the last of my nausea, the fading adrenaline leaving me cold. I glanced over my shoulder, looking up at Alter while she rubbed my back, her eyes thick with compassion. She didn't need to speak to show me she understood. I had killed…maybe not a man. Maybe an Niflin. Did it matter? A living thing. To save Matt's life, sure. But that wasn't me.

At least, it wasn't the old me. Earther me.

They want to kill us. We need to kill them first.

I had a feeling that wouldn't be the last time those words popped into my head. Circumstance had pulled us halfway across the universe and turned us into unwitting fugitives, with no way out and no way home. If we were stuck here, then I had a responsibility to make the best of the situation and do what needed to be done to survive for as long as I could. However long that proved to be.

As if my thoughts had somehow triggered the cancerous cells growing in my body, a wave of dizziness and sudden weakness crashed into me.

I fell forward and the darkness swallowed me whole.

Chapter Thirty-Three

"Ben! Ben, can you hear me?"

The voice echoed my name in the back of my brain, coming at me a second time as if it were racing down a dark tunnel, straight at me.

"Mom?" I asked, searching for the voice in the darkness. My head tingled. My body felt numb. Had I died?

"Ben, open your eyes."

"I don't want to open my eyes. I want to stay here. It feels safe here."

"You are safe. Come on. Open your eyes. I won't bite."

The voice changed as it spoke, losing Mom's rougher tone, gained from years of hard work around sawdust and other contaminants. Consciousness followed with it, rushing toward me down that tunnel like a freight train in a loud whoosh that drowned out whatever it was the voice said next.

My sense of smell returned. Breathing in deeply, I picked up the aroma of freshly brewed coffee. Damn, it smelled good.

"I had this crazy dream," I said, eyes still closed. "Matt and I bought a spaceship. And there was this strange woman on board, and this evil guy who looks like an elf was chasing us. I almost died, but something about it was still fun."

"It sounds like you were having quite an adventure," the woman replied. "How do you feel? Still dizzy?"

"No. I think it's passed."

I opened my eyes. A thin woman with shoulder-length strawberry blonde hair stood over me, dressed in a white flight suit with a red cross patched to the left breast. She had a tray balanced in one hand while the other snapped open a small table, which she placed across my lap before lowering the tray onto it. Looking past her, I noticed I was in a small bedroom. A frosted glass light fixture in the shape of a ball hung from the center of the ceiling. Soft peach walls led to an open hatch, a soft orange-carpeted corridor beyond.

I returned my attention to the woman. "Alter?"

She smiled warmly. "I brought you some breakfast. Coffee and a bacon and egg croissant. Matt said that was the closest thing the assembler had to your favorite."

I continued staring up at her while she picked up a control pad wired to the side of the bed and used it to lift my upper body, putting me into a seated position so I could eat.

"I'm confused," I said. "I heard my mother's voice. And then I thought I was dreaming."

"You passed out," she explained. "I carried you to sickbay and ran a few scans. You have cancer."

"I know."

"I gave you some medicine to help with some of the swelling and moved you here to rest."

"Deck Three?" I guessed.

"Yes. I thought you would be more comfortable. You should eat."

"Thank you for taking care of me." I looked at the croissant. My mouth watered at the sight of the melted cheese running down the side. And the smell of the bacon… "It looks delicious."

"You're welcome."

"How long was I asleep?"

"Nine hours."

I picked up the coffee and took a sip, surprised by how smooth it was. "This is good."

"The assembler has the full atomic structure for multiple varieties of coffee in its datastore. It always makes a perfect cup."

"We need these on Earth. Where are we now? Still in hyperspace?"

"No. We dropped out of hyperspace three hours ago. We're currently at a dead stop in open space. A mote of dust in the eye of a giant. I disabled our identifier to take us off the grid."

"Isn't that risky?"

"The risk is minimized by our position. I chose it for that specific reason. Of course, we can't stay here forever. But at least you can have a little time to get your space legs under you."

"Without being shot at?"

"Yes."

"So I can just relax and eat this sandwich?"

"Yes."

I picked up the croissant. "That's the best news I've heard all day. Where's Matt?"

"He's sleeping also. He refused to rest until I promised I would look after you."

"Thanks, but what about you? You must be exhausted."

"I'm not tired," she replied. She patted my leg. "Now that you're up, I'm going to take care of some other business." She turned to leave.

"Alter, wait," I said. "I have questions. A lot of questions."

"We'll have time to talk later. Eat your breakfast, spend some time on your hygiene. I'll be back."

"My hygiene?" I said, turning my head to sniff my armpit. I needed a shower. Badly. "Okay. How about just one question?"

"What is it?"

"Who *are* you?"

"What do you mean?"

"I mean…who are you? So far, I've met a pink haired killer, a blonde pilot, a brunette karen, and a ginger nurse. Every one of them look different, but they're all you. Or at least, they all answer to the name Alter."

She stared at me like I had three heads. "I don't understand."

I stared back at her like she had four heads. "You seriously don't know what I'm talking about? Did I dream up the whole fight in the hangar? The one where I…" I trailed off, suddenly losing my appetite. "Where I killed someone." I did my best to ignore the tray of food.

"No, that was real," she confirmed.

"And you were there, right?"

"Yes. Of course."

"And you had pink hair and a colorful outfit, just like you did the first time we met, when you crashed the limo into Duke Sedaya's mercenaries."

She shrugged. "I don't know. Did I?"

I stared at her, locking on her eyes. I didn't get the impression she was playing games with me. It was as if she had no idea she had taken on completely different personas. It didn't seem to bother her at all.

"I guess it's not important," I said, forcing myself to look at the food again. I had decided I would do what needed to be done, and that soldier would have killed Matt and probably me if I hadn't shot him first. There was no reason to be so hung up over it. "I'm going to eat this and then find a shower. I'll see you in a bit?"

"There's a phone in the living room. It's connected to the ship's intercom. You can reach me through it wherever I am."

"Okay. Thank you again for helping me."

"You're welcome, Ben." She smiled warmly again before slipping out of the room and leaving me alone with my coffee and croissant.

It took a minute for my appetite to begin worming its way back into my consciousness, and I started with a few small nibbles on the edges of perfectly crisped bacon. If the battle in the hangar had been part of a game like *Jungle Invasion* instead of real life, I wouldn't feel guilty for winning.

That was the bit of logic I needed. The reason that helped me make sense of what I had done and turn it into something good. My appetite returned full force, and I polished off my breakfast in no time.

Chapter Thirty-Four

I hopped out of bed a few minutes later, surprised to find myself in only my boxers. Maybe I was overly shy, but the thought of Alter removing some of my clothes and seeing me in my skivvies sent a flash of heat to my cheeks. Thankfully, Matt wasn't around to see it.

The bedroom didn't have an attached bathroom, but it did have a closet. Flipping a switch on the side retracted the doors, revealing bars and shelves for clothing and nothing else. I groaned at the sight, unsure of where I was supposed to get some new threads. Alter had said the phone in the living room would activate the ship's intercom. I could give her a quick call and get the lowdown.

Making my way from the bedroom to the corridor, I was surprised by how good I felt. Despite the stressors of the last twenty-four hours or so, my head felt clearer than it had for months, my body stronger and lighter. Had Alter done something to me in sickbay that had helped alleviated my symptoms? Or had she just given me the meds I had brought from Earth? Either way, I liked it.

The hallway led to a pair of double doors on the left, suggestive of a master bedroom, and an apparent stairway on the right leading to the living room. A second door sat directly across from mine, with two more on either side of the passage. Like the hallways downstairs, framed classic art prints lined the walls. In this case, a series of Caravaggios, starting with the Conversion of St. Paul. I wasn't much of an art aficionado, but Art History had been an easy elective to score an A.

I had just reached the top of the steps when I heard a soft swish from the opposite end of the corridor, followed by a sharp whistle.

"Looking good, Bennie," Matt called out.

I turned around, chagrined to see him standing there in a pair of silk pajamas and a microsuede bathrobe. "You've got to be kidding me. One, where did you get those PJs? Two, why the hell do you get the master bedroom?"

Matt's spirits seemed vastly improved from the time he had spent strapped to the sofa on the flight deck. A big grin covered his face as he left the master bedroom and came down the hallway toward me.

"One, the assembler makes more than breakfast. Two, because I paid four million dollars for this thing."

"Fifty-fifty, remember?" I said.

"In operational decisions, yes. When it comes to the king sized bed with the crystal chandelier hanging over it, no."

"You have a crystal chandelier? I've got a frosted glass ball that looks like it came from a seventies Sears catalog." I shook my head. "At least you seem to be in a better mood."

"I've reached the acceptance stage of grief. Honestly, the Deck Three creature comforts helped a lot. So did Alter telling me the tech in sickbay can help keep your cancer manageable, at least for the short term. How are you feeling? Most of your symptoms should be gone, or at least reduced."

I nodded, happy to hear the news. "They are. I feel better than I have in months, to be honest. I guess it's a fair trade to have one of the small bedrooms. And by small, I mean tiny. I bet you have your own bathroom, too."

"On a ship, it's called a head," Matt corrected. "And yes, I do." He laughed. "I'd offer to let you use it because you reek like you spent the last nine hours sleeping in a pile of dirty gym socks, but honestly the head downstairs is bigger and nicer. Just a little less convenient. And you need to go down there anyway to assemble some clothes. Unless you want to stick with the boxers. I'm sure Alter wouldn't mind." The comment set my face on fire again, to Matt's continued amusement. "I'm just kidding."

"She's already seen me in the boxers anyway."

He made a face I didn't like. "Yeah. About that."

"What?" I said, the heat building.

"She's seen you in less than your boxers."

"*What?*"

"Don't get your skivvies tied in knots. She had to strip you naked to put you in the full body scanner. If you want to see your tumor, the machine captured a high resolution pic. It's a solid piece of medical tech, better than anything we have on Earth, I think."

"I don't want to see the tumor, I want to get rid of it."

"Alter said she knows a place where there might be someone who can help."

"Really?" I said, all thoughts of embarrassment at having Alter see me naked forgotten by the next bit of good news.

"Yeah. One problem."

"Let me guess, it's going to cost."

He nodded. "According to the scanner, the primary tumor needs surgical removal. Once it's out, apparently they can give you some kind of nanobot injection that will hunt down and destroy any wayward cancerous cells."

"But I can be cured?"

"Alter seemed to think so. But I think we should keep our expectations low, I mean—"

"Wooohooo!" I shouted, too excited by the potential to keep my expectations low. "Matt, this is unbelievable! For everything that's happened already, just that possibility makes it all worth it."

Matt couldn't hold back his grin. "Seeing you so happy, it does."

"I'm more than happy, man. This is beyond unreal."

He put up his hands. "Just hold up a tiny bit. For one thing, the surgery is incredibly complex. That's why Alter thinks there may only be one dude out there who might be able to do it in a system with trillions of ILFs. For another, remember the money part?"

I forced myself back to center, fighting to contain my elation. He was right. There were still some serious problems to deal with. This was far from a sure thing.

But any hope was better than no hope.

"Right. What's an ILF?"

"Intelligent life form. I thought you were a geek?"

"I know you're a jerk. So we've given up on going back to Earth?"

"For now. Let's try to get you better, and then we'll see what happens."

"Sounds good to me."

"Let's try to get you some clothes and a shower first."

"Also sounds good to me."

"This way," Matt said, leading me downstairs, around the corner and into the center door on the right. It was smaller than the other rooms, and empty, with just enough space to stand in front of the back wall, the surface rough with rust and corrosion.

"Are you sure this isn't an empty closet?" I asked.

Matt tapped on the wall. "Assembler H013, initialize the warm up sequence," he said.

"Warmup sequence initiated," a synthesized voice replied.

"By the way," Matt said. "I added a trigger word for the ship's voice control."

"You did? What's the trigger word?"

"Levi."

"Seriously? My never-to-be girlfriend on Earth?"

"Something to remember her by. I thought you would like it."

"Levi. It's not bad, actually. And this is Assembler H013?"

"Yes."

I laughed. "That's a joke, right?"

"What do you mean?"

"Assembler H013. Try shortening it."

"I don't get it."

"I'm not going to help you. Ask Alter. Maybe she gets it."

"Warmup sequence completed," the assembler said. "What can I make for you today, Matt?"

Matt stepped away from me. "Scan non-Matt human, file in your datastore under Ben."

"Okay. Prepare for scanning, Ben."

I didn't really know how to prepare for scanning, so I just remained in place. A trio of green lasers appeared at the top of the wall, creating a triangle that slowly descended over me. I closed my eyes when it hit my face, and then watched as it finished the scan.

"Scan complete. Model constructed," the assembler said. "What can I make for you today, Ben?"

I needed clothes, but I had no idea what kind. I had never cared much for fashion or shopping. Mom still bought most of my stuff when the older duds got too worn or filled with holes.

"A black cotton t-shirt," I said. "A black hoodie. Blue jeans with rips at the knees. A pair of socks. Some boxers. Converse All-stars, size ten."

"Converse All-stars are not in my datastore."

I was surprised the other things were. "Just make me whatever passes as military grade boots for now, I guess. Size ten."

"Size is irrelevant. I will make your boots to fit the specific shape of your foot."

"Okay. Thank you."

"You are welcome."

I couldn't see what the assembler was actually doing, but it started to hum and rumble and whine, serious *things* happening behind the scenes.

"How long will it take?" I asked.

"Not long," Matt said.

The front of the wall slid open a minute later, revealing a large compartment where my starter list of clothing had been thrown in a disorganized pile.

"Assembly complete," the machine said. "What else can I make for you today?"

I leaned into the compartment, scooping up the clothes, amazed by their production and amused by the way they had been spat out onto the deck. I started to laugh.

"What's funny?" Matt asked.

"I can't help imagining an army of Tinkerbells chained up behind the wall, frantically cutting and stitching to make this stuff."

Matt laughed with me. "Alter tried to explain it to me. Something about molecular recombination and atomic destructuring and quantum something or other." He shrugged. "Who cares? It works. That's good enough for me."

"Where's the bathroom?" I asked, cradling the pile of clothes. "I mean, the head?"

"The door on the left next to the elevator. All of the unsecured hatches should open and close automatically. I'm going to stay here and make something to wear, and then I'll be in the kitchen. It's the door right next to this one. Now get out of here. You stink."

"Thanks for helping get me settled," I said. "See you in a few."

"You got it, bro."

I left the assembler and headed back toward the head, a big grin still covering my face.

Maybe this wouldn't be so bad after all.

Chapter Thirty-Five

Matt was right about the downstairs head. It was as big as a bathroom in a suite at the Waldorf Astoria. Decked out in white marble and polished to a reflective shine, the fixtures were all gold-plated, and the toilet was one of those fancy Japanese jobs with the heated seat and built-in bidet. I wasn't too sure about the shower. After stripping off my boxers and opening the opaque stall door, I was surprised to see there were no cleaning agents waiting inside.

And no showerhead.

Instead, a couple thousand pinprick holes lined every side of the shower including the door, offering the smallest hint of how the thing would clean me up. Instead of knobs or handles to turn on water and adjust the temperature, I found only a simple power button.

It took me a few seconds to work up the nerve to press it. Not that I thought the thing would harm me; it was obviously some kind of advanced cleaning tech. But I had no idea what to expect from it, except that it had something to do with the holes.

"Here goes nothing," I said under my breath, tapping the button.

My comment was right on the money. The power button activated the unit, indicating the shower had turned on. But nothing came out of the holes. No weird chemicals, steam, or combination thereof. No sound. No shockwaves. No vibrations. Not even nanobots, though maybe they would be too small to see.

I stayed in place, hesitant to turn the thing off in case it needed a minute to warm up. It occurred to me I might have to throw my dirty boxers back on and go find Matt, since he had already used the shower in the master suite's bath…uh, head. Unless that one was more traditional? If not, he had probably known about this encounter and chosen not to warn me.

The seconds passed with no additional reaction from the shower, so I started counting alligators in my head, figuring when I got to thirty I would give up and get out. I had only reached five when I noticed the tingling sensation on my skin, an icy hot that started at the edges of my extremities and had worked its way across my body by the time I reached ten alligators. By fifteen, I was cradled in a freshly scented warmth I had never experienced before, every nerve ending tingling in zen comfort. Closing my eyes, I kept counting lest the inner silence ruin the moment.

It was over way too soon. I didn't even make thirty alligators before the power light shut off and the tingling immediately began to subside. My skin remained warm, and reaching up to my mop of curly brown hair, it felt softer than I could ever remember, as if I had just finished filming a shampoo commercial. My skin was equally soft, and wrapped in the same pleasant smell I had picked up on Matt.

Nice.

The temptation to run another wash cycle was hard to resist, but I opened the door and stepped out, picking up the fresh boxers the assembler, which I couldn't stop thinking of as Asshole, had made and slid them on. The fit was perfect. Too perfect. Clearly, the machine's scan had gone right through my clothes. The material wasn't cotton, but rather some kind of advanced tech that put modern undergarment wicking materials to shame. Custom made undies. I'm lovin' it.

The black t-shirt was made of the same material and fit like a second skin over my lanky upper body, leaner than Matt's and without the extra muscle to get in the way. The jeans were equally well fitted, though I lamented Asshole's misunderstanding of what I meant by holes in the knees. Instead of designer tears, the openings were perfectly round circles over my kneecaps. What did I expect? The assembler didn't even know what Converse All-stars were.

I pulled on my socks before looking at the boots. Black, ankle high, and made from another material I couldn't identify. It reminded me of rubber, but a lot softer and more pliable. The footwear didn't have laces, only a small tab that looked like it could be pulled across the front. They also had a small button on the side. Having seen Alter in similar boots, I realized they were probably to magnetize the soles in zero-g.

Putting them on, I pulled the tab across and connected it to the material on the other side. As soon as I did, the whole boot tightened around my foot, holding it snugly while remaining breathable. Taking a few steps, the fit and comfort was unbeatable.

"I probably should have asked for something less Earthier," I said, picking up the hoodie and slipping it on. At least it was clean, and I was clean. I felt good. Better than I had in months. The outset of this adventure had me crying for my mother and wishing I could go home. Seeing Matt unconscious and covered in puke had left me distraught.

All of that was in the past. We had survived the initial trouble. We had made it someplace safe. Even better, there was a chance my tumor could be removed and I could be cured. All we had to do was raise some funds to pay for it.

How hard could that be?

I left the head to make my way to the kitchen. The elevator doors slid open beside me as I entered the hallway. I wasn't even that surprised to see Alter looked different again, her nurse outfit exchanged for thick blue overalls, her hair cut short, her arms looking more muscular than I remembered them.

What really took me off-guard was the clear plastic bag on the floor in front of her, and the helmetless dead soldier curled inside.

"Uh…what are you doing?" I asked, staring at the soldier's face. He reminded me of Duke Sedaya, with pointed ears and sharp, narrow features. Another space elf? Niflin, I recalled. I guess that was their natural look.

"Bringing the casualties to the assembler," she replied casually.

"The assembler? Why?"

"Raw materials. Where do you think that shirt you're wearing came from?"

"What?" I tugged at the collar of the shirt, glancing down at it before eying the soldier's spacesuit. No wonder Asshole hadn't given me cotton. It had made what it could with the molecules on hand. My stomach churned as I extended the concept further, my thoughts turning to the croissant. "Wait. Please don't tell me the bacon—"

"The assembler breaks everything down to raw particles," Alter said. "Yes, the atoms came from the soldier. But they were completely reorganized."

"You should have warned me I was eating a Soylent Green burrito," I wheezed, mouth moistening as my stomach threatened to kick back the breakfast.

"It was a croissant, not a burrito. And I don't know what Soylent Green is."

"People," I cringed. "It's made of people."

"Okay. Technically that's true. But in reality, it's more analogous to eating a cow that grazed on grass on top of a grave."

I shook my head, eyes watering. "That's not helping."

"How about this, Ben," Alter said. "We don't have any other food stocked on board, and the assembler only had limited resources remaining. Thanks to Duke Sedaya, we were able to make you fresh clothes and feed all three of us for a month at zero cost. Considering we don't have any money, I'd say we made out pretty well."

I swallowed the bile that came up before it got past my throat, refusing to puke for a third time in a day. She was right. We couldn't exactly be picky about where we got our sustenance from right now. We were lucky to have anything at all.

And the bacon had been crispy and delicious. And at least I had eaten food made of someone who tried to kill me.

"Does Matt know about this?" I asked.

"Not yet."

I smiled deviously. "I want to be the one to tell him."

Chapter Thirty-Six

Alter didn't drag the body down the hallway. Instead, she turned to face the bulkhead immediately to the left of the elevator and tapped on it, revealing a hidden passage.

"Maintenance," she explained before I could ask. "It leads to the assembler's inner workings."

"I'd like to see it," I replied.

"Trust me, right now you don't. Feeding the assembler organic material isn't pretty."

"Did you have to call it feeding?"

She smiled. "This is the last one. I'll drop him off, clean up, and meet you and Matt in the living room."

"Are you going to change your entire appearance again?"

She tilted her head slightly. "What are you talking about?"

"You keep changing your appearance. Even your hair gets longer and shorter. Unless you have a bunch of wigs?"

Alter glared at me like I was insane. "Are you sure you feel okay? I can take you back to sickbay."

"No, I'm fine. I feel great. Nevermind. I'll see you soon."

I waved curtly and retreated down the corridor. I could feel Alter's eyes on my back for a second before I heard the thud as she dragged the Niflin corpse through the secret hatch and it slid closed behind her.

Entering the kitchen, I found Matt sitting at a small table with a bouquet of fake sunflowers resting in a clear vase in the center. He was sipping a cup of coffee and tapping on Keep's phone. His phone now. He glanced up at me.

"I didn't smell you coming. That's a huge improvement." His eyes dropped to the jeans and the holes in the knees. "You trying to become a trendsetter?" he asked, laughing.

"The assembler didn't understand what I wanted."

Matt glanced over at the clothes he had made, folded and stacked on the counter next to a slightly rusted round shutter that reminded me of a camera lens. An assortment of flatware sat in cupboards arranged around the shutter. "I think I need to go back and try again. I asked for rips too."

"Maybe if both of us do it, we can start a trend."

"With who? Alter? She seems to prefer baggier clothes and onesies."

"About Alter," I said. "You have noticed how she keeps changing, right? I'm not crazy, am I?"

"You aren't crazy," Matt confirmed, which relieved me more than I expected. "I asked her about it, and she acted like she had no idea she was any different."

"Yeah, I got that, too. What do you think about that?" I paused. "Where did you get the coffee?"

"Grab a mug, and ask the assembler to make you some. The shutter will open and you can put the mug inside, and then it'll close again. When it opens the second time, you'll have a magic cup of joe."

"Seriously?"

"It's even cooler when you put a plate in and when it opens there's a sandwich on it."

"What kind of sandwich did you have?" I asked mischievously.

"Bacon, egg, and cheese on a bagel," he replied. "The assembler is pretty okay at bagels, all things considered."

The bacon part made me smile. It was mean-spirited, maybe. But I wanted to see his disgusted face when I told him where it came from. Thinking about it, the egg probably came from the same place.

"I thought it was a little strange at first," Matt continued, circling back to my question about Alter as I grabbed a mug. "It definitely confused me. Especially since her whole persona changes with the look. And then I was thinking about that movie with that guy who had split personality disorder."

"Split?"

"Yeah, and the other one, what was it called?"

"Glass."

"That's it. James McAvoy. Great actor. I think it's something like that."

"*Asshole*, I'd like a cup of coffee," I said.

"A*sshole*?" Matt replied. I turned to him and smirked, realizing I had used the wrong name. His expression shifted, the lightbulb switching on. "Oh. I get it. A-S-S-H-0-1-3. You're such a dork. I can add the trigger to the system if you want to call it that."

"I don't think that's a good habit for me to get into. Assembler, I'd like a cup of coffee."

"Mmm," Assembler replied through a hidden speaker next to the shutter. "Coffee. Delicious."

The shutter rotated open, revealing a compartment large enough to fit two plates side-by-side. I put the mug in, withdrawing my hand before the shutter closed.

"It says that about everything you ask for," Matt said.

"So, do you think we should worry about her?" I asked.

"Why? It seems to me that each of her personalities has a different skill. It's like having an entire crew in one person. We lucked out there."

"I doubt it was luck. Have you seen her janitor look yet?"

"No."

I smiled, sensing my chance as the shutter opened again, a hot cup of coffee behind it. I picked it up and carried it to the table, sitting across from Matt. "I ran into her coming out of the shower. She was bringing raw materials to the assembler."

"Raw materials?"

"Yeah." I tugged my shirt again. "Apparently we wouldn't have these clothes without them." I paused dramatically. "Or the breakfast we ate."

He side-eyed me, knowing me well enough to know I was up to no good. "What kind of raw materials?"

I smiled ghoulishly. "You can't make bacon from a spacesuit."

His face paled, and he pushed his chair away from the table. "Oh man. Ugh. Tell me you're kidding."

"Not kidding," I said. "Soylent Green."

He gagged on the idea, shaking his head. "You seem way too okay with this."

I let him cough and make faces for a little longer before replying. "As Alter put it, the assembler breaks the materials down to their raw state and recombines the atomic structures. So it's not really what it started out as anymore. And, it's the only source of protein we have. Since we can't buy any food right now, it's the only way we can eat."

Matt glared at me, thinking about what I had said. Some of the color returned to his face, and he smiled. "You set me up to tell me that."

"Maybe."

"Asshole."

I laughed. "I had the same reaction when Alter told me. I didn't want you to miss the experience. Honestly, I doubt anyone out here thinks much of it. They're just reusing everything they can. Saving resources."

"I need a little time to let that sink in before I ask the assembler to make me anything else." He returned to the table, eying his coffee a bit differently than before. "You don't think this is made from blood, do you?"

I looked at my coffee. "I don't know. I guess it could be, at least in part. But for all we know, it also has molecules from the spacesuit in it. I think the best thing to do is not try to figure out where it came from. Just enjoy that you have it at all."

He picked up the mug. "Cheers to that."

"Getting back to Alter," I said. "Multiple personalities is one thing. But she *looks* different. And not just a little. Her muscle density changes. Her height."

Matt shrugged. "What do you want to do about it? Keep said she was one of the top assassins in the Spiral. She's done nothing but help us since we met her. Who cares how she does it? What if she isn't human? Does it matter?"

I smiled sheepishly. "No. I guess not."

"So why are you thinking about it so much?"

"I don't know." I paused, trying to answer the question internally. "What if she's still working for Keep?"

"What do you mean? Like a spy?"

"Yeah, I guess."

"Why would he spy on us?"

"I don't know. Why would he do anything? The point is, we hardly knew him, and we hardly know her. What if this is a longer con than we think?"

"If it gets you to the guy who can remove your tumor and cure your cancer, I don't care if it is. But you saw how she reacted to Keep taking all the cash. She definitely wasn't happy. She didn't expect it."

"Yeah. You're probably right. Should we go wait for her in the living room?"

"Sure. I'll go change first. Maybe once we've gotten more information out of her, you won't be so paranoid."

"Pot. Kettle. Black," I replied. "Who's paranoid?"

"I'm good now. Kind of glad to be here, even if I do die an early death. Blaze of glory, maybe." He smiled. "You know what I'm really curious about?"

"What's that?"

"What the music is like here. And if they still use guitars."

I smiled. "I hadn't thought about it, but me too. Maybe Levi can play us some modern tunes while we wait for Alter."

"You took to that fast."

"What?"

"Calling the ship's computer Levi."

I shrugged. "That's what you named it. It's probably better than *Asshole*."

"Probably?" He laughed. "I have an idea for the ship's name, too."

"I'm listening."

"Head Case." He froze, waiting for my reaction. "You know, because it's a robot head. And maybe we're a little crazy. After all, we did pick a fight with one of the most powerful nobles in the Quadrant."

"Not intentionally."

"It is what it is."

"Head Case," I said, trying it out before shrugging. "It's better than *ship identifier CUL8TR*," I added, mimicking the Caprum bursar's voice and tone. "That's a mouthful."

"So it has your vote?"

"We are definitely crazy. And this is definitely a robot head. So yeah, sure."

He smiled and pulled out his phone to enter the name. "Head Case it is."

Chapter Thirty-Seven

The Manticore Spiral had music.

It was terrible.

Maybe Matt and I were too far behind the curve. Maybe we didn't understand music that had evolved from whatever it sounded like on Earth four hundred years into the future, when the intrepid explorers had been thrown back in time. Which, come to think of it, was something else I wanted to learn a lot more about. Maybe our ears just weren't seasoned for the even heavier bass than what we were accustomed to, the more deeply synthesized harmonies, and the screeching, overly digitized singing and disgustingly sappy lyrics. It was like K-pop on steroids, with extra candy coating meant to be consumed by robots.

It was bad.

We left it on anyway, playing through speakers spread across the living room, hoping with the end of one song that the next would be better, each time groaning as we tortured ourselves with more of the same. Our only saving grace was that Alter came to save us within twenty minutes of our listening session, sneaking up on us as we stared out the window into the endless expanse of a space filled with thousands of stars.

The view was almost enough to forget about the racket.

"Ben, Matt," she said, shouting over the music.

We turned around. I expected to see another version of Alter standing there. I didn't expect her hair to be up in a bun or with large, thick-rimmed glasses over her eyes, not to mention the light pink tweed jacket and mini-skirt she wore. Her legs were shapely and well toned, a similar skin tone to Matt's light tan. I thought maybe she would be in heels too, but she still wore the ankle-high boots with the magnets in the soles. Just in case, I guess.

"Let me guess, Librarian Alter?" Matt said.

"What?" she replied, staring at him with sincere confusion.

"Nevermind," he said with a slight smirk.

"Planet Candy Kisses," she said, bopping her head to the beat of the background music. "I love this one."

"Please don't start singing," I said.

"Maybe later," she said, smiling. "We need to talk shop. Matt, can you kill the music?"

"Permanently?" he replied. "I wish." He tapped on his phone, shutting it off and exhaling sharply. "I can feel myself getting smarter already."

"You don't like it?" Alter asked. "It's a top one hundred hit."

"Was it produced by AI or something?"

"How did you know?"

"That explains a lot," I said. "Do you have rock and roll in the Spiral?"

"Of course. It's just not that popular here."

"No accounting for taste," Matt muttered.

"Shall we head up to the conference room?" Alter asked.

"Sure," I said.

We headed out of the common room to the elevator, taking it back to Deck Four. The conference room was to the right of the flight deck, a simple space with six seats around a rectangular, black-topped table. Matt and I each took a side, leaving Alter the head. She seemed a little surprised by our deference, but when it came to talking about the Spiral and our place in it, she was definitely in charge.

"Okay," she said, tapping on her edge of the table.

The whole tabletop turned into a large screen, with a set of symbols at Alter's fingertips and a control interface that matched the screensaver on Keep's phone. She tapped on the interface, quickly switching the display to the starmap we had seen earlier.

"I already showed you our position in the Quadrant," she said, using the controls to zoom in until she pinpointed *Head Case* on the map. "Right now, we're as far off the main grid, away from all of the main hyperspace transfer routes, as we could get. We have a few options regarding where we go next, but it all depends on how we decide to prioritize and proceed."

"Hold on," I said. "That's all important, I agree. And I think we have a good idea of our ultimate goal already. But before we get there, I think Matt and I need a bit more of a crash course on what it means to own a starship in the Spiral. More specifically, both Sedaya and the mercenary who talked to Keep mentioned being unaffiliated as if it's something outside the norm."

"Yes," Alter said. "Being unaffiliated is—"

"Just a second," Matt interrupted. "I think we need to clear something else up, first."

"What's that?" I asked.

He turned to Alter. Their eyes met. "Alter, are you a spy for Keep?"

I practically fell out of my chair. So much for being subtle.

"No," she replied without hesitation. "But I do understand why you might have come to that conclusion. I've spent the last twenty years in his company. But I followed him because of this ship. Just like I'm here now because of this ship."

"So your main concern is the ship," Matt said.

"I thought that was understood."

"It is," I said. "We're just confirming. If Sedaya had bought *Head Case*, would you have stayed with it and served him?"

"*Head Case*?" she replied.

"That's her new name."

Alter puckered her lips while she considered. "*Head Case*. I like it." She paused, still thinking about my question. "I don't know. I'm sure Avelus told you I used to work for Sedaya. Until one day I decided I didn't want to do the type of jobs he wanted me to do anymore. I thought after years of serving him, he would appreciate the work I had done and let me move on to become a pilot or a mechanic. Instead, he threw me out with the trash."

"Yeah, Keep did tell us about that," I said. "I'm sorry he treated you so badly. How did you wind up living in the ship's original structure?"

"All of the non-Acheon settlements in Demitrus are crime-ridden slums. No laws. No rules. Most who wind up there don't survive more than a few weeks. The ones that do either become more and more savage or they leave the settlement and venture out into the waste in search of a more peaceful existence."

"I guess you chose that option?"

"As soon as I could. The others on Demitrus didn't know who I was. They wanted to control me. I didn't let them. I killed one of the most powerful bosses on the planet, which caused an abundance of headhunters to come after me, hoping to earn a large reward. They followed me halfway across the planet, until finally I found peace in what remained of a large mech head, clearly destroyed in a battle somewhere. The only entrance was a small gap between it and the sand, down the side of a dune and into a hole in the front where the hangar doors are now. I would push sand into the gap when I slept, completely hidden from the outside world, only leaving to scavenge food and water."

"That sounds awful."

"It wasn't," Alter said, shaking her head. "Not after everything else I'd already been through. All I wanted was peace, and I found it there, living in silence and secrecy. The individuals chasing me finally believed me to be dead and gave up the hunt, and I gained my first taste of true freedom."

"Until Keep showed up," Matt said.

"Not Avelus. The Acheon. They build burrows in the sand, and had a colony near my home. They don't pay any attention to any species that isn't theirs. Whether by bad luck or destiny, when Avelus came to them looking for a ship, they chose this head."

"And you didn't try to stop them?"

"How could I? There are billions of Acheon on Demitrus, and they wouldn't hesitate to harm me if I intentionally harmed any of them. I could have left and found another place to live, but I didn't want that. I met Avelus soon after. He knew who I was right away, just from my reputation. He could have turned me in and collected a huge reward. He chose to allow me to stay with my home in exchange for my help caring for it. I knew he wanted to sell the ship to put the Star out of Sedaya's reach. I didn't know he planned to leave the way he did, though I should have suspected he wouldn't give you time to acclimate before throwing you into the fire. But I suppose forced learning *is* the most effective."

"I don't really understand," I said. "He spent all of those years looking for a buyer just to transfer ownership of the Star of Caprum? An item we could easily sell to Sedaya or the highest bidder?"

"Sedaya would never buy it from you, no matter what the Niflin said. And there won't be any other bidders as long as it's known that he wants the Star."

"And so we have to play keep away with it," Matt said.

"That was his plan all along, wasn't it?" I asked. "That's why he needed someone who showed skill as a pilot. He needed someone with a chance to evade Sedaya's forces."

"It's also why he needed someone from Earth," Alter agreed.

"Because we're unaffiliated," I guessed.

"Yes."

"What does that mean?"

"Who cares what it means," Matt said. "Keep set us up, and you knew he was setting us up." He thrust his finger at Alter. "It doesn't matter if you expected him to pay for parking or not. You knew what would happen with Sedaya and what it would mean for us."

"Matt," I said, trying to calm him down as his volume increased.

"You didn't say anything," he continued, shouting now. "You didn't warn us of what we were getting into."

Alter was unruffled by both his raised voice and his accusations. "Why would I warn you?" she asked. "If you hadn't bought the ship when you did, it would be in Sedaya's hands right now. So would I."

"So you're looking out for yourself."

"Again, I thought that was understood."

Matt froze, his entire argument shattered by the fact that Alter had made the best decisions for herself and not a couple of strangers. His face flushed, and he slumped in his seat, silent.

"Besides," Alter continued. "I'm not going to just let Sedaya capture or destroy us. I think I proved that already. Your best interests and my best interests are the same."

"Right now," Matt grumbled. "What if that changes?"

"As long as you don't intend to turn the ship over to Sedaya, that won't change."

"What about if we give him the Star?" I asked.

"You'll need to replace it as a power source. It won't be quick or inexpensive."

"But you don't have a problem with that?"

"Why would I? The Star is a tool. A unique tool, but it still serves a specific purpose and can be replaced. Not as easily because of the nature of the ship. But before you get any ideas, understand that it won't be as simple to appease Sedaya as turning over the Star. He's a man who holds grudges, and our escape is an embarrassment to him."

"So we're screwed when it comes to getting him off our asses," Matt said.

"That might not be a bad thing."

"Why not?"

"Sedaya is powerful, but he also has plenty of enemies. You have a reason to dislike him. You're unaffiliated. That means you can move against him without drawing attention to anyone who might hire you to make those moves."

I glanced at Matt. He looked back at me. I could tell by his face he wasn't totally comfortable with the idea Alter had just floated. Neither was I. My gaze shifted back to our strange companion.

"There's only one problem," I said. "I don't think we want to be, what? Mercenaries? Guns for hire?"

Alter wasn't fazed. "What do you want to be, then?"

"What other options are there?" I replied.

"To put a starship to good use? Cargo hauler. Salvage crew. VIP transport."

"I kind of thought we would just fly around and check out all of the different planets."

Alter raised an eyebrow over the rim of her glasses. "And how are you going to pay for these excursions? For food and water and maintenance? And ultimately for surgery?"

"I know, we need to do something to make money. What pays the best?"

Her eyebrow had dropped, but it went up again just as quickly. "I'll give you one guess."

"Gun for hire," I said, not all that thrilled with the answer.

"Or smuggler," Alter said. "Which is almost as dangerous. The greater the risk, the bigger the reward."

"Right. How big a reward do we need to convince your contact to fix me?"

"One good job should be enough."

"I assume you know where to find that job?"

"Of course."

I looked at Matt again. "What do you think?"

He shrugged. "I think we don't have a lot of choices. Can you go into more detail about what being unaffiliated means? Keep went through a lot of trouble to sell this ship to Earthians."

"The Hegemony is a modern feudal society," Alter answered. "That means every individual that's born within it is subject to the noble whose flag their planet falls under. It's a deeply ingrained part of living in the Manticore Spiral."

"Is that how you wound up working for Sedaya?" I asked. "You were born on one of his planets?"

"Not exactly," she replied, somewhat cryptically. "But you aren't wrong about the general idea. When a noble conquers a planet from another noble, there are no riots or efforts to overthrow the new government. The new rule is accepted and all individuals born on the planet become subjects of the new ruler. Many take pride in the flag they were born under, even Sedaya's. They won't take jobs with rivals without explicit permission. And they will never work against the best interests of their leader."

"Okay," I said. "I think I understand. So by being from Earth, we don't fall under anyone's flag. We're completely independent and can pretty much do whatever we want."

"As long as it doesn't disrupt the flow of the overall Hegemony, yes."

"What do you mean by that?" Matt asked.

"The Empress' Royal Sentries monitor activity across the Hegemony. They prefer not to intervene in any small affairs, but cross them or make enough noise and you'll attract their attention. It's better that they never know you exist."

"That seems straightforward enough," I said.

"So, what do we do now?" Matt asked.

Alter scrolled her fingertip down to another planet and tapped on it, shifting the new planet to the center of the interface and zooming in on it. "This is Cestus Alpha," she said. "It's one of a few dex planets."

"Dex planets?" I asked.

"Dark Exchange," Alter answered. "Where mercenaries go to pick up work."

"Why not just post the jobs on the hypernet?" Matt questioned. "Or the *dark* hypernet? I guess you don't have LinkedIn here." He smirked, thinking he was funny.

"The jobs available at a dex are sensitive enough that if their origins were discovered, wars would break out and thousands of innocents would die. Digitized comms always leave a trail, and even the best encryption may be vulnerable in time."

"Oh," Matt said, the smirk wiped from his face. "Yeah, I guess that would be bad."

"Verbal agreements, on the other hand, are known only by the parties involved."

"How far is Cestus Alpha?" I asked.

"Three days in hyperspace," Alter replied.

I eyed the map. "That's all? The planet seems pretty far away."

"About three thousand light years."

"So we move a thousand light years per day. Forty-one light years per hour. That's Earth to Trappist in less than an hour. To Proxima in minutes. Wow."

"We went from Earth to Caprum in three hours," Matt said. "That's more impressive. How'd we do that?"

"I don't know," Alter replied. "Keep made it happen. He refused to tell me how."

"That's...strange," I said, looking for a good word. "You went to Earth with him, but you don't know how you got there?"

"No. Everything you saw on Caprum except the ship was a hologram to make you think you were still on Earth. As soon as we entered or exited the hangar, we were on your planet. Keep would always sit in the back out of my sight, so I never saw what he did to make the transfer happen."

"What if he's the only one who can get there?" Matt said. "What if we can't get back without him?"

"We'll worry about that later," I replied. "We're not about to go home yet, anyway. Three days. That'll give us time to finish our tour of the ship. If you don't mind?" he asked Alter.

She shrugged. "I think you've seen pretty much everything."

"I haven't seen Deck Five."

"There's nothing important on Deck Five," she answered.

"Then it's not a big deal if I see it," I replied.

Alter's expression told me she didn't want to show us the deck. "Deck Five is my quarters."

"Not Three, with us?"

"No. I prefer solitude when I'm not occupied caring for the ship."

I wasn't going to push her to see her room. "Okay.

You could have led with that. We respect your right to privacy."

"Thank you. Do you have any other questions?"

"Not a question," Matt said. "More of a request."

"Go ahead."

"Well, if we're going to be smuggling or doing whatever illegal stuff that'll make us a big payday in a short time, I think it's important Ben and I are better equipped to protect ourselves if need be. I have a lot of martial arts training, and I've shot a gun before, but I'm sure there's a lot we could learn from you."

Alter smiled. "You need a teacher."

"If you wouldn't mind," I said.

She bit her lower lip thoughtfully before nodding. "Okay."

"I want to learn other things too," I said. "Like how to fix the ship."

"There's no need. I can handle maintenance."

"What if something happens to you? What if you're killed or disabled or something?"

"If I'm dead, it'll mean you're also dead."

The statement sent a chill down my spine. Dark, but also true. "I'd still like to learn at some point. I'm interested in how everything works."

"Let's start with making you less of a liability in a fight," Matt said. "Then you can nerd out to your heart's content."

"Fine. When do we start?"

"We need to put *Head Case* into hyperspace," Alter said. "Then we can begin."

"Great. Can you go straight to the flight deck, or do you need to change first?"

Alter's eyebrows lowered as she glared at me, confused. "What do you mean, change first?"

I almost laughed out loud. "Nevermind. We'll meet you on the flight deck."

"Of course."

Matt and I stood up and left the conference room, making the short trip to the flight deck. I lingered through the hatch, hoping to catch Alter as she exited the room, but she remained behind until the doors had slid shut, blocking my view.

"Give it a rest," Matt said, noticing my antics.

"I'm just curious how she does it," I replied.

"It's maaaagggiiccc," Matt said, wiggling his fingers. "Let it go."

"Fine. Are you sure you want to do this? Become a smuggler or whatever?"

"I'm sure I want to save your life if we can. It doesn't matter how we get there, as long as we get there. Besides, I wouldn't mind sticking it to Sedaya a few more times in the process."

"It could get dangerous."

"*Could*? No. It will be. But what's the adventure of a lifetime without a little danger? I'm more worried about the music here."

We both laughed as we took our seats, me in the pilot's seat, him on the sofa. The flight deck hatch slid open and Pilot Alter walked in, dropping into the co-pilot seat. I held back my comment on her change in appearance, which she had managed in under two minutes.

Magic. Right. I doubted that. But I also accepted it.

"Are you two ready?" she asked.

"We're all set," I replied.

"Then let's get to it."

Chapter Thirty-Eight

The next three days passed in a hurry. Being on board *Head Case* felt more like a vacation. Matt and I spent three hours each day learning about the different weapons, armor, and other gear stored in the ship's armory, practicing their use and going through some basic self-defense moves with Alter. According to her, Keep had bartered for all of the equipment at the same time he negotiated the construction of the ship with the Acheon. All of it was rebuilt, reconditioned, or recreated from the piles of garbage the Quadrant dumped on the planet, returned to usefulness by the resourceful aliens.

The education and exercise left me feeling great, especially when combined with both the medication I had bought on Earth and the added chemicals available in sickbay. For the first time in months, I could get my heart rate up and my blood pumping without dizziness, and practice kicks and punches, holds and grabs without falling flat on my face from the exertion.

Not that it really improved my aptitude for fighting. While Matt was able to hold his own against Alter when she pulled her punches, my skills were more than a little lacking. Her simplest maneuvers often found me flat on my back, unsure of how she had put me there. Anyone could become good at anything given enough time and dedication, but we had only three days. Yet, with the hope of surviving my cancer putting my focus through the roof, the training left me happily exhausted.

The downtime set me to exploring the compartments of the ship I had yet to see. Wandering through *Head Case*, I opened every hatch, cabinet, drawer, and panel, save for Deck Five. It still seemed odd to me that Alter chose to live there instead of Deck Three, and that she had the whole deck to herself. Matt had described seeing piles of random stuff there, storage, and I wondered if maybe she had recreated her environment on Demitrus, holding tight to the one place she said she felt safe.

What had happened to her before Demitrus? Keep said she had been an assassin, but that reaction indicated something deeper and more damaging than a weariness of killing. I tried inviting her to join Matt and me at mealtimes, but she always declined. Whenever she wasn't training us or fixing something, she withdrew to her quarters. She lived on the ship, took care of it, and helped us as best she could. Even so, I had the impression she only tolerated our presence in what she considered *her* ship. *Her* home.

Whenever I wasn't training, exploring the ship, sleeping, or eating, I could be found either in the pilot's seat on the flight deck working on mastering the interface, or with Keep's phone, trying to learn all of *Head Case's* controls. Matt was more than happy to pass the settings over to me. He had never been much of a techie, preferring to spend his free time in the small gym or in the living room. He was dismayed when he learned the hypernet didn't work in hyperspace and the onboard datastore didn't have a wide selection of media content. Instead of getting a feel for society in the Fertile Quadrant, he was left zoning out to Alter's favorite picks. It seemed she had a thing for cats and dogs and had saved hundreds of videos from YouTube.

I moved my bedroom from the small cabin where I had awoken to a slightly larger one closer to the stairs, mainly because the overhead light fixture looked more Ikea than fifties kitsch and it was closer to the downstairs head. I slept like a baby on the foam mattress in that room, and woke up sore but satisfied every morning of the trip.

Fresh out of the shower on the third day, I found Alter in the kitchen with Matt. She was in her pilot persona, which I hadn't seen since we had entered hyperspace. Over the last few days we had primarily spent time with Sensei Alter, in long white robes and barefoot, her hair pulled tight into a geisha bun and held by sticks he had used as an effective teaching aid. Sensei Alter was both calm and demanding, zen in her instruction, determined to see results. She had carried a different personality into our weapons training, presenting as Drill Sergeant Alter. Loud and brash, quick to admonish, firm and strong. To be honest, I liked that Alter the least of any I had seen so far.

"What are you wearing?" Alter asked, eyes flicking over my outfit.

"What do you mean?" I asked, straightening my coat. "I'm trying to fit in. You know, not to look like an Earther."

"In that?"

"Like Han Solo. Star Wars? He was from a galaxy far, far, away. That's where we are now, right?"

I glanced at Matt. We had both gone that route, him the older version of Han, me the younger, both in futuristic jackets, a long sleeved shirt with an open collar, dark trousers, and boots that came up just below the knees. I wore the gunbelt too, though I hadn't pulled a blaster from the armory to finish the outfit.

He wasn't wearing his jacket, and his pants and boots were obscured by the table, evading her discernment.

"You think the Quadrant is like an Earth movie?" she asked.

"I don't know what the Quadrant is like," I replied. "Come on. This has to be better than jeans with a perfect round hole over the knees and a hoodie."

"Yes, it is an improvement over that. But the lack of space boots will draw attention."

"Are you sure they aren't called hyper boots?" Matt quipped.

We both ignored him. "These are space boots," I said. "I just had Asshole bring them below the knee." I had tried not referring to the machine that way, but it rolled off the tongue so much easier than calling it the assembler.

"Lose the boots," Alter suggested. "That will help."

I shrugged. "Are you here because we're almost there?"

"Yes. We'll arrive at the drop point in twenty minutes."

I moved past her to the assembler. "Asshole, please make me bacon and egg on a bagel, with extra cheese."

"You got it. One bacon and egg on a bagel, coming right up."

"Did you do something to the assembler's voice modulation?" Alter asked, glancing at the round aperture as though it were broken.

"I played with the settings," I replied. "It should sound like a Brooklyn accent."

"Brooklyn accent?"

"You know. Hey yo, yo hey," I said, presenting my best version of it. Mom was born in Brooklyn, and the effect had still snuck out from time to time even though she had been out of New York for years. "Do you like it?"

"Not at all."

"I told you," Matt said. "It's not even a good Brooklyn accent."

I laughed. "I'm still messing around with it. But the original response phrases were way too stiff. It felt like talking to a machine."

"It is a machine," Alter pointed out.

I smiled as the aperture rotated open, the sandwich waiting inside. My mind had already put a mental block on where the protein on the bagel had actually come from, allowing me to not only eat it, but enjoy it. I pulled the plate out and grabbed a mug, sticking it inside.

"You won't have time for coffee," Alter said. "We'll drop pretty close to Cestus Alpha's orbit. And there's no food or drink allowed on the flight deck."

"What? No drink on the flight deck? Whose starship is this?"

"It took me four hours to repair the damage Matt's vomit did to the underdeck wiring."

"No food or drink on the flight deck," Matt said, finishing his coffee. "You lose the vote."

"We didn't have a vote," I replied.

"Sure we did. Alter said no. I said no. Quorum reached. You lose."

"Damn it," I said. "Asshole, just some water, please."

"You got it, Bennie. One water, coming right up!"

I picked up the sandwich and took a big bite, chewing quickly. I didn't have much time to eat.

"I'm heading up to the flight deck," Alter said. "I'll see you two there."

"Okay," Matt said.

Mouth full, I settled for a wave.

The aperture opened and I retrieved the mug of water, swallowing my bite. Damn, it tasted good. Probably too good. I reminded myself not to think about it.

"Are you ready to start our new life of crime?" I asked.

Matt smiled. "It's only a crime if you get caught."

Chapter Thirty-Nine

"Go ahead," Alter said. "Bring us out of hyperspace."

I leaned forward, positioning my pinkie on the toggle switch beyond the throttle that controlled hyperspace. As she had explained, the trick to dropping out of the FTL bubble wasn't so much the act of slowing down, but rather regaining immediate control of the ship. While the hyperspace lanes and drop points were predetermined for all inhabited planets, there was no way to control the arrival of multiple vessels at one time, meaning there was always a chance of a collision. Then there were the drops into contested areas, war zones, and the like. You never knew what you were flying into until you got there and it was always better to be prepared.

As a dex planet, Cestus Alpha's biggest risk came from the authorities, either those of the nobility controlling the area of space or the Empress' Royal Sentries. The latter would be the worst case. It would not only mean dropping into a death trap, it would mean the dex no longer existed, exterminated because someone there slipped over the thin red line.

All of that swirled in my head as I knocked the toggle off, immediately grabbing the throttle as the hyperdrive disengaged. My heart pounded harder than it probably should, my nerves tense. Alter had offered to handle the flying for the initial drop. I refused. This was my and Matt's ship. I had to be responsible for it.

Eyes first, as Alter had instructed. Primary sensors second. Secondary sensors last. The starfield ahead of us decompressed, and while I spotted a handful of ships in the distance, they were little more than specks against the backdrop of what I assumed was Cestus Alpha. The immediate space ahead remained clear. I glanced at the HUD, quickly taking stock of the other ships in the area. There were two more within the drop zone and about thirty in orbit around the planet. Still good. I tapped on the HUD's grid, switching it to energy readings. Ships moving into the drop zone would come in hot, giving us a few seconds to get out of the way.

Nothing. We were safe. I kept *Head Case* on course for the planet, setting the throttle to half. It would take only a few minutes to reach orbit, where we would need to ping Cestus Orbital Control for permission to land.

"Good entry," Alter said. "Smooth and stable."

"Thank you," I replied. "I have to admit, I was nervous about it."

"That's not unreasonable your first time."

She had already described Cestus Alpha to Matt and me, complete with images and video. Eighty percent the size of Earth and circling a red dwarf star, Cestus was ninety-eight percent ocean. In fact, water was its largest legal export, a series of space elevators visibly rising from the planet. Many miles long, tubes carried the water to satellites that processed the abundant liquid and filled waiting supertanker starships with the finished product. Those ships would carry the water across the Quadrant, mostly supplying dry worlds occupied by mining companies.

The entire sequence was fully-automated, save for a small crew of maintenance workers who were easy to bribe into silence. As far as they and the rest of the Quad were concerned, the planet remained uninhabited. Which was easy to believe since the only dry land on the planet was the caldera of a massive, active volcano and the small portion of land around it revealed by half a century of water removal.

"Very cool," Matt had said when Alter showed us the media, and again now that we were here in person.

"Very cool indeed," I added. "All of the ships in orbit here are smugglers?"

"Or other ships available for dark ops," Alter replied. "Of any kind. Being an assassin may be one of the cleanest of the professions of the individuals you'll see planetside."

"Do you think we'll be able to find a job pretty easily?"

"A job, yes. The right job, perhaps. Perhaps not. I think it would be in your best interests to earn as much as possible from a single run."

"But the adage remains true, right? The greater the risk, the greater the reward?"

"Yes."

"Are we ready for that kind of risk?"

"Probably not. But it could take months to earn what you need relatively safely. Months you may not have."

"I feel great."

"You only have enough medications for a month.

And the sickbay treatment might not be enough to keep your symptoms at bay. Neither is a cure."

"We can't get similar meds here?"

"Possibly. But that won't stop the cancer from spreading."

"Understood."

"Also remember what I told you about the other mercenaries here. If any of them are under Sedaya's flag, which is likely, there's a good chance they'll try to earn the bounty for your capture. They won't know who I am, which will allow them to be bold until we give them a reason not to approach us."

"So we're pretty much assured of being attacked down there," Matt said.

"I think it's best to be prepared. It's what you've been training for."

I could hear Matt swallow nervously behind me. "Yeah, but that doesn't mean I'm looking forward to it."

"Good," Alter replied. "We should never invite or initiate violence. But if it comes to us, we should be ready to utilize it to maximum effect."

"That's a good one, Confucius," I said.

"Who's Confucius?" Alter replied.

"Do you have fortune cookies in the Spiral? Little cookies with messages inside them?"

"I've seen cookies on Aleshem with microbot capsules in them, and when you break open the cookie they write a message in the air with colored lights."

"Fortune cookies two-point-oh," Matt said.

"On Earth, Confucius is the one who comes up with all the messages," I added.

"I see. So you approve of my message."

"Yeah."

"Why didn't you just say so?"

"I thought I did."

A light on the console flashed orange, indicating an incoming encrypted, short-range comm. Alter leaned forward and flipped on the toggle, opening the channel and transmitting both the ship's identifier and special codes she said we needed to acquire approval to land.

"*Head Case*, this is Cestus Orbital Control, I have you on sensors. Are you a maker or a taker?"

"Taker," Alter replied.

"And what level are you seeking?"

"Level five. Or higher if there's anything NV available in that range."

"Standby."

"NV?" Matt asked.

"Non-violent," Alter replied.

"What's your current maximum storage load?" Control asked.

"Four hundred cubic meters," Alter answered.

"RID?"

Alter glanced over at me. It was the first time since we met that she looked uncomfortable. She exhaled as she tapped on the console between our seats, entering a screen I had never seen before through a pattern of taps rather than an icon on the interface.

"Transmitting," she said.

Control's voice, suddenly shaky, followed a short silence. "Is this authentic?"

"Very," Alter replied coldly.

"Uh. Okay. Um. I have two available contacts."

"Flags?"

"Huron and Nakata."

"I'll see Nakata's maker first. Huron if that doesn't work out."

"Confirmed. Transmitting connection identifier."

Matt held up Keep's phone, which vibrated as though it had gotten a text message.

"Identifier received," Alter said.

"Permission to land granted," Control said. "Welcome to Cestus Alpha, Enigma."

The comm link disconnected.

Chapter Forty

"Enigma?" I asked, looking at Alter.

"My pseudonym on the dex," she replied. "Everyone who's accepted a job through a dex has a pseudonym and a unique identifier. One is easy to fake, the other impossible. You'll receive both when you sign your first contract. But only someone with a lot of experience has any chance of meeting a maker for a level five-plus job."

"So we're riding your coattails," Matt said.

"I don't know that term."

"Using your reputation to benefit ourselves."

"It would appear that way, but I also have strong motivation to keep *Head Case* under your ownership and away from Duke Sedaya. We both benefit."

"Fair enough. What were you asking about flags?"

"Baron Huron and Baron Nakata. Two of the ten noble houses in the Quadrant. There used to be twelve, but Sedaya has swallowed two of them. Nakata has a reputation for offering better terms, and he's part of the silent opposition to Sedaya. That's why it's our first choice. We're fortunate to have an option."

"We're fortunate to have you," I said. "Is Alter your real name or another pseudonym?"

"Avelus gave me that name," she replied.

"Can I ask you a personal question?"

"What's my real name?"

"Yes."

"I don't know."

"You don't know your name?"

"No."

"Did you end up with amnesia or something?" She threw an icy glare at me that told me I had stepped over the line. "Sorry. I don't mean to be a jerk."

"We're approaching the ingress," she said, changing the subject. She tapped at the air, but this time I knew exactly what she was doing. "Shields are active for atmospheric entry."

I cut the throttle by half, keeping a loose grip on the stick as I guided *Head Case* around the field of starships orbiting the planet. They all had a more traditional shape, mostly long and rectangular with a couple of more rounded designs. A few had bright paint jobs, but most were an unpainted gray or gunmetal. The sizes varied with a range from fifty to three or four hundred meters.

"Are they still waiting for permission to land?" I asked.

"The larger ships are too big to land," Alter replied. "Their emissaries likely took a skiff to the surface to deal. The smaller vessels are probably waiting for hire. Sometimes it can take a few days to land a suitable contract, and not every captain wants their crew loitering in the settlement."

"Let me guess," Matt said. "A hive of scum and villainy?"

"I wouldn't call them scum or villains, considering we're about to join them. Individuals who make a career on illicit activity tend to promote vice. Prostitution, gambling, drinking, drugs, and black markets. You'll find all of that and more down there."

"Sounds great," I said sarcastically. "How long do you think we'll need to be there?"

"We already have a meeting set up. Hopefully not more than a few hours. Being on the ground leaves us exposed."

I guided *Head Case* into the atmosphere, only aware when we had contacted the thermosphere when the shields began to register the friction against them. Falling onto a planet was a lot easier than running away from one, and we broke through into clear skies, the singular landmass against the endless waves of ocean immediately visible through wispy cloud cover. The only other thing to see were the space elevators rising from submerged rigs anchored miles beneath the surface. Normally, the technology would have left me in awe, but I was growing increasingly nervous about touching down. Alter had said confrontation was pretty much a given, and I hated confrontation.

My thoughts turned to orbital control's reaction to Alter's identifier. The man had sounded terrified, her reputation undoubtedly preceding her. I felt stupid to be worried when we had her at our side, and I did my best to calm down while we finished our descent.

"Where should I land?" I asked, looking down at the collection of ships arranged along the natural terrain of the island. Matching the ships above, they were an assortment of shapes, sizes, and in a few cases colors. While I could easily find similarities with starships from different sci-fi series—Battlestar Galactica here, Star

Wars there, the Expanse a little further out—none of them looked anything like *Head Case*.

"Anywhere there's space," Alter replied.

"Which should be almost anywhere," Matt said. "Only those little ones have a smaller footprint than us."

"The skiffs."

"I can't believe we're about to touch down on another planet," Matt continued. "You should be a little more excited."

"It is awesome," I agreed. "But I'll feel better when we're on our way out rather than in."

"We'll be fine."

I appreciated his confidence and the fact that he had gone all-in on the adventure. It seemed knowing there was a chance to cure my cancer had left me more risk-averse than when my actions had led us here in the first place. Nothing ventured, nothing gained. I let myself enjoy the sight of the other starships as I found a landing zone between them, even smiling by the time Alter extended the landing struts and we gently settled onto the dirt.

"Welcome to Cestus Alpha," Alter said, releasing her harness and standing up. "I'll meet you two in the armory. Make sure you set the ship to hibernate before you leave the flight deck."

"Wilco," I said, tapping in the air to bring up the augmented reality interface. I navigated to the security settings, putting the ship in hibernation. The primary control system would keep everything warm and ready to activate at a moment's notice should we need to make a quick escape. That done, Matt and I got out of our seats and left the flight deck, taking the elevator to Deck Two.

"Levi, open the armory door," Matt said as we

approached. It had taken us no time to get used to calling the ship's computer Levi. Even Alter had taken to the name. Of course, now when I thought of the PCS I saw a sweet round face in thick glasses instead of an ugly metal box, but it was probably better that way.

The heavy blast door swung inward, revealing the large arsenal of death.

Unlike the other storage areas that seemed haphazardly arranged, the armory was impeccably organized, a place for everything and everything in its place. Spacesuits, body armor, and other tactical gear lined the shelves along the immediate portside bulkhead. At least one of everything was sized for Alter, while a couple of the suit designs were one-size-fits-all in a stretchable, rubbery material that hugged the body. Matt and I had both tried on the vacuum-protected gear. Neither of us wanted to turn around to face Alter when we did, though it didn't matter as much in my case since she had already seen me fully unwrapped. While the suits had a codpiece to hide our junk, they were still too tight to be comfortable in her presence. On further reflection, it was a stupid attitude to take, especially because I was looking forward to having a reason to put it on and venture directly into space.

Small arms waited on the shelves beyond the armor and gear, the assortment of remade weapons impersonating a museum of antique guns. A range of deadly output was available, from more conventional bullets to plasma toroids like the rifles we had used, to ion blasters and energy beams to ray guns. They took an array of appearances, from a small plasma pistol I could hide in my palm to a larger pulse gun that I could barely lift in one hand. A few of the weapons had grips that clearly weren't intended for human hands. Alter explained how the Acheon delivered the guns in one big lot, and they were included in the pile.

Past the small arms were the rifles, similar to the pistols in the randomness of their design, but bigger. The plasma rifles carried more charge and fired larger toroids. The railguns featured much larger magazines, higher calibers, and greater stopping power. And so on. My favorite of the group was a long gun that looked like a single-shot rifle from the American Civil War, but had been converted to a ray gun that couldn't be used on the ship because it would instantly put a hole through every deck and even the hull. I had no idea where the Acheon had gotten it, but every time I entered the armory my eyes drifted to the gun.

A set of six large containers sat beside the long guns, neatly stacked. During our first full tour of the armory, Alter had taken the top container down and opened it, revealing a projectile launcher inside. Fancier than any bazooka or RPG launcher I had ever seen, it had a large foldable LED screen on the side, which the shooter could use to guide the explosive munitions after firing. Military grade and probably an accidental dump to Demitrus, she said it was the most valuable ordnance on the ship, easily worth a hundred thousand electros on the black market. She had been surprised when she found it among the Acheon's delivery.

The other containers held lesser ordnance. Grenade launchers, explosives, and the like. The last racks and shelves beside them were the melee weapons. Knives, short swords, kukri, nunchucks, and other short-range weapons. There was nothing like the batons ICP Alter produced from her baggy clothes, but I really didn't want anything to do with stabbing or slicing someone anyway. If anyone got that close to me and Alter didn't step in, I was already screwed.

I made a straight line to the small arms, trying a few of the guns before I found one that fit the holster well. A simple gun, it had a square body and a triangular barrel. Alter had taught us how to identify the type of ordnance the guns fired by the location of its power source. A plasma pistol in this case, it held a cell inside the grip the size of a USB drive that plugged into a slot designed for it as though the gun were a computer.

Matt picked out a blaster, a little larger than mine with a more conventional look save for the square battery that snapped into the top of the body. It fit his holster a little awkwardly, but securely enough that he would be able to grab it if needed and it wouldn't fall out.

"Are you gentlemen ready?" Alter asked in an almost unfamiliar voice, drawing our immediate attention.

She had changed again, into a persona that immediately brought Catwoman to mind. Or maybe, Enigma. A fitted black outfit lined with what looked like matte black armor plating. A dark utility belt with a pair of blasters and her batons hanging from her hips. Dark skin, wide nose, full lips, and short, curly hair. Her purple eyes were explosively venomous in contrast, the serious set of her jaw and her posture in the doorway overloaded with confidence.

She hadn't just made minor adjustments to her outward appearance. She was almost another person altogether. One that unnerved me just looking at her.

I was glad she was on our side.

"You look…" Matt said, trailing off as he tried to find the words.

"Different," I finished for him, figuring it was preferable to what he was probably thinking. "We're ready."

She eyed the guns in our holsters. "Good selection. Let's go."

Chapter Forty-One

I squinted as soon as we exited *Head Case* through the smaller hatch in the hangar bay doors, the sun unexpectedly bright, especially compared to the lighting inside the ship. My heart thumped with excitement as we descended the ramp to the layer of limestone that formed the outer bed of Cestus Island. I immediately took a knee so I could reach out and touch the alien soil. Another planet. Another life. A fleeting moment of worry about Mom's worry for me sent a chill of homesickness rushing through me before it was once again drowned out by amazement.

"Act like you've done this before," Alter suggested, putting a gentle hand on my shoulder.

I shot back to my feet, looking around to see if anyone had noticed. The shore was lined with starships, but they all seemed abandoned.

Glancing at Matt, I saw he had Keep's phone in hand, in the middle of activating the ship's full security lockdown. The inner hatch slid closed, a slight shimmer offering notice that the shields were active. Nothing

257

would get through without a lot of effort and a signal to the device that *Head Case* was under attack.

Even better than Sentry Mode on a Tesla.

"This way," Alter said, leading us from the ship and along the shore.

I looked out at the ocean as we walked. With no moon orbiting the planet, the tides remained almost flat, the water like glass all the way to the horizon. Incredible.

We covered half a mile on foot before reaching a heavy gate at the edge of the cliff, the island's original waterline. A pair of men in slightly ragged blue uniforms waited in front of the open gate, rifles in hand, obviously bored by the lack of activity. Their visages brightened, and they straightened as we approached. One of them drew a small, clear slab from a pocket.

"ID?" he said.

Matt tapped on the phone. "Transmitting."

"Received," the guard said. "Confirmed." He and the other guard stepped aside to let us pass. A stone stairway beyond the gate brought us up and away from the beach.

"They didn't seem to know who you are," I said to Alter as we ascended.

"Everyone is anonymous here, unless they choose not to be," she replied. "The identifier tells the guards we have scheduled business here. It doesn't matter who it's with or what it's for."

"What if we didn't have business?" Matt asked. "What if we just came for the vice?"

"You'd have the same type of identifier for that too. Like I said, it doesn't matter what you do here, the ID just registers your arrival and departure."

"The guards didn't take our guns or anything," I said, surprised.

"Don't expect them to help you if you get in a bind, either," Alter replied. "Yi's hired plenty of guns, but only to defend Cestus' immediate interests, not to keep the peace. Making trouble with the two on the beach is asking for a lot worse trouble."

"Yi?"

"Yi runs the place. Not someone you want to cross."

"But he isn't in with Sedaya?"

"*She* falls under Duke Arnid's flag, but she also doesn't take sides. It would do too much damage to the business."

"I get it. So who do we need to worry about?"

"We won't know until we know."

"I love the sound of that." I groaned.

Reaching the top of the steps, a worn dirt path led through heavy vegetation, thick enough to further obscure the settlement ahead. Even so, I could hear the faint sounds of awful music, shouting, and laughter in the distance. The thick canopy of trees overhanging the island had made the settlement invisible from above, aiding to its secrecy. Now, I couldn't wait to see it.

A pair of larger men in worn spacesuits came into the view on the path before we reached the brush. Both more than six feet tall and heavily muscled, they carried large pistols on their hips and wore tense, angry expressions. Watching them come toward us, the stagger in their walks suggested they were drunk.

Alter moved aside to let them pass, so Matt and I did too. I didn't sense any worry from her so I did my best to stay calm as they reached us, their size completely intimidating.

I thought they would go right past. The way they were walking, it felt like they didn't even know we were there. But as they came perpendicular to us, nearly at the stairs, one of them wordlessly lunged at Matt, the other at me.

I reacted instinctively, ducking under their grab and falling to the dirt, rolling aside as the bull stumbled over where I had just been. Matt managed to avoid the clumsy attack too, leaping aside before grabbing his attacker's arm and holding on, using it as an anchor while he threw a hard kick at the bent over behemoth's jaw.

When Matt's foot connected with a loud crack, I figured the guy would drop. But all the blow did was turn his head sideways, leaving him off-balance. I didn't see what happened next, because the other attacker tried to stomp me with his size twenty boots. I managed to catch his massive foot and push it aside, reaching for my gun as he straddled me, looking down.

HE SUDDENLY FLEW OFF me as Alter planted one of her fiery batons in his throat before kicking him away. I rolled to my feet in time to watch Matt shoot his attacker point-blank in the chest, the round doing little to slow the asshole down. Alter made up for it, jumping on his back and drawing her baton across his neck. He gurgled in surprise, clutching at his sliced open throat as Alter jumped off and he collapsed.

I closed my eyes, fighting nausea from the violence, my heart pounding so fast I couldn't make out one beat from another. Matt holstered his gun, eyes wide from the adrenaline-driven fight.

"Geez," he said, breathing hard and shallow. "What the hell? Why did they attack us?"

"Drunken bastards," Alter replied, turning off her baton and putting it back on her hip. "They saw you two, took us for amateurs, and probably decided they wanted our gear."

"Even if we look like amateurs, you don't," I said.

"That's why they went for you first. They were hoping for two quick kills, and then they could team up on me. Not that it would have worked, especially in their drunken state. But then, that's what made their decision-making so poor to begin with. They got what they deserved."

I glanced over at the two corpses, spilling blood onto the rock. It still churned my stomach to see them like that, but I had a feeling they wouldn't be the last and I needed to get used to things as they were, not how I wanted them to be. Everything had its positives and negatives. "Do you think they had a ship? Maybe we could claim it as salvage."

Alter smiled. "Now you're thinking like a smuggler. These two are more likely crew. Captains usually dress the part to attract business."

"Are we dressed the part?" Matt asked.

"Well enough, except you didn't take my advice and change your boots. We might not have been attacked if you had."

"Seriously?" I said. "Because of our boots?"

"Everything is a signal. From your clothes, to your posture, to the set of your eyes. You want to signal confidence here, even if you don't feel it."

"Confidence. Right." I glanced at Matt. He had already updated his posture, giving the same impression of control he had when he walked out on a stage to sing. I envied that ability a great deal.

A second group of individuals rounded the corner of the path from the settlement, drawing our attention. It took a lot of effort not to stare at one of the four members in the group. Humanoid, but definitely not human, the alien had large eyes and ears on a small face, four arms along a furry torso, and four legs, its spine turning upward like an insect's. A tube ran from its mouth to a canister on its back, which I assumed was filled with whatever mixture of chemicals it needed to breathe. The other three were human. One of them wore a crisp uniform, a gun hanging from one hip, a long dagger on the other. The other two were also clean and neat in ordinary gray flight suits.

Their attention turned to the two bodies as they approached, offering only quick notice before meeting our eyes. Confidence. I did my best to project strength and arrogance, as though I was pleased with the kills.

"Good day," their leader said, nodding to us.

"Good day to you, sir," Matt replied with a mischievous smirk. The furry alien turned its head toward him and chittered something beneath its breather, drawing smiles from the other two. They passed without incident, continuing to the steps and down toward the beach.

"Come on," Alter said. "We don't want to be late."

Chapter Forty-Two

The path through the jungle stretched another kilometer, winding through alien brush not incredibly different from what I expected the Amazon to look like. Plenty of green plants with large leaves, tall trees with thick canopies, and an assortment of small brushy plants. Considering the atmospheric composition and climate, maybe it shouldn't have been surprising. Even so, I kept my eyes peeled for signs of alien birds and insects and other creatures, hoping to spot something as weird and wonderful as the furry spacefarer that had passed us.

I did manage to catch a glimpse of something large and bright red flying between the trees, and I heard plenty of calls and chirps from the surroundings. But it seemed the wildlife knew to stick to the outskirts of the small landmass, giving the more intelligent life forms space to do their business.

The Dark Exchange didn't so much change the landscape as it was an almost natural part of it, its presence taking me by surprise as we reached the last turn in the path.

While the buzz of activity had been audible from the stairs, it intensified to a harsh murmur as the first of the structures appeared. The rounded tops of the metal structures were painted in a camouflaged green pattern, making the buildings look like they grew from the jungle floor. Open-air lifts anchored to the tall trees carried riders from the ground into the lower levels of the canopy, where it seemed like most of the action took place. From the ground, I could see dozens of individuals standing up above on rigid walkways between the trees or on platforms surrounding their trunks. Additional structures lined the branches, some as large as a house.

"Act like you've done this before," Alter reminded us, Matt and I quickly returning our amazed eyes to ground level.

As we moved into the maze of structures. I could sense the sharpness of her focus. Not that the individuals on the ground paid us any mind. We were nothing special here. Just another group of mercenaries looking for work. Even so, Alter's promise that we would be tested remained at the front of my mind. But what if the two brutes near the steps had been a test? Did they recognize us from somewhere? Or maybe someone in one of the ships had seen us leave *Head Case*? We could be relatively anonymous here, but our ship would stand out anywhere.

A large, round structure rested in the center of the open area beneath the trees, its metal roof stained in places with what I anxiously classified as blood spilled by others who had fallen or were thrown from overhead. The rough nature of the idea gave me shivers, though I was relieved when we made a straight line to that building instead of the lifts, happy to stay on the ground.

The guard at the entrance to the structure reminded

me of a medieval knight. Adorned in thick gray armor with a heavy helmet, a sword rested on his hip, with a plasma rifle slung to his back. He eyed us warily as we neared, but didn't block our path as the door into the building slid open.

The same awful music we had avoided on the ship blared out from the open entry. Looking inside, it was easy to make out the nature of the place. A round bar sat at the center, stocked with a huge array of bottles and containers, half the seats around it occupied. Smaller tables circled it where a few more groups drank and ate. Nearly naked women of all shapes and sizes wandered the enclosure, some carrying trays, others pausing to strike a suggestive pose. At the outer perimeter, glass walled enclaves offered silence and secrecy, though only one that I could see from the front appeared to be occupied.

Matt and I followed Alter into the bar. She had only made it a few steps when one of the women approached her, wrapping an arm over her shoulder and whispering something in her ear.

"Take your arm off me or lose it," I heard her reply.

The prostitute quickly pulled back her arm and wandered off while Alter turned and scanned the private booths. She ignored everything else in the place so we did too, sticking close as we crossed the floor.

"Matt, transmit the meeting ID to this booth," she said.

"Okay," Matt replied, taking the phone out of his pants pocket and tapping on it. The door to the glass booth slid open. There were two unpadded metal benches, one on each side of the simple metal table, inside the booth. Each was only large enough for two people. Matt slid in first and Alter moved in beside him, so I sat opposite them. The door slid closed behind us, drowning out all of the exterior noise.

"Now what?" I asked.

"Now we wait," she replied. "Nakata's maker should be along soon enough. The identifier will lead him to this booth."

"Should we get a drink or something?" Matt asked.

"No, no drinks. We're here for business, not pleasure. The faster we can conclude it, the faster we get off this planet. The safer it is for us."

"Right," I agreed, pausing. "They don't have any blue milk, do they?"

"Blue milk?" Alter asked. "I don't think I've ever seen anything like that. But we aren't drinking."

"Oh, I don't want to drink it. I just wanted to know if it existed."

"I don't understand you sometimes, Ben."

"I don't understand him most of the time," Matt said. "I think he keeps trying to use nerdy sci-fi pop culture references, but nobody here understands them."

"I was just curious," I said. "Tell me you weren't thinking it."

"I wasn't thinking it."

"Liar."

We both clammed up when a figure paused in front of the booth. He used his glass slab to open the door, sliding in beside me.

He smelled good at least, a dab of cologne or after-shave quickly filling the small space. Short white hair, with dark eyes and light skin that seemed to cling to his bones. His strong jaw and calm expression exuded confidence and comfort.

"Enigma, I presume?" he said, looking across the table at Alter.

She nodded. "And my associates."

"Do your associates have names?" He glared across the table at Matt.

"Stang," he said, too damn quickly as I realized I needed an alias. He had always used Stang for everything.

Nakata's maker side-eyed me. "And you?"

I didn't know what to say, so I blurted out the first thing that came to mind. "Hondo."

I spotted Matt's wince out of the corner of my eye. I didn't really like the name either, but it would have to do.

"I'm Vicar Lo," the man said, returning his attention to Alter. He reached a gaunt hand under his coat, pulling out a thin slab of clear plastic similar to the one Matt had in his pants pocket, and placed it in the center of the table. "Privacy." The booth's glass turned opaque, wrapping us in total secrecy. "Your reputation precedes you, Enigma. But I have to admit, you aren't what I expected."

"What did you expect?" she replied.

"A man for one. Not to sound misogynistic. But there are a lot more men than women in your line of work. More enhancements, for another." I noticed his eye twitch, and staring into it I spotted what looked like a small glint of metal shifting behind his iris. "Again, the vast majority of your ilk have at least two or three physical modifications."

"Like your eye," Alter said.

"Yes. Third, I thought you would be older. The last I had heard, you were supposed to be dead. You disappeared almost twenty years ago, and yet you don't look a day over thirty, if that. Perhaps you inherited your father's identifier?"

"No. The identifier is mine. But a good assassin never reveals their true face. *You* should know that."

"Is it still that obvious?" Lo said.

"To the ones who know."

He glanced over at me. "I used to be an assassin too. A contemporary of Engima's," he explained before looking back at Alter. "With that said, it's an honor to meet you, Enigma. Your exploits are well known across the Family, even if you were never a member." He paused. "Where have you been, all of these years?"

"Enjoying retirement. Much like you."

"There is no retirement for people like us. When you're too old, they find another use for you or throw you out with the trash."

My eyes shifted to Alter. Somehow, she managed not to give even the slightest hint of a reaction to the statement.

"In any case," Lo continued. "What brought you back?"

"It doesn't matter." She reached for the clear slab.

"Not so fast," Lo said, stopping her before she picked it up. "You do understand, I'm hiring smugglers, not killers."

"I do," Alter replied. "Hondo is one of the best pilots in the Spiral. Stang's ship is the fastest in the Quadrant, guaranteed. My team is the best you'll find."

"Your team? People like us always work alone."

"I'm not like you anymore. I told you, I retired."

Lo smiled. "Of course. Well then, if you say Hondo is the best pilot in the Spiral, I believe you. And I certainly don't need to worry about pirates with you on board." He motioned to the slab. "That's the cargo."

Alter didn't ask what it was or what might be on it.

She knew better. My curiosity begged me to put the question to Lo, but I held my tongue.

"Where is it going?" she asked.

"Kasper. The courier is expecting it to arrive in nine days. He'll be at the spaceport with an active identifier linked to the device. Leave it somewhere it won't be stolen and he'll pick it up within minutes. Don't linger to keep an eye on it. If you see the courier, it will be considered a breach of contract."

"Okay. What's the rate?"

"Twelve million."

"That's a lot of electro to move a personal slab from one side of the Quadrant to the other. You'd be better off sending it with a whore on a pleasure cruise. More subtle."

"The data on the slab is too sensitive to risk any attempt to access it. In fact, without the proper key, the slab will self-destruct when turned on. The high rate is to mitigate the temptation, as failure to deliver the slab is a breach of contract. Also, the recipient's enemies are aware of the slab's existence. They may be waiting on Kasper, or they may try to capture it ahead of your arrival."

"You mean they may already be *here*?"

"Possibly."

Alter nodded. "The contract?"

Lo retrieved his smaller slab. The interface was visible through the back, though I couldn't read the text. He tapped on it a few times.

Alter held her hand out in front of Matt, and he placed our phone on her upturned palm. She quickly scanned the contract before looking up at Lo. "Eighteen million," she said firmly.

Lo didn't bat an eye. "The contract is for twelve."

"You didn't know who you would have the opportunity to hire. Now you do. Eighteen million."

"Twenty-five years out of action and off the map," Lo said. "And you believe you're still worth that much?"

"We can go outside and you can try me."

He smiled. "That won't be necessary." He tapped on his slab again.

Alter glanced down at the phone before smiling back. "Not in the mood to bargain, then?"

"I consider your offer a bargain for *your* services."

Alter entered something on the phone before handing it back to Matt. "It's always a pleasure to do business with Duke Nakata."

Lo bowed his head. "Payment will be transmitted automatically when the slab's identifier is linked to the courier. End privacy."

The glass didn't have a chance to clear before the bullets started raining in.

Chapter Forty-Three

We were lucky the privacy glass offered a split second of protection against the rounds that suddenly punched through it, allowing in the thudding sound of rifle fire. The first bullet caught Lo in the left side of the head. His skull snapped toward me absorbing the last of the slug's kinetic energy before it could explode from his skull and hit me. More rounds followed, all of them striking Lo in the side, riddling him with bullets while he inadvertently protected me from the barrage.

"Get down!" Alter shouted.

I was already moving, sliding from the bench to the floor under the table, hoping the thin metal was at least some insurance against taking a bullet. I didn't think to reach for my gun, but I couldn't see where the shooter was anyway.

Alter's legs disappeared from beneath the table as the bullets swept across the booth, my heart skipping as the thought of Matt being shot whipsawed through my mind. I looked up to see that he'd dropped belly down on the bench where Alter had been sitting. He had his gun in hand but couldn't raise up to shoot it as rounds zinged through the air just above his body. They struck the far wall, punching through to the outside.

The glass finally shattered as something much larger than a bullet slammed through it, shaking the entire booth as the small fragments of the barrier fell to the floor like raindrops. The shooter came into view through them. He didn't look special in any way, though his clothes gave him a definite military appearance. He also wasn't alone. An entire group of similarly dressed and equipped assholes had fanned out behind him, just the sight of them clearing out the bar ahead of the violence.

That was all I had time to process before Alter landed between me and the shooter, having dived through the glass, without so much as a scratch. She swung her batons in a blur, absorbing or redirecting the rounds coming at us and then leaped in the air, leading with her foot as she cracked the lead shooter in the jaw. The rest of his fighters raised their rifles, all taking aim at Alter.

"Come on," I said to Matt, pulling my blaster as I crawled to the front of the booth and opened fire on them. Matt started firing from his prone position. Most of our shots went over their heads, but at least we were able to take some of the heat off Alter.

I took aim, getting a bead on one of the men, my finger resting on the trigger. A split-second of uncertainty and then I squeezed the trigger, the blast hitting him square in the chest. He turned toward me and I fired again, hitting him center mass a second time, the round enough to paralyze him. He shuddered and fell unconscious to the floor, continuing to quiver.

Of course, shooting at the bad guys also told them

we were still there and still alive. A few of them turned their guns toward us, prepared to blow us to hell. Matt and I both made a break to escape the confined space, my eyes fixed on the attacker most likely to kill me. I fired a couple of blasts at him, missing by a lot as the first of his rounds came in, hitting the floor just in front of me.

The bullets stopped coming at me as a metal disc, like a ninja star, zipped in, burying itself in his neck. He dropped his gun and sank to his knees, both hands grasping at the sudden wound.

Staying low and moving laterally to the booths, around the curve of the structure, I sent a series of blasts at an adversary hiding behind an overturned table. The metal surface absorbed the first three shots, but the last one punched through the weakened metal, knocking that attacker down.

Alter easily took out the last attacker as she ran for the door. "Stang, Hondo!" she shouted. "Grab the slab and let's go!"

"Got it!" Matt shouted, scooping up the device, amazingly still intact after the attack. He tucked it under his left arm like a football, jumping over one of the bodies and running to where I waited.Both of us headed for the exit, Alter meeting us there.

All three of us came to a stop as the hatch slid open, revealing an armored guard standing there, rifle in hand. "Drop your weapons. Put your hands up." Alter had already returned her batons to their holsters, but Matt and I still had our blasters in hand. We both looked to her for guidance. When she nodded, we dropped the guns.

"What is this?" Alter said. "These jokers attacked us. The meeting place is supposed to be secured. What do you think will become of this DEX if it isn't safe to do business here?"

I couldn't see the guard's face behind his helmet, but I could hear a thin, muffled voice spilling out of a speaker inside it.

"The Viceroy wants to speak to you," he said.

"Yi? Why? We've done nothing wrong. We were finalizing a standard contract."

"I don't ask questions. I follow orders. This way." He turned to the side to give us space to pass him. Closer to the path, a larger contingent of armored guards were making their way toward the building.

"That's a lot of guards," Matt muttered beside me. "I don't have a good feeling about this."

"Murphy's Law," I replied softly. "If it can go wrong, it probably will."

Alter glanced at us, her eyes narrowed and sharp, her hand moving slowly toward one of the hard cases attached to her belt. She had told us nobody was dumb enough to pick a fight with Viceroy Yi. But what if the Viceroy picked a fight with us first?

The only question was why. Did it have something to do with the slab Matt had under his arm? Or had he spoken to Sedaya? Either way, we were screwed.

A shrill tone blared from Matt's pocket as the alarm he had set on *Head Case* went off, signaling that someone was trying to get into the ship. The unexpected noise caused the guard to flinch.

Alter didn't waste the distraction.

She lunged at him, batting his rifle away before he could fire. A baton slipped into her grip and acti- vated. With her free hand, she pushed the guard's helmet up and away, leaving the base of his thick neck bare. She sliced the baton across it before pulling his head back down and climbing onto his shoulders. Pushing him to the floor, she took his rifle as he fell.

"Fall back!" she snapped, holstering her baton and bringing the rifle up. I paused to pick up my blaster before sprinting across the room as she opened fire, sending a barrage of plasma at the approaching reinforcements.

"This is ridiculous," Matt said as we ran. Alter moved aside as return fire poured through the door, the plasma blasts passing on either side of us. Matt and I reached the bar and vaulted over it, dropping down behind it to avoid the plasma toroids peppering the room. I found the bartender still cowering there.

"Hello," I said to him, offering a quick smile.

He stared at me for a second before thrusting a knife at my face. I jerked backward, and the knife missed me. Before he could turn and come after me again, I grabbed a bottle off the bottom shelf and smashed it against his skull. He fell on me, out cold, the knife dropping from his hand.

"Loser," I said, shoving him off and getting back up into a crouch. Bent over, I followed the backside of the bar around to the end of it, Matt right behind me.

"Where's Alter?" Matt asked.

"She can take care of herself," I replied.

"I hate this again."

"Me too."

We made it to the other side of the bar as the rain of blaster fire slowed, the guards becoming more cautious as they approached the entrance to the building. I could hear their heavy boots on the ground outside, along with the clacking of their armor against itself at the joints. It didn't surprise me that I couldn't hear Alter. If she dressed like a ninja and threw stars like a ninja, she was a ninja.

"Get ready to run," she said from somewhere in front of us. How had she gotten there? I poked my head up over the bar just in time to see her throw a wad of goop against the far wall at the back of the booths. She dove away before it exploded, blowing a hole in the wall and sending a thick wave of smoke and steam into the room. "Now!"

I ran around the end of the bar, and Matt vaulted it a second time, both of us sprinting into the thick smoke, heading for the hole behind it as the guards poured into the front of the bar. They fanned out and once again opened fire. Plasma sizzled through the smoke, hitting the wall around us as we escaped through the hole.

Alter waited outside.

"What the hell is going on?" I asked, breathing heavily. Whatever had made the smoke, it didn't bother my lungs at all. Another ninja move.

"Sedaya," Alter replied. "It has to be. Only he has the power to convince Viceroy Yi to sacrifice his exchange to capture us."

"But Yi isn't under his flag."

"That doesn't always matter. Anyone can be bought for a high enough price."

"Wouldn't it have been cheaper to just pay us for the Star?" Matt asked.

"That's not the point. Come on."

Alter led us away from the path toward the surrounding jungle. Shouting drew my attention upward, just in time to see more guards taking aim at us from the overhead walkways.

"Move!" I shouted, practically pushing Matt ahead. We raced away from the center of the settlement, darting into a narrow alley between two of the buildings that were high enough to force the shooters up above them to move to a better position.

Still running, we were nearly slammed when an Niflin mercenary swung out in front of us. Instead of a helmet, he wore a breathing apparatus on his back, with a small tube leading to his mouth. He had a pistol in each hand, his first round hitting Alter in the shoulder. She grunted and stumbled, nearly falling to her knees, when the second round struck her thigh. Raising my gun was almost instinct as I aimed and fired, catching the Niflin in the abdomen. The first blast slowed him down. My follow up round put him on the ground for good.

"Alter," I said, catching up to her. She was bent over, one hand clutching her leg.

"I'm okay," she replied. "Flesh wounds."

"How are we going to get back to the ship?" Matt asked. "They'll be waiting there for us."

"We don't need to go to the ship. We can bring the ship to us. First, we need to get away from security."

"This entire island can't be more than a hundred acres," Matt said. "How are we supposed to get clear?"

"The jungle's small but dense. It'll be easy to disappear. We need to make a break for the foliage." She pointed to the edge of the jungle, just past another open gap behind the buildings we were tucked between. "I'll put down smoke to hide us. Go as fast as you can, and don't stop until you see the water. Are you ready?"

"Ready," I said.

Alter reached into the case on her belt, withdrawing a small black marble and underhanded it across the alley into the intersection. It activated when it hit the ground, spewing thick smoke in every direction.

"Go!" she said, turning around as the guards reached

the opposite end of the alley. Matt and I both hesitated as she raced toward the soldiers, shouting back over her shoulder. "I'll catch up! Do it!"

I didn't want to leave her, but she was probably better off without us weighing her down. We broke for the smoke and the jungle beyond, sprinting away as plasma fire sizzled behind us.

We escaped into the jungle, leaving Alter behind.

Chapter Forty-Four

I ran as fast as I could through the brush, doing my best not to trip on the roots or get tangled in thick branches. Matt's footsteps confirmed he remained close behind, following me through the dense vegetation and away from the settlement.

The gunfire stopped behind us, and for a moment I was ready to slow down, take a breather, and wait for Alter to catch up. I couldn't believe this was happening. That a short excursion to a planet where we should have been relatively anonymous had gone sideways so quickly and completely. It seemed like fate decided it had a cruel joke to play and had picked me to act it out. Buy a real, working spaceship and go to another galaxy, only to wind up a criminal being hunted at every turn. Maybe it would make for a good movie, but otherwise it sucked.

And yet, a part of me was really enjoying this. Had the tumor done something to alter my emotional state?

The gunfire started again, only it was closer now. The plasma rounds hissed through the brush, hitting the trees to my left. The bad news was that the guards had followed us. The good news was that they apparently had no idea where we actually were. They were firing blindly, perhaps hoping to scare us into surrendering.

Fat chance.

We kept running, delving deeper into the greenery. I heard the guards moving into the jungle behind us, giving chase as we ran but already a good distance behind. Their armor was too heavy and clunky to let them traverse the thick vegetation with ease. There was no way they would catch up. That didn't stop them from trying, and it didn't stop them from shooting. Plasma continued lighting up the mild darkness beneath the dense canopy, rounds streaking through nowhere near the mark. The effort was so poor it would have been comical if only one hit from a round in the back wouldn't be fatal.

A minute passed. Then another. Then another. After five minutes, we were still running hard, navigating the jungle as best we could. It occurred to me that I would never have been able to run like this before the sickbay treatments and my meds. Maybe the cancer was still in me, but I felt completely well. That was my silver lining.

The guards fell further back, finally giving up shooting at us. I kept going anyway, breathing hard, my stamina beginning to fade. Alter had said not to stop until I saw the water, and I trusted her advice. And hoped she was okay. It felt awful to abandon her, and I had to remind myself she was better off without having to worry about me and Matt.

Light began shining through the trees ahead, signaling we were near the edge of the jungle. I slowed a little then, just enough to be able to shoot if guards waited on the other side of the last line of trees. The water had to be close. I could smell the salty air. Only another few hundred feet to go.

Reaching the last stretch of vegetation, I pushed through a growth of large leaves, the water coming into full view, the ground dropping off into a steep, rocky slope right in front of me.

I frantically hit the brakes, almost nose-diving over the edge. My gun flew from my hand and bounced over the cliff as I turned and dropped to my hands and knees. I grabbed at loose pebbles and embedded rocks to keep from sliding off what had to be a hundred-foot high cliff. I lost purchase when the pebbles rolled beneath my left hand. My right slipped off a larger embedded rock. I dug my fingers into the dirt, fighting to hang on as my toes slid over the edge, the rest of me threatening to follow.

"Ben!" Matt shouted, diving out of the woods and stretching his hand out toward mine, only to come up a few inches short. I gritted my teeth, finding just enough arm strength to propel myself forward and grab hold of his wrist. "Hold on," he grated, grasping my wrist. He twisted around to dig in his heels and push while he pulled himself back with his free hand, bringing me up with him. Within a few seconds, I was sitting on the ground next to the cliff edge.

"Shit, that was close," I wheezed, doing my best to catch my breath and calm my racing heart.

"Alter said see the water, not jump into it," Matt replied. "You scared the hell out of me."

"I scared the hell out of me." I paused to breathe. "Do you think they're still following us?"

"I don't know. I hope not. I left my gun back at the bar."

"I dropped mine over the cliff when I fell."

Matt reached down to his boot, retrieving a long knife. "I still have this. These boots weren't completely useless."

I laughed off some of my tension as quietly as I could. "Are you okay with stabbing somebody with that thing?"

"Kill or be killed," Matt replied. "They were shooting at us. I thought you were over that?"

"It's different to shoot someone versus stabbing them. Stabbing is more up close and personal."

"If you say so. And yeah, I'm ready to use it to protect us."

A rustle in the brush captured our attention. I moved into a crouch, and Matt did the same, holding the knife out in front as though it could magically ward off whatever was coming at us.

"It might be Alter," I suggested.

"I hope so," he whispered back.

We moved back to the trees, tucking in behind a trunk as the rustling moved closer. We both waited there, pressed against the bark, Matt ready to swing out and stab whoever turned the corner.

The rustling stopped on the other side of the tree, disappearing as if it had never been there at all. I turned my head toward Matt's. Our eyes met, both of us confused. We strained to hear any movement, but the jungle had gone silent. Too silent. There should have been chirps and squawks and other noises. Someone was definitely there. Waiting for us to come out?

Neither one of us moved. Let it come to us; we weren't about to reveal ourselves.

A minute passed. Another. The silence remained, keeping me on edge. I looked at Matt again, about to whisper a suggestion that we attack the area where we had last heard movement from both sides of the tree. Something dripped onto my forehead, thick and wet and smelly. I tipped my head back and stared up at a catlike creature with the largest teeth I'd ever seen.

Seeing me seeing it, the creature's jaws opened further, no doubt ready to snap forward and take my entire head off in one bite. Before it could, a blue creature no more than six inches long—it reminded me of a cross between a tarsier monkey and a flying squirrel—sailed in and glommed onto the side of the bigger creature's head, clinging there, over its left eye, as it made a high pitched buzzing sound. The big creature gurgled, went stiff, and fell out of the tree, bouncing off my shoulder and onto the ground. The blue creature remained attached to the now dead one, covering its eye.

"What the hell?" Matt whispered, pressed tight against the trunk. He hadn't seen the thing over our heads before it fell.

"We need to get out of here," I replied softly. "That blue thing just killed it."

The blue creature moved before we could, raising its large head to look up at us with huge eyes. It would have been one of the cutest things I'd ever seen if it didn't have a pair of fangs sticking too far out of its tiny mouth.

"Don't move," I suggested to Matt, now that it was looking right at us.

"Yeah, because it can't see us with those softball eyes," he replied. "What the hell is it?"

"Well, based on its coloring and the size of its teeth," I said sarcastically, "how the hell should I know? It bit that thing in the eye, and now that thing is dead."

"But wasn't that bigger thing about to bite you?"

"Yeah, I think so."

"So it saved your life."

"I guess. Probably so it could devour us instead."

"Why would something that tiny want to eat something our size?"

"I don't know. Maybe it only eats brains or something."

Before I knew what it intended, the tarsier squirrel leaped away from the catlike creature, lunging right at me. With only a second to react, I closed my eyes and turned my head away, expecting to feel the fangs sink into my cheek.

I didn't feel anything. Keeping my eyes closed, I started counting the seconds, still waiting for the killer bite.

"Huh," Matt said when I got to five. "I think he likes you."

I turned my head back and opened my right eye, finding myself staring into one of the alien squirrel's huge orbs. The sight almost made me laugh out loud with nervous tension, but I was afraid any sudden noises or movements would spur it into action.

The creature perched on my shoulder, its hind claws dug into my jacket. I watched it watching me until it bent its head down, a long, narrow tongue flicking out and sliding across its underbelly as it began cleaning itself.

Matt moved away from the tree, drawing the thing's attention.

"Stop moving!" I hissed.

Matt froze, both of us watching until it started cleaning itself again.

"There you are," Alter said, coming around the side of the tree and practically scaring me to death. I froze stiff in surprise, while the creature on me made a high pitched buzz and launched itself at Alter.

Somehow, she caught it in mid-air, her reaction time

ridiculously fast. Its head stuck out past her fist, trying to bite her finger with its long fangs. She almost as quickly opened her hand, letting the alien rodent rest in her palm.

"Oh, I'm sorry," she said. "But you shouldn't be so quick to go on the offensive."

The tarsier squirrel turned on her hand and jumped back to my shoulder, perching there again.

Alter stared at me. "Where did you get the Jagger?"

"You know what this thing is?" I asked.

"It's good to see you, by the way," Matt added.

Her eyes shifted to the catlike creature. "He killed the Aslink for you?"

"That thing almost bit my head off, until this thing bit it in the eye."

"I don't think he appreciates being called a thing."

"You mean it speaks English?"

Alter laughed. "Look at it, Ben. Of course he doesn't *speak* English, he doesn't have the proper vocal structure. But he understands it well enough, I'm sure. Isn't that right?"

The Jagger's buzz sounded almost as if he said "Mmm-hmm."

"Wait," Matt said. "You're saying the blue squirrel is an ilf?"

"Very," Alter said. "Though I have no idea how he got here."

"Why is he sitting on my shoulder?" I asked.

"If I had to guess, he saw you running through the jungle, noticed the Aslink hunting you, and decided to intervene. He probably needs a ride off Cestus. Is that right?"

The Jagger buzzed again, in the same way he did the last time.

"How do you know he's a he?" I asked, glancing at him.

"Females are yellow and twice his size," Alter replied. "And you really should stop talking about him as if he's a wild animal."

I froze, turning beet red. "Oh. Shit. Yeah. I'm sorry. I've never seen a Jagger before. I've never seen much of anything that isn't human before. Thank you for saving my life."

When the Jagger buzzed again, it sounded to me like he said "No problem."

"You need a ride?" I asked.

He buzzed in affirmation.

"You've got it."

"Speaking of a ride," Alter said. "Where's *Head Case*?"

"What do you mean?"

"I thought you would have brought the ship over by now. I slipped the guards, but the island isn't that big."

"How am I supposed to fly the ship without being in the ship?" I asked.

"Stang, phone."

Matt pulled it from his pocket and handed it to Alter. She tapped on it a few times before handing it to me. The view on the screen mimicked what I would expect to see in the pilot's seat, looking through the augmented reality of the helmet. It was just like a video game.

"You're telling me we have remote control?"

"Yes," Alter said impatiently.

"Why don't you fly the ship over?" I suggested, holding the phone out to her.

"One, I don't know how to fly the ship," she said, confusing the hell out of me.

"Since when?"

She ignored me. "Two, I need to go back and slow down the guards. You should have taken care of this already. Stang, you're with me."

"I lost my gun," Matt said.

She passed him one of hers before looking at the Jagger. "Are you in?"

The Jagger buzzed noncommittally for a moment before changing its tone to an affirmation. I flinched when he licked the side of my face before leaping to Alter's shoulder.

"I think you've made a new friend," she said. "Get the ship up here. The faster the better. We'll hold them back."

Chapter Forty-Five

I looked down at the screen, a little nervous about trying to fly *Head Case* remotely. Sure, I had played plenty of games on my phone before, and this wasn't really all that different except that this time a real starship would respond to my commands. In better circumstances, that would be very, very cool. With half the island hunting us, the pressure was on.

I dragged the throttle open just a little, easing my way into things. Pulling back on the stick, the view shifted as *Head Case* began shifting up and forward. Tilting the phone allowed me to look down, and I cursed when I spotted a team of Niflin mercenaries about to do something drastic to crack open the shields, and a second ship I was about to collide with.

"Here goes nothing," I said, dragging the throttle all the way open and pulling hard on the stick. Without anyone inside, there was no limit to the inertia that made it through the counter-systems. The only question was whether or not the superstructure could take the heavy flex.

My view through the phone shuddered as the ship made the maneuver, rocketing away from the mercenaries on the ground. That didn't mean the ship was going to get away. The mercs fired a large projectile, a net erupting from it and opening up to clip the bottom of *Head Case* as the ship rose over it. Like a spiderweb, the net clung to the hull, but as beginner's luck would have it, I was able to successfully scrape the web off on the the irregular superstructure of a merc ship. Tilting the phone more to look down as the ship rose, I saw the web turn red with heat and energy, beginning to sink into the second ship's currently unshielded hull.

Too close for comfort.

Flipping the phone to landscape so I could see a greater area around the ship, I couldn't hold back my smile. Free and clear. At least for the moment.

I turned *Head Case* and slowed down. I also took a second to glance up from where I stood, looking for the ship out over the ocean. I didn't see it. I also didn't see myself from the flight deck, but we had to be on the western side of the island. I added back some thrust and sent *Head Case* zooming along the shoreline, listening for the sound of the thrusters from my spot at the edge of the cliff.

What I heard instead was gunfire echoing out of the jungle some distance away. A heavy barrage, followed by a short burst. When the next barrage came, it sounded a little lighter. And closer.

Go Alter!

Returning my attention to flying the ship, I finished the course correction and focused on gaining altitude while circling the island to the west. At the same time, I walked backward to the tree Matt and I had hid behind. Forgetting about the dead Aslink, I tripped over it and nearly fell on my face. But my luck held. The tree trunk was there to break my fall.

I kept my back pressed against the tree. Although it lowered my ability to see the sky overhead, it also improved my level of security. Besides, *Head Case* was big enough that it would be hard to miss once it flew into the range of my vision.

I continued steering the ship around the island, gaining enough height to see nearly the entire island. The settlement at the center was hard to spot through the overgrowth, but the flashes of light from the guards' rifles stood out on the western side, helping me direct the ship that way. Descending again, I nearly brushed the treetops on my pass.

The swooshing roar of the thrusters hit my ears, bringing a smile to my face as I looked up past the branches of the tree. The ship came into view a moment later, sending an excited chill through my body. We were going to make it! Looking through the phone, I cut the thrust and twisted the stick while holding the ship level. I rotated *Head Case* as it drifted forward, clearing the edge of the jungle and the cliff. I cut the thrust to almost nothing and let it slowly descend.

Behind me, the gunfire increased in volume and intensity, indicating the guards were closer than I thought they would get before I brought *Head Case* in level with the top of the cliff, letting her hover there as the ramp slid down onto solid ground.

Huffing and puffing, Matt stumbled through the brush and fell on his belly behind the tree, literally at my feet. I glanced down at him and then at the phone, spotting a pair of guards following Matt's obvious trail through the brush. I didn't even think about what I was doing when I tapped on the upper half of the phone, activating the HUD and selecting the fire control system. I deactivated the starboard side cannon before exiting the menu, and then quickly tapped on the two incoming guards. I could only see them through my connection to *Head Case*, but that was more than enough.

They reached Matt as he finally rolled over. Fortunately, they couldn't see me standing behind the tree.

"Duke Sedaya sends his regards," one of them said, leveling his rifle at Matt.

"And I send mine," I shouted, loudly enough for them to hear me. They froze as I hit the trigger button on the screen. The port side cannons opened up, the heavy blasts ripping through the two guards with such force they simply vanished beneath the assault.

I eased off the trigger, exhaling sharply.

"Shit," Matt said, looking up at me. "Nice save."

"Come on," I said, helping him up just as another guard rounded the tree behind us.

"Gotcha!" the man growled.

I glanced down at Matt. He had his pistol in hand, aimed between my legs.

"Don't miss," I whispered, wincing as he fired. I felt the heat of the bolt sizzle past my delicates and into the guard, taking him by surprise. I jumped out of the way as Matt fired another half-dozen rounds, desperately trying to punch through the man's armor.

The guard stumbled but didn't fall as he recovered his aim. A high-pitched buzz preceded the Jagger as he slammed into the guard's neck and dug his head under the man's helmet. Like the Aslink, the guard went stiff as a board before toppling over backward.

The Jagger leaped from the body like an arrow,

catching my jacket with his hind legs and neatly spinning around.

"Thanks, buddy," I said.

"No problem," he buzzed.

"Go! Go! Go!" Alter shouted, breaking out of the foliage and sprinting toward *Head Case*.

Chapter Forty-Six

I didn't hesitate, turning and running after Alter as Matt jumped to his feet, following us. A loud thud and crashing brush behind us threatened to steal my attention. I glanced down at the phone instead, catching a brief glimpse of a large metal foot amidst the greenery.

"Open the hatch!" Alter shouted.

"Levi, open the hangar door hatch!" I said, hoping the command would reach through the phone. It did. The hatch slid open, the ramp extending a few feet from the cliff's edge.

Alter reached it first, leaping the gap easily. She whirled around, eyes widening as whatever was coming through the jungle smashed past the foliage. Looking down at the phone while I ran, I saw a large, bipedal robot striding toward us. A huge cannon was slung under its bullet-shaped upper torso, and racks of missiles rested on a pair of racks on top.

Still running, I quickly tapped on the HUD and hit the trigger button. The cannons spewed energy at the mech. It sidestepped the initial barrage as Matt jumped onto the ramp and ran up into the ship.

The Jagger buzzed in my ear, warning me of the approaching gap. I had to stop shooting at the mech to look up. "Alter," I said, tossing the phone at her without warning.

She had to jump to catch it, leaping like a ballerina and grabbing it, doing a neat pirouette in the sky before landing and again hitting the trigger. I made the mistake of looking down when I jumped, watching the sea crash against the shore below while flailing across the gap. I hit the ramp hard, falling and clutching at the grated deck to keep from sliding off. The rough landing knocked the Jagger from his perch, sending him flying into the ship.

"Get to the flight deck!" Alter said, still firing on the mech.

"No time; pass me the remote."

She didn't so much hand it to me as grab my shoulder and throw me into the hangar before tossing the remote at my chest as she ran past where I sat on the hangar deck. The hangar hatch slid closed, the first batch of shells striking it without punching through. My hands shook as I turned on the shields, deflecting the assault.

I opened the throttle and pulled back on the stick, sending *Head Case* blasting off and away with such immediate force that I was thrown backward, rolling and flipping chaotically until I hit the starfighter pinned to the deck. I dropped the phone, and it rattled away, leaving me out of control of the ship as it accelerated and climbed, keeping me pinned to the deck.

"Shit!" I shouted, looking to where the phone had settled against the rear bulkhead. There was only one way to get back there.

Growling the entire time, I gritted my teeth and pulled myself free of the starfighter, the G's rolling me sideways. I flew backward again and slammed into the back wall hard enough to knock the wind out of my lungs. Gasping for air, I picked up the phone, leveling the stick and lowering the thrust enough that the dampeners were able to keep up. Still breathing hard, I got to my feet and rushed to the stairs, climbing them quickly to meet Alter at the elevator. We jumped into the cab together, headed for the flight deck.

In that fleeting moment of forced pause, I noticed the wound she had taken earlier was gone. In fact, not only had her skin healed, but her ninja suit had healed, too.

"Special fabric," she said, noticing me.

"And special skin?" I asked, our eyes meeting.

"Yes," she replied, clearly uncomfortable with my discovery.

The elevator doors opened on Deck Three. I ran out, but she didn't follow. I knew why. She had to go do whatever she did to change personas. I still didn't understand it, and her earlier claim she couldn't fly *Head Case* left me less willing to accept that lack of clarity. Even so, it was something for another less chaotic time. Of course, once things settled down I probably wouldn't care anymore.

"Levi, open the flight deck hatch," I said. My voice was programmed into the security system now, and the doors slid open on my command.

I vaulted the sofa, catching myself with my hands on the center console between the two pilot seats before face-planting into it. I threw myself into my seat and strapped in. Grabbing my helmet off the headrest, I yanked it on and reached for the controls, my eyes immediately drifting to the sensor map in the corner of the

HUD. We were well away from the island, shooting across the planet at twenty thousand feet. The collision alert sounded in my ears, startling me. One of the space elevator cables appeared suddenly, dead ahead.

"Shit," I cried again, twisting the stick as I pulled it hard left. The force threw me against my right-shoulder restraints as *Head Case* swung away from the cable, just barely slipping past without losing one of its ears.

Again, too close.

I angled the ship upward and slowly regained thrust, climbing steadily away.

The forces on the ground didn't give chase. I hadn't seen any ships in orbit that I thought would give us trouble, but if Sedaya had already gotten to Yi, who knew how many mercenaries he might have hired. It seemed we were still a step behind the noble when we needed more than anything to get a step ahead.

The flight deck hatch opened. Pilot Alter hurried in, the Jagger on her shoulder.

"Where's Matt?" I asked.

"I sent him to sickbay," she replied as she sat. "His shoulder was wounded during the fighting."

The Jagger leaped from her to the headrest of my seat, perching there.

"Will he be okay?"

"Yes. It's a minor injury, easy to heal."

"Easier than your injuries?" I asked suggestively.

"Ben, I'd rather not talk about it."

"Why not?"

"I…" She paused. I had never seen her look so unsure of herself. "Can we please drop it for now?"

"One of the guards said Sedaya sends his regards. How did he know we would go to Cestus? You said it would be safe."

"What are you insinuating?"

"You've been so helpful to Matt and me. So valuable. But your mercenary pseudonym is too accurate. You're an enigma to me, and normally that might be okay but whether it's all circumstantial or not, I'm having a hard time trusting you right now."

"You think I told Sedaya where we were headed?" she replied, offended and angered by the suggestion.

"How else would he know we would be on Cestus? If there's another way that makes sense, I'm happy to be wrong. I'll be happy to apologize."

She opened her mouth, but no other excuse came out. She shook her head. "I don't know. It wasn't me, Ben. I promise. I hate Sedaya as much as anyone. Probably more."

"I want to believe that so badly, but nothing about you makes sense. I accepted it because it didn't seem to matter, but right now it does. You have multiple personalities. Maybe one of them betrayed us. And you without your pilot persona knowing it."

Her face tensed at the idea, as though there was a chance it was true. Then she shook her head. "No, that's not possible. There's only one me."

"Then how do you only sometimes know how to fly a starship?"

"It's…complicated. Ben, please don't ask me to explain. We knew Sedaya would have eyes and ears on Cestus. We knew an attack would come."

"But from the guy in charge of the entire exchange?" I replied. "Did you expect that?"

"No. It shouldn't be possible. Sedaya has no jurisdiction here. All he has to offer is…" She trailed off.

"Is what?"

"He may be planning to seize Cestus, and perhaps

other planets under Duke Hoka's rule. Buying Yi out ahead of time would be a simpler solution for a world like Cestus. But that doesn't make a lot of sense. This territory is so far from his own."

"Distance wise maybe. It was only three days. Could that be possible?" I was fishing for an alternative. I wanted to believe that Alter had nothing to do with it, and her pleading for me not to pry had left me feeling guilty for even mentioning her nature.

"It's definitely possible," she replied. "But I can't promise that for sure. Don't use that as a reason to believe me."

I looked over at her. Our eyes met again. I couldn't help it. For better or worse, I still trusted her. "I believe you," I said. "Not because of that. Because...I just believe you. Gut feeling I guess. Now, can we get out of here without having to fight our way out?"

"The ships I saw orbiting the planet are no match for *Head Case*," she said. "They won't try to stop us."

"What if they gang up on us?"

She smiled. "They're mercenaries, not military. They don't work well together. We aren't being chased. We should be safe."

I exhaled sharply, letting my body relax. "Whew. Okay. So, where do we go next?"

"Kasper," she replied. "We've still got a job to do."

Chapter Forty-Seven

Kasper wasn't close to Cestus. According to Alter, it sat at the farthest side of the Quadrant, one of what she referred to as the Edgeworlds. Under the flag of Duke Nobukku, it was an Earthlike planet in every way, from the composition of the atmosphere to the percentage of land to ocean and an abundance of evolved wildlife.

And it would take almost all of the nine days Lo had given us to get there.

After putting *Head Case* into hyperspace, I removed my helmet and safety restraints, careful not to accidentally elbow the Jagger as I did. The small blue ilf had resumed cleaning himself and didn't seem bothered by my movements, though he stopped preening to look at me as I got to my feet.

"I'm going to check on Matt," I said.

"I'll be down there soon," Alter replied.

I almost asked her if she was going to change personas again, but I already knew the answer and bringing it up would only reignite her discomfort from our prior conversation. So much about her was so strange and hard to understand, but I had decided I trusted her. And the truth was, we needed to trust her. Matt and I would have been dead three times over without her experience and multiple skill sets.

I glanced at the Jagger instead. "Are you coming?" He buzzed an affirmative and jumped onto my shoulder again. I was already starting to get used to having him there, his adorable blue rodent shape just visible in my peripheral vision. "Do you have a name?"

His buzz sounded something like "Shzzzk."

"That's not too easy for a human to say," I said. "Do you mind if I call you Shaq?"

His buzz sounded accepting. I smirked at the idea of naming the tiny alien after a seven foot tall basketball player.

"Great. I'm Ben. It's nice to formally meet you."

"You too," Shaq buzzed.

I left the flight deck and Alter, taking the elevator to Deck Two. Instead of going forward to the armory, I turned right off the cab, the hatch opening directly into sickbay. I had been here a few times already to receive treatment for my cancer, and already knew the simple layout well. Three rooms with glass doors that could turn opaque like the booth on Cestus.

Inside each of the rooms, a well-padded seat with an AI-driven full body scanner hanging over it, able to diagnose most ailments and provide treatment instructions for quite a few. Against the far bulkhead of sickbay, one regular cabinet filled with medical supplies, including medications, as well as a fridge and freezer combo for less stable concoctions. While it was probably the most advanced setup of anything on the ship, it still had one major weakness in that it couldn't measure and administer the drugs. Just another reason Alter was so vital to our continued success.

Matt was in the first room, visible behind the clear door. Shirtless and alert, he used his uninjured arm to wave to me when I entered sickbay.

"Ouch, that looks nasty," I said upon entering the room and getting a better look at his arm. The skin around the wound was burned, the damage itself a puss-covered mess. "Does it hurt?"

"Yeah," he replied. "I need some painkillers."

"Nurse Alter will be here soon."

Shaq hopped off my shoulder onto the end of the bed, slinking up Matt's blanket-covered leg on all fours.

"Uh, what are you doing?" Matt said.

I couldn't understand Shaq's longer buzz. He continued up Matt's leg to the edge of the blanket before jumping onto his arm, right next to the wound.

"Shaq?" I said as Matt raised his other arm, presumably to swat the Jagger away.

He buzzed again before a line of spittle dropped out of his mouth onto the wound.

"Shit," Matt said. "What are you trying to…oh." He calmed down, smiling as Shaq continued drooling onto the damage. "Wow. Weird, but okay. Our little bro's spit is a natural painkiller, I guess."

"Not exactly," Alter said, entering the room in her nurse persona. "His spit paralyzed the nerves so you don't feel the pain. Normally, they use it to numb the area they're about to bite when attacking their prey, so that it doesn't even know it's being bitten before the venom in their fangs kills it. I don't think he intends to bite you, though."

Shaq made a higher pitched buzz that I took as a

laugh. Done paralyzing the wound site, he scurried back to Matt's leg and returned to my shoulder.

"Thank you," Matt said.

"No problem," Shaq replied.

Matt glanced at me. "You named him Shaq?"

"His real name sounds kind of like Shaq. It's a natural fit."

Alter looked at the screen on the side of the autodoc. "You're lucky it's only a flesh wound. A few millimeters lower and you would have muscle damage. As it is, you'll need some salve and a wrap. I'll be right back."

She left the room, heading for the cabinets in the medical storeroom to retrieve everything she needed.

"Since we're still alive, I assume we got away," Matt said. "Where are we headed?"

"Kasper," I replied, suddenly remembering our cargo. "Tell me you still have the slab."

"Yeah, it's over there, under my shirt," he replied.

Shaq jumped off me to the table where Matt's slightly bloody shirt rested. He pulled it away, revealing the clear device. I was relieved to see it wasn't damaged.

"You wanted off Cestus, right Shaq?" I asked.

"Mmm-hmm," he buzzed in reply.

"We need to go to Kasper first to fulfill our contract and get paid. But where can we drop you off after that?"

He answered with a quizzical buzz, like he didn't understand the question.

"What planet do you want to go to next?"

Shaq didn't make a sound.

"Are you okay?" I asked, frustrated with our inability to communicate.

"Mmmmm," he buzzed noncommittally.

"You want to stay with Ben?" Matt asked.

"Mmmm-hmmm," Shaq replied in a higher-pitched, more excited buzz.

"Really?" I replied. "Why?" I didn't understand the Jagger's reply. He liked me for reasons I couldn't begin to guess at. I shrugged. "It's fine with me. Matt?"

Shaq turned to look at him, his big eyes growing bigger and causing Matt to laugh. "I don't have a problem with it. But I'm with Ben. I have no idea why you like him so much."

"Thanks," I said.

Matt laughed. "It's probably just the shape of your hunched shoulders that he likes. They make a good perch."

"My shoulders aren't hunched."

"Yeah, right. Whatever Quasimodo."

"They aren't," I insisted, looking at Shaq. "They aren't, are they?"

Shaq emitted another high-pitched laugh, but didn't answer the question.

"Turning on me already?"

Alter returned with a rolling table. A pair of scissors, a scalpel, gauze, bandages, tape, and two tubes of some medicine or another rested on it.

"Shaq's joining the crew," I announced as she pulled the table up beside Matt's arm.

"I believed he would," she replied, not at all surprised. "But what happened to your last crew?"

Shaq buzzed out what sounded like a whole back-story while Alter squeezed out the contents of one of the tubes onto Matt's wound.

"This is a probably unnecessary numbing agent," she explained. "Next, I need to cut away the damaged skin, but you won't feel it."

"Do you know what Shaq just said?" I asked.

"Yes. He said he worked for the two drunk morons we killed."

"And you saved me instead of killing me?" I asked.

"They were assholes," Alter said. "They treated him like a pet instead of an equal, and never split the electro evenly when he did most of the work. He followed you from there, hoping to earn a place."

"You totally earned a place," I said to Shaq "The thing is, we can't afford to pay you right now. We're pretty much broke."

Alter translated as Shaq buzzed. "That's okay. You won't be broke forever. Besides, I don't really have much use for electro. It's the principle of the thing."

"I hear you," I said.

"Alter, is there anything you can't do?" Matt asked.

"There are a lot of things I can't do. Understanding Jagger isn't one of them."

"Can all of you speak Jagger?" I asked. It was a bit of a smart-ass question, but I was honestly curious.

"I don't know what you mean," she replied. Of course not.

"How did you learn the language?" Matt asked.

"Sedaya has a Jagger assassin on his payroll. We taught one another. They make excellent killers, for obvious reasons."

Shaq buzzed excitedly in response to the statement.

"He says not to worry, he won't kill any of us. He likes us."

I smiled. "Thank you."

"No problem," he buzzed.

Alter finished cleaning the wound. She picked up the second tube, squeezing out a dark salve that looked like dog poop onto the damage. Then she covered it with bandages and gauze, taping it around his arm to secure it.

"It should heal in about twenty-four hours," she said. "Don't get it wet until then. The pain shouldn't return. If it does, I need to know immediately."

"Got it," Matt said. "Twenty-four hours. That's impressive. Thank you for patching me up."

"Of course."

I leaned over and grabbed his shirt from the table, tossing it to him. "You probably want to go home again," I suggested, figuring getting shot would be a real turnoff toward this whole adventure.

He surprised me, shaking his head. "No. I'm not letting that asshole Sedaya scare me off. But I am more determined than ever to stick it to him somehow. You?"

"I've never been more scared or felt more alive. This feels like where I was always meant to be."

Shaq buzzed out something that had an inflection at the end, suggesting a question.

"He wants to know how a pair of Earthians wound up as mercenaries in the Fertile Quadrant," Alter said.

"How do you know we're Earthians?" I replied.

He buzzed and pointed at Matt's foot, jutting up beneath the blanket.

"The boots," Alter said, laughing.

I laughed with her, letting the pent up tension release. "Let's head down to the living quarters and I'll tell you all about it."

Chapter Forty-Eight

The days in hyperspace flowed smoothly from one to the next. Like before, every day started with a few hours of training, Sergeant Alter putting us through our paces and teaching, mostly me, how to defend myself. On top of that, she began giving us educational sessions on the different ilfs in the Fertile Quadrant and across the Manticore Spiral. I was somewhat surprised to learn that the majority of spacefaring intelligent life forms were humanoid in nature. While that made sense for sci-fi movies and tv shows, it had always seemed to me that evolution should be more random than that. Then again, it also made reasonable sense that similar planets with similar atmospheres, climates, and molecular and chemical composition would result in similar evolution.

Not that there weren't exceptions. Exotic planets produced more exotic life forms, non-carbon based aliens with stonelike or crystalline appearances, for example. Since they couldn't survive well beyond their own environments, they didn't interact as much with the wider Hegemony.

Then there were the aliens like Shaq, part of a subclass of ilfs that had evolved higher intellect alongside a primary advanced life form. His homeworld, Dasker, was outside the Fertile Quadrant, and was also the homeworld of the Eitnid, a larger humanoid race that bore a generalized resemblance to bigfoot.

As before, I also took to learning more about *Head Case*'s computer systems, including trying to understand the source code that made everything work. Since it had origins in the same programming languages and styles I had been learning in school, I wasn't at a complete loss reading the code. At the same time, the paradigms had evolved so much I still felt lost most of the time.

I spent the rest of my time hanging out in what we decided to start calling the lounge rather than the common room, hanging out with Matt and Shaq. While we couldn't understand most of what the Jagger said whenever Alter wasn't around, we gained enough of an understanding of the different tones of his buzzing and some basic vocalizations that he wasn't completely left out in the cold. Even as the days passed and we grew closer to Kasper, it continued to amaze me that creatures like Shaq even existed, and that I had started thinking of one of them as a friend.

As for Alter, she continued doing her various jobs as *Head Case*'s primary caretaker, though I did manage to convince her to let me help with some of the more basic tasks, like running daily checks across all of the ship's systems, isolating discrepancies, and logging them for her to make repairs. Keep had claimed the ship didn't require much maintenance, but that turned out to be a matter of perspective. No more than a day or two went by before Alter had to tweak something, leading me to start thinking *Head Case* was held together with duct tape and paperclips. By helping her, I managed to start chiseling away at her otherwise aloof presence aboard the ship, and by the eighth day finally got her to accept an invitation to pizza and a movie with the boys.

Which is what found Matt, Shaq, and I in front of Asshole's primary assembly unit, waiting for it to finish my latest request. Fully comfy in a t-shirt, hoodie, sweats, and a pair of maglock-capable sneakers, my heart pumped in anticipation.

"I hope this comes out right," Matt said, waiting with me. He had gone a different route, dressed in a long-sleeved black velour rocker button-down, properly ripped jeans, and also maglock-capable steel tipped boots.

"I hope Alter likes it," I replied.

"Don't get those hopes up too high. She likes that syrupy crap that's popular here. I'm not sure the two are compatible. I still don't know why you're going through all this trouble. She's way too old for you, and she doesn't seem at all interested."

"I'm not trying to date her. I just want her to feel like part of the crew. A real part of the crew, not just here because *Head Case* is her safe place."

"I'm not sure she wants that, though."

"Me either, but there's no harm in trying, right?"

"You know, I just noticed. You're starting to look a little more buff under there." He reached out and squeezed my bicep, which I had also noticed had started to build up a little in response to the daily exercise.

"Jealous?" I asked. Of course, he was still a lot more cut than me. While I was a nerd getting in better shape, he was a jock upping his game.

"Totally." He laughed. "I'm happy for you. The treatments are slowing the cancer, you're getting in the best shape of your life, and in a few more days maybe you'll be cured for good."

"I'm glad we decided to do this," I said. "I'm glad we stuck with it. No matter what happens from here, in my mind it was worth it."

"Mine too. I didn't think I would ever say that when we first left Caprum. I'm not even that nervous about getting shot at anymore."

"Probably because it seems to happen any time we aren't in hyperspace."

"We were shot at in hyperspace too."

"Probably because it seems to happen all the time," I corrected, laughing.

"Assembly complete," Asshole announced. I turned my attention to the wall as it slid open, eyes widening and heart leaping when the contents were revealed.

"It looks perfect," I said, stepping into the assembly closet and picking up the guitar. A classic acoustic six-string, it felt great in my hands. Closing my eyes, I strummed it lightly.

"It sounds good, too," Matt said.

I opened my eyes, smiling. "Now we have a band."

"Rock on."

Shaq buzzed on my shoulder, reflecting my excitement. I slung the guitar over my shoulder and we headed from the assembler to the kitchen.

"I really hope this works," Matt said. "This is more important than the guitar."

"No it isn't," I replied.

"Blasphemy." He pushed back the sleeve of his shirt, revealing a gold watch underneath. "She'll be here in a few minutes."

"Asshole, gimme a pizza, extra cheese," I said.

"Did someone say pizza?" Asshole replied, his accent

a little more refined thanks to my tuning. "One pie with extra cheese coming right up."

"You got the voice commands right," Matt said.

The assembler hadn't contained a profile for pizza, so I had needed to go into the source code to train it to make the food, and to understand a request to assemble it. That consisted of breaking down the ingredients, finding matching recipes already in the databank, and merging them together into the design. Thankfully, pizza was a relatively simple construct.

"One pizza, get it while it's hot!" Asshole announced, the aperture spinning open. The smell wafted out immediately, making my mouth water.

"Two for two," Matt said, sliding on a pair of thick cloth potholder gloves with chickens embroidered on the back and retrieving a wide spatula. "Although, I think we'll need a few more. Your size is a little off."

"Personal pizza," I agreed. "I could eat two of those myself."

"Try one with pepperoni."

"I didn't have time to program in pepperoni. We can do bacon."

"Close enough."

"Asshole, we need six more pizzas. Two more with extra cheese, three with bacon."

"And pineapple," Matt added.

"What?" I said. "Nobody wants pineapple on their pizza."

"Sure they do. It's especially good with Canadian bacon."

"No, it isn't. We want Alter to like the pizza, you know."

"Come on. It's not like I'm asking for anchovies."

"Asshole, scratch the pineapple," I said, glancing at him. "Maybe next time."

"Fine."

"Six pizzas?" Asshole said. "You must be hungry. Order received. Coming right up!"

Shaq hopped off my shoulder, landing on the table next to the pizza. He leaned over it, giving it a sniff before turning away, buzzing out in disgust.

"It's not my fault you only eat meat," I said. "There's bacon coming."

He buzzed happily, giving me a tiny thumbs-up.

Asshole assembled the pizzas one at a time, Matt lifting them out and putting them on individual plates. I found a knife in one of the drawers and set about making slices. I would need to make a pizza cutter for next time too.

"That's all of them," Matt said as Shaq picked a piece of the bacon off one of the pies. "Dude, wait for Alter. Didn't your mother teach you any manners?"

He shoved the bacon into his tiny mouth, devouring it in seconds as a response.

"Don't make me call you wildlife."

Shaq buzzed in amusement, hopping onto my shoulder as I picked up two of the plates to bring them into the lounge.

Making the round trip, the first pitcher of beer was ready by the time I got back. Matt had already poured a small sample into his mug.

"How is it?" I asked.

"Tastes like Schlitz," he replied. "But it'll do."

"I hope this is a resource problem," I said. "And not a case of people in the Spiral preferring the cheap stuff."

We brought the rest of the pizza and beer into the lounge. Matt turned on the television, pulling *That*

Darned Cat up from the datastore. Not a great movie. At all. But we figured it was in there because Alter liked it.

I left the guitar leaning against the piano in the corner and headed to the sofa. Shaq hopped off my shoulder and onto the couch. He perched on the arm, intensely interested in the cover image for the movie—a cat wearing sunglasses.

"Oh wow!" Alter exclaimed, appearing at the top of the step into the lounge. "You picked *That Darn Cat*? I *love* that movie! The cat is so cute and funny."

I stared at her, uncertain if I was more surprised by her attitude or her outfit. Unsure of which persona to expect, I definitely didn't plan to see her in adult onesie unicorn pajamas, a rainbow horn sticking up from the top of her hood. She wore a playful, innocent smile on her face, more youthful than any of the others I had seen.

"Hey Alter," Matt said. "Nice PJs."

"Thanks," she replied. "I thought this was a pajama party?"

"Come as you are," I said. "We've got pizza and beer, but I'm not sure you're legal for the alcohol."

"I don't understand," she responded, not getting my joke.

"You just look a lot younger than usual."

"I do?" She grabbed the front of her onesie. "Do you like it?"

"Yeah, it's great. The food, drink, and movie are ready to go, but Matt and I have a surprise for you first."

"Really? I love surprises!"

Matt dropped down on the piano bench while I picked up the guitar. "We thought you might like to hear some real live Earth music."

"Justin Bieber? He's my fave."

I glanced at Matt. "Uh. No. Not exactly."

She dropped onto the sofa, putting her legs up on the cushions and lounging comfortably, facing us. Shaq hopped from the arm to her lap, curling up there. "I'm sure I'll love it, whatever it is. I'm ready when you are."

I strummed the guitar, Matt tickled the ivories, and we went into the opening riff for *Johnny B Goode*, an oldie but still awesome. Keeping my eyes on Alter as we played, her face went from relaxed and happy, more so than I'd ever seen it, to pained in about three seconds. By the time Matt started singing, she practically smacked Shaq off her lap as she leaped from the sofa and ran out of the room.

We both stopped playing, turning to look at one another. "What the hell?" we said at the same time.

My heart sank. So much effort to make her feel welcome and we had inadvertently done the opposite.

"I'll go talk to her," I said, putting down the guitar to chase after her. Shaq hopped to the arm of the sofa to leap onto my shoulder, but I put my hand out. "Not this time, bud." He buzzed understanding, and I hurried from the room.

Chapter Forty-Nine

I ran back to the elevator, too slow to catch Alter before she left the deck. I didn't understand why she had reacted the way she did to the music. Did she hate it that much and didn't want to say anything? Did she decide she needed a different personality to enjoy rock and roll? Was there something else we had done to offend her?

It took a few seconds for the elevator to return. I jumped in and guided it to Deck Five, desperate to apologize to Alter and make sure she wasn't mad at Matt and me. While I knew she wouldn't leave the ship no matter what we did, I really wanted her to feel like we were all one crew, and that we would have her back when needed. While I had questioned her loyalty before we'd entered hyperspace, I'd felt stupid for that as soon as the adrenaline wore off and I calmed down. I couldn't believe I'd even suspected her to begin with. I couldn't believe she'd ever want to go back to Sedaya after what he had done to her.

The cab reached Deck Five, opening to the wall of miscellany Matt had mentioned. This was my first time

on the deck, and I stopped at the threshold of the elevator, using my body to keep the door from closing.

"Alter?" I said. "It's Ben. Are you here?"

She didn't respond, leaving me to wonder if she had
come back to this deck or gone to Six or Seven.

"Alter?" I asked again. "Can I come in?" One thing I
knew for sure. I wasn't going past the barrier without her
permission.

A soft sob came from the other side of the wall of
stuff, threatening my resolve to respect her privacy.

"Alter, I'm sorry. Matt's sorry too. We didn't mean to
upset you. We were trying to entertain you. To have
some fun. We just want you to feel like you belong. Be
part of the team, not just the ship's caretaker. And our
caretaker, for that matter. Because, you know, we care
about you." It sounded sappy, like one of the modern
songs she liked listening to. But it was also true. "Alter,
can I come in?"

The sobbing stopped, leaving a few seconds of
silence hanging between us. "Ben," she said softly. "You
don't understand."

"I'd like to," I replied. "You're my friend."

"No, I'm not," she answered faintly. "I know you
want to pretend we can be one big happy family, but we
can't."

"Why not?"

"I'm not like you."

"I know. So what?"

"I've done things, Ben. Bad things. A lot of bad
things."

"I know that too. You don't become a well known
assassin by doing good things. But you wanted to get out.
You did get out. It doesn't matter who you were twenty
years ago. It matters who you are today. We see you as a

friend and a valuable part of our team. We care about you. Please let me come in."

Another round of silence followed. I didn't say anything else. I didn't advance or retreat. I waited for her to decide. If she had told me to go, I would have gone.

"I don't deserve your friendship," she said at last.

"That's for us to decide, isn't it?" I replied. "I haven't deserved a lot of crappy things in life. I don't think Matt and I deserve you either. But here we are."

"Here we are," she repeated softly.

A third silence persisted, nearly a minute passing while I waited. I could tell whatever had happened in the lounge was about more than the music. We had accidentally triggered something deeper and more meaningful. And now that I was standing there, maybe it was a good thing.

"Are you still there?" she asked.

"Yes. I won't leave unless you want me to. Do you?"

"No."

"Can I come in then?"

She hesitated, and when she spoke again I could tell the word was hard for her to say. "Okay."

"Are you sure?"

Another pause.

"Yes, I'm sure. You can come in, Ben."

I didn't realize how nervous I was until I rounded the corner of the barrier. I didn't know what I expected to find there, but a huge pile of sand definitely wasn't near the top of my list.

The largest pile was in the center of the deck, though the motion of the ship had created ripples and dunes as it shifted back and forth. An endless sea of stuff covered the periphery from floor to ceiling, while even more objects lay scattered along the sand. There was no obvious rhyme or reason to the things Alter had collected. A teddy bear, a piece of an airplane wing, a Barbie doll, at least a thousand different stuffed animals. A katana, bo staff, boxing gloves, heavy bag, a number of small metal cages, and some things I couldn't recognize at all. She even had a large piece of driftwood nestled within the grains.

The one thing I didn't see was her.

"Where are you?" I asked, standing at the edge of the tiny desert. I realized it wasn't just *Head Case* that was her home. It was the sand itself, which had probably filled at least part of the head's shell when she had discovered it. Maybe all of the junk had been there too, garbage discarded on Demitrus.

Just like her.

The thought left me ready to shed tears. "Alter?" I asked.

The sand shifted a few feet away. Surprised by it, I jumped back, watching as it sank within itself. A clear tendril appeared in the center, only a few inches long. It stretched forward and split apart, branching out into more tendrils, the ends becoming wide to support itself on the sand.

I backed up another step, watching the tendril. It couldn't be. Could it?

More of the sand shifted, a multitude of tendrils stretching out and planting themselves against the pile. They spread forward, pulling a larger clear mass out of the sand until a three-foot diameter blob of gelatin that resembled a nerve cell rested on top.

"Alter?" I whispered, still uncertain. Matt and I had both considered that she might be an alien, but this was a step beyond anything I could have imagined.

The blob continued changing shape as it rose from

the sand, gaining height, stretching and expanding. My heart pounded as it began to gain a more definitive form, the confirmation leaving me speechless.

"Alter," I said again softly, staring at the clear human form as it finished constructing itself.

"I told you, I'm not like you," she said, the gelatin gaining color and texture, becoming not only skin, but also clothing and hair, continuing to alter until a new version of her stood in front of me. No more than fourteen, with olive skin and dark hair, she was dressed in a flowing nightgown that stretched down to the floor.

"What are you?" I asked, mesmerized by how she had just made her entrance.

"My race is called the Aleal," she replied.

I continued staring at her. Not knowing what else to say, I blurted out the next thought that came to mind. "That is so freaking awesome!"

She flinched in response to the statement, expecting a different reaction. Tears formed in her eyes as she processed what I had actually said. "Awesome?"

"Yeah. You know, cool, wicked, amazing. You're a shapeshifter."

Her smile carried too much sadness. "Ben." She paused, shaking her head. "You still don't understand."

"What do you mean? You just showed me your true form, and I think it's incredible. What's there to understand? I want to know so much more about you. About the Aleal. About how you do the things you do. Did Keep know?"

She laughed, but it remained heavy with misery. "No, he never knew for sure, but I think he suspected. Very few people know the Aleal even exist."

"Why are you so sad? I'm sorry. I just don't understand."

"Because you don't know anything about me," she replied.

"I know you've saved my life more than once. I know you take care of the ship. I know I want to know more about you. Matt and I already thought maybe you were an alien. I just didn't realize how cool you would actually be."

"It's not cool," she snapped. "It's not amazing or awesome."

"Yes, it—"

"Ben, an Aleal can only take the shape of something it's consumed."

I froze where I stood, staring at her as my brain tried to catch up to the statement. I frowned, giving Alter a look she must have thought was disgust, because she turned away, her silent tears becoming audible in more soft sobs.

Every persona she had exhibited was someone she had killed. I didn't know what to say. I didn't know how to feel.

Yes, I did.

I stepped forward, wrapping my arms around her from behind. I had never actually touched Alter outside of martial arts practice, and her young form didn't make it any easier, but I hugged her anyway. "I don't care," I told her, holding her close.

She turned her head and tipped her chin up to look at me. "Ben, I don't think you heard me. This form. This child. I murdered her. I devoured a part of her brain so I could capture her essence. So she would become part of me."

"Did you kill her because you wanted to, or because Sedaya made you?"

"Does it matter?"

"Doesn't it?"

She gently turned to face me, my arms falling away. "She was one of my jobs. All of them were." She changed form again, needing only a handful of seconds. This time, to a large man in a military uniform. "Sedaya found my homeworld. He captured me. The others fought him. He brought me back to his castle. He wanted me to feed on this man. I didn't want to. He tortured me." She started crying again, tears rolling down her cheeks into her beard. "He broke me, Ben. He used me. He turned me into a killer. And when he was done with me he threw me away."

"I'm sorry, Alter. I'm sorry you had to go through all that. Why would I reject you because he made you kill people? So what if you ate them? Asshole turned the Niflin we killed into bacon for me. Same difference."

She shook her head. "No, Ben. He made me become an assassin, and it was horrible. But then, for a while, I enjoyed it. I liked gaining new personalities. New skills. I felt important. Special. Powerful."

"But that wouldn't have happened if Sedaya hadn't stolen you and pushed you into it. If that's all you knew, if that was the sum total of what you thought you were, then why wouldn't you enjoy it for a while? You told me you wanted out, and that's when Sedaya dumped you. Obviously, you didn't enjoy it anymore."

"No. I didn't."

"So what's the problem?"

She looked down at me, our eyes meeting. I kept our gaze locked as she changed again, back to the younger woman in the unicorn onesie. Her sadness faded, her smile returning. "You don't hate me?" she asked, sounding more like a child than an infamous assassin.

"As long as you don't play any more of that overly sweet techno pop, I don't hate you," I replied.

She laughed. "I'm sorry I ran away. I just… You wanted to play your music for me. You invited me to come down and were going to watch *That Darn Cat* with me. No one's ever actually cared about *me* like that before. They only cared about what I could do for *them*."

"Well, I guess you can't say that anymore," I said.

"Ben… there's something else."

"Okay."

"I can't eat the pizza. Or anything that comes out of the assembler. It has to be raw and organic. I can store it temporarily, but I can't actually digest it or use it as fuel."

It took me a second to realize what she meant. "Oh. So you have a supply of mice or something that you feed on?"

"Normally, yes. Something like that. But I ran out, and once we left Caprum I had to find an alternate source."

"Sedaya's soldiers?"

"Yes." She lowered her head, ashamed.

"They deserved it. We'll make sure you get whatever you need as soon as we can."

The shame faded as she looked at me again. "Thank you, Ben. For being such a good guy. For being my friend."

I smiled. "That's what friends are for, right? Come on, we've got a song to finish, a movie to watch, and pizza for you to pretend to eat."

She laughed. "Let's do it!"

Chapter Fifty

"Kasper Orbital Control, this is *Head Case*," I said as we drifted toward the field of starships waiting to drop to one of the spaceports scattered around the planet. "Requesting atmospheric landing at Persephon Spaceport. Transmitting customs identifier now."

I tapped on the center screen, sending the identifier that had broadcast to the PCS the moment we activated Lo's slab. The identifier should confirm we had legal business in Kasper's capital city and that everything was on the up and up.

Because everything wasn't on the up and up, I waited with baited breath for control to respond. Glancing over at Alter, she nodded in firm support of both my landing request and confidence in our credentials.

Movie night had been a blast and had changed so much so quickly with Alter. While her different personalities remained, the fact that I knew her secret had made it easier for her to share her alien nature with both Matt and Shaq, and in turn had allowed her to be more comfortable in it. She shifted from one persona to another right in front of us now instead of retreating to her quarters, and she was even thinking about moving to Deck Three with us.

While we hadn't spent a lot of time discussing her race and origins, I had learned that the Aleal were one of the Spiral's best kept secrets. An intelligent race of outwardly primitive organisms with a massive potential for both growth and abuse. Exposed to the wider universe, every Aleal was a tabula rasa. A blank slate. Able to absorb what she called essence from other intelligent life forms, it meant she gained the ability to become that form, albeit without their distinct individuality. While an essence allowed her to gain an individual's learned skills and mimic physical attributes, it didn't include personal memories or experiences. She didn't know the name of the soldier Sedaya had forced her to absorb, if he had a family, where he grew up, or anything like that. Before absorbing him she had no language and no true understanding of the universe beyond her kind's natural habitat. But through him, she could speak, recite history, shoot a gun, and the like.

Though the Aleal didn't have a definition of gender, it was clear Alter preferred utilizing female essences, as she only revealed the soldier to me the one time. I was sure she had more males in there, along with essences of other races. As she had explained, the personas were tools, and she already had a well-defined box of them. It was only in unfamiliar situations where a new essence might emerge, like when we spoke in her quarters. No one in the galaxy knew what she was except for Matt, Shaq, and me.

And, of course, Duke Sedaya.

She hated that he knew, and hated more that he knew where her homeworld was located, especially since she didn't know herself. I had asked if it was possible he had gone back for more Aleal like her. The idea frightened her. She couldn't know that for sure, and the thought of him subjecting another of her kind to the same treatment he had put her through was a horrible, infuriating thought. There was nothing we could do about it, and I regretted mentioning it afterward.

"*Head Case*, this is Kapser Orbital Control," a man with a flat affect replied. "Customs tag received. Permission to land at Perspehon Spaceport granted. Transmitting flight plan now. Follow the markers to join the queue."

"Copy that, Kasper Orbital Control," I said as the PCS received the flight plan and displayed the path and markers on my HUD. "Moving into position now."

I exhaled my relief that the codes we transmitted passed muster, and also likely alerted the courier we were on our way. I was eager to finish the job and earn some electro, both to pay for the contact that might be able to cure my cancer and to stock up on fresh supplies and resources for Asshole. I had accepted the dead Niflin as raw materials out of need, but once the need was gone I didn't really want to continue eating the Soylent, reconstituted or not.

In stark contrast to Cestus, the entire orbit was ringed with ships of every shape, size, and configuration, at least a thousand in total that I could see and no doubt more on the other side of the planet. The activity from space to ground remained constant, arrivals and departures moving in a smooth flow.

At nearly a dozen points around the world, space elevators rose to large stations where the biggest of the ships were docked, including a Hegemony Royal Sentry, even more massive from our much closer approach than it had been when we left Caprum. The long, wedge-shaped white spacecraft stood out against the sea of smaller, darker ships, its power and prestige undeniable.

I adjusted the throttle, firing the retro thrusters and slowing us down as the marked path brought us around the station where the Sentry was parked. We were tenth in line to land, our ETA a little more than thirty minutes away.

"Any sign of trouble?" I asked Alter, who had set about scanning the other ships nearby, both visually and with the ship's sensors.

"Not so far," she replied. "And even Sedaya knows better than to start trouble beyond his jurisdiction, especially when there's a Sentry in orbit."

"So the Hegemony doesn't have one stationed on every planet?" Matt asked from the sofa behind us.

"No," Alter replied. "The Hegemony consists of over five thousand occupied worlds in total, covering thousands of light years. It would be impossible to build enough ships to cover all of it adequately. Though the Royal Sentries tend to keep to the outer Quadrants rather than the inner Spiral, where the Empress' power is more consolidated. They're here as a symbol of her power more than anything. That one's probably resupplying before it will sweep across the Quad again. It's lucky for us that it's here right now."

"You really think they'd get involved if Sedaya went after us again?"

"We have a valid customs identifier. They can't touch us while we're onboard. Once we depart is a different story. But the risk is probably too high to make it worthwhile. Better to be patient and act with more certainty."

"What are the chances we can get him off our backs for good?" I wondered.

"If it becomes more costly to him to chase us than to leave us alone," Alter answered.

We settled back in our seats. Alter used the center console screen to load a video game where the objective was to walk a corgi across a busy park without making contact with anything, like a cuter version of Frogger. We each took turns, including Shaq, who wound up being the best of us. That wasn't a big surprise to me. The Jagger seemed to operate at a higher frame rate to begin with.

"We're up," I said as the markers expanded, providing a flight path to bring us down to the surface. I adjusted our heading and velocity, dipping us toward the atmosphere and activating the shields.

I couldn't help gawking at Kasper's landscape as we descended. At one level, it reminded me strongly of Earth in terms of geography, with all of the same geological features just arranged in a different pattern. But if it was like Earth, it was a utopian Earth a thousand years in the future. Glass tubes crossed the lush countryside, conduits for long bullet trains that floated in the center of the tubes, rocketing around the landscape at high speed. Massive glass structures jutted out from fields of flowers surrounding sparkling blue lakes, connected by bridges that overhung the natural features, flowing with foot traffic. Beyond the cities, smaller domed structures dotted the countryside, accessible by other floating vehicles that darted back and forth from place to place.

"I would have guessed the edgeworlds would be more like the Wild West," I said, taking it all in.

"The Wild West?" Alter asked.

"Yeah. No real authority, not a lot of people, settlements instead of cities. More like Cestus maybe, but on a larger scale."

"There are places like that, but they're beyond the edgeworlds. Occupied by undocumented colonists hoping to evolve an economy that gains them recognition with the larger Hegemony. Or in some cases, run by dissidents or criminals escaping the Empress' justice."

"She doesn't send the Royal Sentries after them?" I asked.

"There's no need. Their positions are already so weak they can't harm any of the recognized territories. It's a convenient way for criminals and dissidents to lose themselves."

The spaceport came into view as we drifted closer to the city. Dozens of what looked like solar-collecting hexagons surrounded by lush grass, streams, and flowers formed the landing pads for incoming ships. Various sized floating barges waited to carry passengers and cargo to the central terminal—a huge, glass domed structure in the center of the pads. From the air, the spaceport had the shape of a sunflower, no doubt intentional.

The PCS painted our assigned landing pad on the HUD for me, using the data Orbital Control had transmitted. I updated our vector for the approach while trying not to get distracted by other nearby ships landing and taking off. This was the experience I had daydreamed about when Keep had sent me the link to his ad for the ship, not getting chased off one planet only to be shot at on another.

I don't think I had ever been happier.

It showed in my flying. I touched *Head Case* down gently on the pad, almost dead center. Immediately, Alter and I removed our helmets and unbuckled our restraints.

Shaq hopped from the headrest of my seat to my shoulder as we all got up, all four of us heading from the flight deck as a group.

By the time we reached the elevator, Alter had switched to her Enigma ninja form, only instead of the black body armor she wore what I took for regular street clothes. Black pants, a black halter top, and a black faux leather jacket that nearly matched my brown one. I didn't see her batons anywhere, but that didn't mean much. She could store them inside her gel-like form. Or rather, wrap herself around them. I knew she had firearms for herself, some for Matt and me tucked away in there as well.

The perfect assassin.

Even though I knew she was on our side, the thought of how easily she could infiltrate security and kill someone sent a chill down my spine.

We rode the elevator to the hangar, crossing the deck to the outer hatch.

"All right Shaq," I said. "Time to make yourself scarce."

He buzzed affirmation before scampering down my arm and jumping across to the small bag Matt held, which also contained the slab. Matt unzipped the bag, reaching down to turn the slab on again so it would broadcast its identifier. Shaq slipped inside with it before he zipped it closed again.

The Jagger was our insurance, just in case something went sideways and someone other than the courier captured the slab before he picked it up. Once Matt made the drop, Shaq would climb out and stay hidden somewhere until they were gone. Since he wasn't on the contract, he could legally see the courier without negating the agreement. Not that we really cared about the individual's identity, but Shaq might not have a chance to clear the area completely before he arrived.

The smaller hatch opened at our approach, and we stepped out onto Kasper. The foliage around our landing pad was even more amazing from ground level, the flowers blooming in bright reds, yellows, purples, and blues. Exotic looking birds flitted around them, while equally odd, colorful insects clambered along the stalks.

The customs identifier had also emitted the general weight of our cargo, and a smaller skiff had been left for us to cross the landing area. Reaching it, I discovered it was fully automated rather than manually controlled.

"Ready," Alter said once the three of us had hopped on board.

The skiff pulled away from the landing pad, rising slightly to clear the tops of the flowers as it charted a path toward the terminal.

And to being eighteen million electro richer, and more importantly, closer to saving my life.

Chapter Fifty-One

We split up after the skiff reached the entrance to the terminal, where a group of armed and armored guards were set up at scanning stations, checking all of the arrivals from our terminal, which appeared to include an incoming transport. A decent crowd waited at the queue, composed of humans dressed in a range of fashions. To be honest, the entire setup didn't stand out as much different from an airport on Earth. At least my slightly toned down young Han Solo look played pretty well among the rest of the arrivals.

Matt picked the line in the middle, so I moved to one a few rows over while Alter went in the other direction. We processed quickly, the line continually moving as more arrivals filled in behind us. I did my best to keep my eyes forward, tempted to check on Matt and Alter more than once. What was I worried about? Between the security forces and the crowds, there was no way anyone was going to attack us here.

That didn't mean we weren't being watched or followed. The large payday Lo had agreed to suggested there might be more than a little bit of trouble waiting. Just like we expected the courier to notice our customs identifier, any potential counterparty would see it too. While they might not be able to track the slab directly, they only needed to identify us as the carriers to get a bead on us.

I reached the scanning station within a few minutes. The guard didn't say or do anything as I approached. He kept his hands on his rifle, stiff as a board, while I stepped through a wall of green lasers. I didn't realize I was holding my breath until I passed through the lasers without incident. I continued forward toward the exit while trying to indiscreetly locate Matt. A beeping behind me got my attention, and I looked back half-expecting the scan to have caught Alter with her internalized contraband. Instead, I spotted her along the wall, moving in the same direction as me. One of the guards had stopped a woman with a large bag, seizing it from her while she complained. I didn't linger to get the rest of the story, falling in a few people deep behind Alter, who I was certain had already gotten a bead on Matt.

A long, glass covered corridor followed the scanning station, leading to the central concourse. Looking up as I walked through it, I could see more ships coming and going in the background, while different types of small, flying lizards and birds passed directly overhead. Other colorful lizards and insects clung to the glass, soaking in the heat of Kasper's sun. Amazing.

The concourse was even more amazing. Upon entering, I could immediately see how it was arranged in multiple levels of platforms that followed the round shape of the structure. A waterfall accentuated the large, open center, while a dozen glass elevators ringed the circle, carrying passengers to the different levels. Storefronts lined the perimeter, and holograms floated over-head, advertising different products as calm electronic music emanated from everywhere. It worked to subdue the overwhelming sense of scale.

I was so caught up in gawking at the construction that I nearly lost sight of Alter, leaving me to scramble after her as she slipped between a pair of travelers and was gone. We should have had comms, earpieces or walkie-talkies, anything really, but we didn't have the right resources for Asshole to assemble any; a problem we could correct as soon as we scored the electro. Fortunately, she slowed before she had gone too far, not only allowing me to catch up, but backtracking past me.

"Keep an eye on Matt," she whispered to me as we crossed paths. I watched her for a split-second as she headed for a bathroom, likely to change form, and then scanned the floor for Matt. I found him waiting for one of the elevators.

Lo had instructed us to leave the slab somewhere it couldn't be stolen right away. Without a full under-standing of the spaceport's layout, we hadn't decided on a specific spot, instead leaving the location up to Matt's discretion. I didn't know if he had already found a place to dump the bag or if he was still looking. Either way, he didn't seem to be in a rush.

It was a good thing, too. It gave me a chance to put eyes on a pair of women on the opposite side of the lift. Dressed in tight, sparkling outfits that reminded me of leotards, their military standard boots looked out of place. Observing them from the corner of my eye as I neared the line for the elevator, I noticed they kept glancing in Matt's direction. Then one would lean in close to the other as if whispering a private comment.

The second would smile or laugh, and the process would repeat.

I made sure I was at the railing when Matt boarded the cab, leaning over it and forcing myself not to gawk at the landscape, where a large pool of water was surrounded by rocks and greenery. A bridge passed over the rocks and through the waterfall while an invisible shield prevented anyone crossing the concourse over it from getting wet. Peeling my eyes from it, I saw him get off on the second floor, which seemed a little less crowded than where we had entered.

I glanced back toward the two women. Gone. Of course.

Scanning the floor, I found them moving to an adjacent elevator. If they got off on the second floor, it would confirm they were following Matt like I suspected. Of course, they could just be looking for a friend, but something told me that wasn't the case with these two.

I went in the other direction, to the elevator ninety-degrees from the one Matt had taken. Glancing over the edge of the railing every few seconds, I spotted him standing near the railing, turning his head as if he was looking for something specific. Then he looked up, ostensibly to track the source of the waterfall, then sweeping his eyes over me before he leveled his gaze again.

Reaching the elevator, I squeezed in with a large group of travelers, ending up pinned between an older woman and a tall man in a dark suit.

"Nice day, isn't it?" I said to the man, meeting his eyes as he glared down at me without speaking.

The cab stopped on the fourth floor, and most of the passengers departed there, freeing up space. I moved to the side of the cab until it stopped again on the second floor. Lurch hurried off the ride ahead of me, going in the same direction.

I fell back a little from him, wondering if he was a bad guy too. The icy glare he had given me suggested as much. Looking past him, I saw Matt rounding the concourse, coming toward me with the bag still in his possession.

I wanted to ask why he was taking so long to dump it somewhere when I got my answer. A couple of men in long jackets were a little further back, trailing him.

Closing the gap between us, Matt bumped his shoulder into me. Handing over the bag, he whispered, "I think they're following me."

"I think you've got a pair of Jazzercise rejects watching you too," I replied, taking the bag and moving toward the railing to avoid his tail. I leaned over it, keeping my peripheral vision on them as they stayed with Matt. "Shaq, I've got the bag," I said, dipping my head closer to it. "If it gets rough in there, be ready."

He buzzed in affirmation.

I turned around, leaning against the railing and looking at the storefronts across from me, searching for somewhere to leave the bag.

"Hey kid, what's in the bag?"

The two leotards moved away from the other pedestrians, coming at me. One of them slid a small card from under her sleeve. With a quick wrist movement, it folded outward into a tiny gun.

"Give us the bag, and we won't hurt you," she said, pointing it at my face.

I didn't have a chance to say or do anything. One second, the two women were threatening me. The next, they were on the ground. Knowing Alter had gone to the bathroom to change her persona, I didn't know which of the passersby was her, but I was certain she was responsible for the save.

I needed to drop the slab somewhere, fast.

A shout from the floor above stole my attention. I started turning to look just as a woman in a red jacket fell past me, grabbing the bag as she did. I managed to get my hand on the strap, pulled to the railing as her momentum yanked hard on my shoulder, offering me a choice to let it go or hang onto it and either jerk my shoulder out of its socket or take me down with her.

I didn't get to make the decision.

The strap snapped, the bag still in the woman's grip as she continued the drop, hitting the ground and rolling to break her momentum. She leaned over the bag to unzip it.

I barely saw Shaq emerge from the bag and dive back inside. One second, the woman was crouched over the package. The next, she was on her side, stiff as a board.

And the slab was out in the open, unguarded.

Someone on the ground floor screamed when they realized the woman was dead. I planted my hand on the railing, ready to vault over it, momentarily held back by the idea of breaking both legs. How had the woman managed the feat from higher up? I had to try. That tablet was my chance at survival. It was worth the risk.

I had one leg over the railing when Matt appeared from under the overhang. He quickly scooped up the slab from inside the open bag as Shaq scaled the back of his leg and tucked himself under his coat. The two men following him appeared, still on his tail as security reached the dead woman.

Where had Alter gone? She had the guns, and I needed one right now. Then again, there was no way to shoot the guys chasing Matt without causing a panic and risking security getting their hands on him.

Matt reached the edge of the bridge, using it to cross to the other side of the concourse. The two men split up, one of them hurrying around the bridge to cut him off. Damn it, Matt had gone the wrong way, positioning himself with no means of escape. Nowhere to run.

I left the railing, sprinting past a group of onlookers gathering around the downed leotards and shouting for the guards. Pushing my way past the other travelers, I went full speed around the circle, desperate to get ahead of the bad guys.

A guard emerged through a door between two of the storefronts, his head immediately turning my way. I slowed my run, looking away and trying to appear inconspicuous as he started in my direction. Damn it again. Glancing back to the bridge, I saw Matt standing in the center, the slab in his hands. My guy had reached the bridge well ahead of me, the two thugs converging on him from both sides.

Triple damn.

"Alter, wherever you are, that's your cue," I whispered.

Matt glanced one way, and then the other, identifying the thugs.

Out of options, he held the slab over the side of the bridge.

And dropped it.

Chapter Fifty-Two

I watched the slab fall, end over end, my hopes of collecting the money and being cured falling with it. Hitting the pool with a soft splash, pushed under by the force of the waterfall, I lost sight of the device.

I didn't lose sight of the two men. They had frozen in place when Matt dropped the slab, and now they turned around, trying to get off the bridge to find the discarded slab. They shoved their way past upset pedestrians moving in the opposite direction, the traffic on the bridge slowing them down.

Seeing them retreating, Matt smirked and followed the one on the far side, easing his way through the people.

I didn't waste time wondering what Matt was thinking. He and I had been best friends since we were in kindergarten. I didn't need him to tell me why he had dropped the slab. I knew why, and that knowledge sent me rushing to the nearest elevator.

We were supposed to drop the device somewhere the courier could find it. Somewhere it wouldn't be taken by the other players in this game of four-dimensional chess before they could pick it up. Matt had sent it to the bottom of the waterfall, the rushing white water shoving it elsewhere in the large pool. Maybe it would surface near the edge where one of the two thugs could grab it. But not likely. Only the courier, able to directly track the device, would be able to find it quickly. Hopefully, he could swim if needed.

I heard a splash and the murmur of surprise from a number of people just before I stepped into the elevator. Remembering the terms of our contract, I spun away from the pool, making sure I didn't see the courier. I could only hope Matt and Alter, wherever she was, had done the same.

The elevator opened on the ground floor a few seconds later. I risked a glance at the bridge when I stepped out, finding Matt had reached the far end, just behind the thug. The man must have sensed him coming, because he spun around and threw a hard right hook that should have connected with Matt's jaw. Matt sensed the punch coming and sidestepped it. He grabbed the thug's arm, using the momentum of the punch to throw the man onto his back. The thug however wasn't going down that easily. He caught Matt's leg as he tried to kick him in the ribs, twisting it until Matt fell against the bridge railing. The thug hopped back up, drawing his arm back to throw a punch as he yanked Matt back around to face him.

Sliding my gaze to the other side of the bridge, I didn't see if thug one connected with Matt's jaw. My attention was on thug number two as he shoved a woman off the bridge and into the water.Breaking free, he reached into his pocket, withdrawing a gun and swinging it toward me.

I froze, caught in the open, dead to rights.

Except he wasn't aiming at me.

He opened fire, blaster rounds zipping past the elevator to where the courier had to be making his escape. The security guards who had responded to the dead woman were only a dozen feet away from the guy, but they didn't react to his shots, even as the nearby travelers screamed and fell to the floor, trying to stay out of the line of fire. Whoever the thugs were, they were tight with security.

A small blue blur caught my attention, charging fast along the bridge railing. Shaq leaped the twenty foot gap to the shooter, spreading his arms to allow his webbing to carry him through the air. The thug started to turn as the Jagger approached. Too late. Shaq grabbed onto his neck, teeth digging in.

The guy didn't have a chance.

I looked back at Matt just as he planted a hard jab to his thug's nose, sending him reeling. He followed up with a kick that sent the man into the railing, his momentum carrying him up and over and into the pool, temporarily out of the fight.

I turned around, half-expecting to see the courier dead on the floor, the slab missing once more. Instead, I caught a glimpse of Lurch's back as he opened one of the maintenance access doors and vanished through it.

I knew he was the courier!

And he had gotten away.

Or had he?

Before I could turn around again to regroup with Matt and Shaq to find Alter, a bald-headed newcomer in a long brown jacket approached the door, pulling it open and trailing the courier through it.

Damn it.

"You! Don't move."

I swiveled my head in the direction of the order. A security guard jogged toward me, rifle aimed at my chest. I slowly raised my hands as the guard pulled up directly in front of me.

"Shhhh," the guard said, drawing the blaster and holding it out to me, grip first. Not a guard, then. Alter. "Help the courier. I'll keep security off your back."

I took the gun with a smile. "On it."

Alter turned toward the other guards as I broke for the door, sprinting across the concourse as fast as I could, my seesaw emotions threatening another hard crash. Pushing through the door, I was confronted by a long, sterile, and unfortunately empty corridor, with an inter-section fifty feet away. I charged forward, racing to the split and freezing when I reached it, head whipping in both directions. A pair of moving shadows against another wall to the right suggested the courier and his tail had gone that way.

Rushing along that corridor brought me to another t-junction, a door on the left, another long and empty corridor on the right. Obviously, they had gone through the door. I opened it slowly and stepped into what I assumed were the inner workings of the spaceport's HVAC system. Massive tubes surrounded me, dripping condensed moisture to form growing puddles on the floor. A low roar echoed from somewhere deeper in the system.

Running footsteps splashed through the puddles further ahead.

I moved more cautiously, trying to remain quiet as I continued the chase. While my heart pounded and my nerves were taut, I impressed myself with my overall ability to still think clearly and the knowledge that when

I got the drop on browncoat I wouldn't hesitate to shoot. It was a big step up from my first hours on Caprum when Alter's violence against Sedaya's goons had ended up with me puking, and it lent me confidence now.

Moving through the tight, damp passageways, I continued tracking the footsteps, winding through a maze of intersections in pursuit, hoping to gain on the pair while doing my best to stay silent.

The footsteps ahead of me accelerated suddenly, and for the first time I heard the courier's feet too, echoing from a spot too close to browncoat.

"Shit," I hissed, picking up my pace. At least they wouldn't be able to hear me over their own noise. Of course, it got harder to hear them too. I raced along the passages, desperate to reach browncoat before he reached the courier. Everything was riding on making sure he got out alive. Not because I cared if he lived but because he still had to transmit the payment.

Coming around a corner, I nearly froze when I saw browncoat in a silhouetted profile, hand outstretched, aiming his gun. I swung my blaster toward him, stifling a cry as he fired three rounds. He didn't see me coming as he advanced between two thick pipes and out of view.

I slowed down, moving quietly toward him, a lack of footsteps proof he wasn't on the move. Peering around the corner, I found him hunched over the courier's body, holding the slab in both hands.

"Don't move," I hissed, pointing my gun at the back of his head.

He froze in place.

"Put the slab on the ground, stand up and face me. Don't even think of going for your gun, you won't make it before I put a blast through your skull."

He lowered the slab to the courier's stomach, placing

it there before raising his hands. He stood up slowly, head turning to look back at me over his shoulder.

I nearly dropped my gun. "What the hell?"

"Hey, kid. Funny meeting you here like this. Entirely unexpected. Badabing badaboom."

"Keep?" I said, staring at the man who'd sold *Head Case to* Matt and me and then stiffed us on the parking fees.

The man who had just killed the courier and cost me eighteen million electro.

The man who may have just killed me.

"What the hell did you do?" I growled.

"Took care of a potentially major headache," he replied flatly, as if he had just finished mowing a lawn or changing a lightbulb. "Say, I know this probably isn't the best timing, but how would you like to help me save the galaxy?"

THANK you so much for reading Starship For Sale! For more information on Book Two, please visit mrforbes.com/starshipforsale2.

Other Books By M.R Forbes

Want more M.R. Forbes? Of course you do!
View my complete catalog here
mrforbes.com/books
Or on Amazon:
mrforbes.com/amazon

Forgotten (The Forgotten)
mrforbes.com/theforgotten
Complete series box set:
mrforbes.com/theforgottentrilogy

Some things are better off FORGOTTEN.

Sheriff Hayden Duke was born on the Pilgrim, and he expects to die on the Pilgrim, like his father, and his father before him.

That's the way things are on a generation starship centuries from home. He's never questioned it. Never thought about it. And why bother? Access points to the ship's controls are sealed, the systems that guide her automated and out of reach. It isn't perfect, but he has all he needs to be content.

Until a malfunction forces his wife to the edge of the habitable zone to inspect the damage.

Until she contacts him, breathless and terrified, to tell him she found a body, and it doesn't belong to anyone on board.

Until he arrives at the scene and discovers both his wife and the body are gone.

The only clue? A bloody handprint beneath a hatch that hasn't opened in hundreds of years.

Until now.

Earth Unknown (Forgotten Earth)

mrforbes.com/earthunknown

Centurion Space Force pilot Nathan Stacker didn't expect to return home to find his wife dead. He didn't expect the murderer to look just like him, and he definitely didn't expect to be the one to take the blame.

But his wife had control of a powerful secret. A secret that stretches across the light years between two worlds and could lead to the end of both.

Now that secret is in Nathan's hands, and he's about to make the most desperate evasive maneuver of his life -- stealing a starship and setting a course for Earth.

He thinks he'll be safe there.

He's wrong. Very wrong.

Earth is nothing like what he expected. Not even close. What he doesn't know is not only likely to kill him, it's eager to kill him, and even if it doesn't?

The Sheriff will.

Deliverance (Forgotten Colony)

mrforbes.com/deliverance
Complete series box set:

The war is over. Earth is lost. Running is the only option.

It may already be too late.

Caleb is a former Marine Raider and commander of the Vultures, a search and rescue team that's spent the last two years pulling high-value targets out of alien-ravaged cities and shipping them off-world.

When his new orders call for him to join forty-thousand survivors aboard the last starship out, he thinks his days of fighting are over. The Deliverance represents a fresh start and a chance to leave the war behind for good.

Except the war won't be as easy to escape as he thought.

And the colony will need a man like Caleb more than he ever imagined...

Starship Eternal (War Eternal)
mrforbes.com/starshipeternal
Complete series box set:
mrforbes.com/wareternalcomplete

A lost starship...

A dire warning from futures past...

A desperate search for salvation…

Captain Mitchell "Ares" Williams is a Space Marine and the hero of the Battle for Liberty, whose Shot Heard 'Round the Universe saved the planet from a nearly unstoppable war machine. He's handsome, charismatic, and the perfect poster boy to help the military drive enlistment. Pulled from the war and thrown into the spotlight, he's as efficient at charming the media and bedding beautiful celebrities as he was at shooting down enemy starfighters.

After an assassination attempt leaves Mitchell critically wounded, he begins to suffer from strange hallucinations that carry a chilling and oddly familiar warning:

They are coming. Find the Goliath or humankind will be destroyed.

Convinced that the visions are a side-effect of his injuries, he tries to ignore them, only to learn that he may not be as crazy as he thinks. The enemy is real and closer than he imagined, and they'll do whatever it takes to prevent him from rediscovering the centuries lost starship.

Narrowly escaping capture, out of time and out of air, Mitchell lands at the mercy of the Riggers - a ragtag crew of former commandos who patrol the lawless outer reaches of the galaxy. Guided by a captain with a reputation for cold-blooded murder, they're dangerous, immoral, and possibly insane.

They may also be humanity's last hope for survival in a war that has raged beyond eternity.

Man of War (Rebellion)
mrforbes.com/manofwar
Complete series box set:
mrforbes.com/rebellion-web

In the year 2280, an alien fleet attacked the Earth.

Their weapons were unstoppable, their defenses unbreakable.

Our technology was inferior, our militaries overwhelmed.

Only one starship escaped before civilization fell.

Earth was lost.

It was never forgotten.

Fifty-two years have passed.

A message from home has been received.

The time to fight for what is ours has come.

Welcome to the rebellion.

Hell's Rejects (Chaos of the Covenant)
mrforbes.com/hellsrejects

The most powerful starships ever constructed are gone. Thousands are dead. A fleet is in ruins. The attackers are unknown. The orders are clear: *Recover the ships. Bury the bastards who stole them.*

Lieutenant Abigail Cage never expected to find herself in Hell. As a Highly Specialized Operational Combatant, she was one of the most respected Marines in the military. Now she's doing hard labor on the most miserable planet in the universe.

Not for long.

The Earth Republic is looking for the most dangerous individuals it can control. The best of the worst, and Abbey happens to be one of them. The deal is simple: *Bring back the starships, earn your freedom. Try to run, you die.* It's a suicide mission, but she has nothing to lose.

The only problem? There's a new threat in the galaxy. One with a power unlike anything anyone has ever seen. One that's been waiting for this moment for a very, very long time. And they want Abbey, too.

Be careful what you wish for.

They say Hell hath no fury like a woman scorned. They have no idea.

About the Author

M.R. Forbes is the mind behind a growing number of Amazon best-selling science fiction series. He currently resides with his family and friends on the west cost of the United States, including a cat who thinks she's a dog and a dog who thinks she's a cat.

He maintains a true appreciation for his readers and is always happy to hear from them.

To learn more about M.R. Forbes or just say hello:

Visit my website:
mrforbes.com

Send me an e-mail:
michael@mrforbes.com

Check out my Facebook page:
facebook.com/mrforbes.author

Join my Facebook fan group:
facebook.com/groups/mrforbes

Follow me on Instagram:
instagram.com/mrforbes_author

Find me on Goodreads:
goodreads.com/mrforbes

Follow me on Bookbub:
bookbub.com/authors/m-r-forbes

Printed in Great Britain
by Amazon